Gwendolen

GWENDOLEN

a novel

DIANA SOUHAMI

A HOLT PAPERBACK   HENRY HOLT AND COMPANY   NEW YORK

Holt Paperbacks
Henry Holt and Company, LLC
Publishers since 1866
175 Fifth Avenue
New York, New York 10010
www.henryholt.com

A Holt Paperback® and ® are registered trademarks of
Henry Holt and Company, LLC.

Library of Congress Cataloging-in-Publication Data
Souhami, Diana.
Gwendolen : a novel / Diana Souhami. — First edition.
    pages cm
ISBN 978-1-62779-340-7 (pbk.) — ISBN 978-1-62779-341-4 (electronic book)
1. Social classes—England—Fiction.   I. Eliot, George, 1819–1880. Daniel
Deronda.   II. Title.
PR6119.O6775G93 2015
823'.92—dc23   2014030247

Henry Holt books are available for special promotions and
premiums. For details contact: Director, Special Markets.

First U.S. Edition 2015

Designed by Kelly S. Too

Printed in the United States of America
1   3   5   7   9   10   8   6   4   2

For my brother
Mark Jacob Souhami
(1935–2014)

A woman's heart must be of such a size and no larger; else it must be pressed small, like Chinese feet; her happiness is to be made as cakes are, by a fixed receipt.

—George Eliot, *Daniel Deronda*

Contents

Gwendolen

I · Grandcourt

I was winning when I met your gaze. Its persistence made me raise my head then doubt myself. It broke my luck.

That was our first encounter. A Saturday in September, toward four in the afternoon, the day still light but cool and fresh, Homburg so pretty, so dull, swallows in the eaves of the houses, grapevines on the walls. Little to do but stroll the main street and glance in shop windows at gifts for the rich to give to the rich: ribbons, perfumes, baubles. Only the long, red, stuccoed building in the middle of the street enticed: the Kursaal, the town's social hub. Madame von Langen, my second cousin, accompanied me. Through the great door another far door opened to a garden, beyond the garden was a park, beyond the park the Taunus Mountains wooded with fir, birch, beech, and oak. It was a vista that promised escape from the tight little town and my own despair; a vista that suggested good fortune. A vista that deceived.

In the gilded rococo gaming room naked nymphs cavorted on the ceilings; the players—old, powdered, and engrossed—multiplied in the walled mirrors. There was a reverential silence, a sanctity; red or black, the spin of the wheel, the nasal whine of the croupier: "Faites vos jeux, mesdames et messieurs." My hand, gloved in pale gray, stretched out to rake gold napoleons toward me. I was twenty and born to be lucky. My numbers were Mama's birthday, the day I was born, my father's age when he died (thirty-six), the date Mama then married the hateful Captain Davilow. That September day at the Kursaal I thought my life might transmute into luck. I began with pittance money, but the more I won the bolder I became. I felt destined to win a million francs before the end of play. I was blessed, the most important woman in the room. Then your gaze deflected me. Your judgmental eyes.

I see that gaze now. It mixed attraction with disdain. Your eyes drew me in but implied I was doing wrong. I was beautiful but flawed, you seemed to say. I felt the blood drain from my face. It was the *coup de foudre* (as in Bellini's *Romeo and Juliet*), the start of my unequivocal love for you and your equivocal love for me.

Perhaps all that followed I in a moment saw. As if I knew I was to be excluded from where I so desired to belong.

I was capricious, reckless, and in need of guidance, my life waiting to be defined.

I began to lose heavily. My mood plunged, then rose in defiance. I put ten louis on my chosen number; my stake was swept away; I doubled it, again then again. It took so little time for the croupier to rake from me the last heap of gold. My eyes burned with exasperation. Madame von Langen touched my elbow and whispered we should leave. In my purse only four napoleons remained. As I left, I turned to meet your eyes, which I knew were still on me. My look was defiant, yours ironic. Did you respect my daring, my courage to lose?

Mine is a gambling temperament, impulsive, reckless, hopeful. I so wanted the high stakes, the winning chips. To win was to defy the familiarity and fear of loss. Or to court it. It took a punishing journey for me to reach a point of balance between elation and despair.

I HAD FLED to the von Langens from horror at home. I stayed with them in their hired apartment. They took scant notice of me. The baron, tall with a white clipped mustache, liked to sit in the gardens of the Kursaal and read the court columns of the *Times*. Madame von Langen liked a flutter at the tables, though no more than a ten-franc piece on *rouge ou noir*.

That evening after dinner we returned to the Kursaal for the music. I wore a sea-green dress, a silver necklace, a green hat with a cascading pale green feather fastened with a silver pin. I anticipated seeing you again. The rooms shimmered with heat from the flares of gaslights; a trio of strings played Mozart and Weber; thick-necked men with cigars talked in groups; women with fans reclined on ottomans. I felt that all who were there admired me—my retroussé nose, almond eyes, pale skin, light brown hair. I heard Vandernoodt say a man might risk hanging for Gwendolen Harleth. "There was never a prettier mouth, a more graceful walk," his companion said. I was used to hearing such things.

I flirted and charmed, but what I wanted, hoped for, was again to see you. Then you appeared. You stood in the doorway, that detachment you have, your way of observing, your tall, still figure, dark hair, dark eyes. In a nonchalant voice I asked Mr. Vandernoodt who you were. "Who's that man with the dreadful expression?" He answered he thought you looked very fine, your name was Daniel Deronda, and the previous evening he had sat with you and your party for an hour on the terrace but you spoke to no one and seemed bored. He said you were English and a relative of Sir Hugo Mallinger, with whom you were traveling. You were staying at the Czarina, the grand hotel in the Oberstrasse.

DANIEL DERONDA. I still love your name. Here in violet ink is my admission of love and pain, hope and struggle.

You will never read it, though all is written with you in mind. I know now that I kept a place in your heart and that in a way you loved me, though not as I hoped to be loved, or as I loved you. I hoped I was the woman from whom you might have felt unable ever to be apart, the girl, the woman whom you might have chosen, not to take with you to the other side of the world, but to love and be with until parted by death.

I ASKED THE Vandernoodts to introduce you to me. You were related to Sir Hugo, so Madame von Langen agreed. The baron looked for you on the terrace and in the café, but you were gone. I waited, but you did not return. It was the first of the disappointments you caused me. Each left me bereft and alone. You had hovered at the threshhold, surveyed the scene, and found it not to your liking. Then you left.

That was the start of my habit of anticipation: looking for you but not finding you. How often in the city crowd have I mistakenly believed I saw you: your walk, the way you turn your head.

It was midnight when we got back to the von Langens' apartment. A letter had been left by a servant on the table in my room. It was from my mother, Fanny Davilow. She chastised me for not having written, feared this letter might not reach me, and that I had traveled on to Baden with the von Langens without telling her. "A dreadful calamity has befallen us all," she wrote. She, I, my half sisters, all of us were ruined. Our agent, Mr. Lassman, had gambled the firm's fortunes on which our entire income depended; the business had collapsed with debts of a million pounds. Whatever money I had with me I must use to return home at once for she was unable even to send my fare. I must not borrow from the von Langens for she could never repay them. We must leave our house, Offendene, immediately. A Mr. Haynes would take over its rental. We had nowhere to go; we should have to live in "some hut or other." There was no money to pay tradesmen or servants. The calamity affected my uncle (Mama's brother-in-law, Henry Gascoigne), and his family too. My four half sisters were in tears; they and Mama would have to sew or mend for a pittance wage; I must find work as a governess.

I read the letter twice. I was annoyed and unconvinced by it. I was used to Mama's laments and exaggerations and unwilling to jump to her anxious command. I had never known Mama to be happy. I feared contagion from her gloominess. My uncertain plan had been to return home at the end of September, but even before this letter I was afraid to do so. On impulse I had fled the muddle and shame that beset me there: the rich man determined to marry me, whose proposal I had almost accepted, not because I loved him or knew what love was before I met you, but to provide for Mama and be exalted in Society. And then his concubine, "the snake woman," who lay in wait for me, told me he should marry no one but her; that she had left her husband for him, and their son should be his heir.

SO MUCH HAD happened so quickly; I was in a maelstrom of temptation and fear. And now it seemed penury and homelessness threatened too. I did not know what to think or do, or where to turn. I was aggrieved by Mama's letter, aggrieved by you. Had my luck at roulette stayed unbroken, I might have won enough to pay for everything: my return home, the rent on the house, the servants' wages. But even as I read of this latest disaster, I suspected it was not money I gambled for.

I pondered whether to leave for home immediately or go to the Kursaal, win to counter my misfortune, and perhaps again see you. I decided to pawn my turquoise chain. The pawnbroker at least might give me enough to pay for an afternoon at the tables and my fare home. The chain had no sentimental attachment. It had belonged to my father, of whom I had no memory. He was killed when I was a year old, thrown from his horse as it jumped a brook.

I was impatient for morning and for the pawn shop to open. I did not go to bed. A cold bath revived me. I was traveling without a maid, so I packed my own case and put on my gray traveling dress. I pondered my reflection in the long mirror between the two windows in my room. Despite this deluge of disaster, I felt I was charmed. My happiness and good fortune must prevail.

BEFORE MY HOSTS came to breakfast I stole out unobserved to Mr. Weiner, the little Jew pawnbroker in the Oberstrasse. The morning air of late summer was sweet with roses and lavender. On my way I passed the Hotel Czarina. No one was about. As I went into the shop I thought if anyone sees me they will think I am going to buy some jewel or bauble as a gift. The chain was pretty but frivolous, and I felt no remorse at parting with it, only annoyance that the greedy little Jew priced it at a mere four louis.

Within half an hour I was back at the von Langens' apartment. My hosts were still not up, so I waited in the salon. I intended merely to tell them Mama wished me to return home and to make no mention or revelation of trouble. And now that I had eight louis, I so wanted to gamble again. I was wondering how much I could risk yet still have enough for my fare, when a servant brought in a packet, addressed to me, which had just been delivered to the door.

I took it to my room. It was the necklace I had pawned less than an hour before, wrapped in a linen handkerchief from which the initials were torn. Enclosed on a scrap of paper was a scrawled penciled note in capital letters: A STRANGER WHO HAS FOUND MISS HARLETH'S NECKLACE

RETURNS IT TO HER WITH THE HOPE THAT SHE WILL NOT
AGAIN RISK THE LOSS OF IT.

SO IT BEGAN. You as my conscience. I knew it was your
doing. Rebuked once more, chastised by your view of how
I ought not behave. It was as if you sought proof of my
transgressive ways. What did you mean you had *found* the
necklace? You must have watched me from a window in
the Czarina, seen me enter and leave the pawnbroker, waited
until I was out of sight, then hurried to quiz him. Why
did you wait? What did you know of my reason for going
to his shop in the early morning? I had shown no particular distress. I might have been buying presents for my half
sisters. And why the ripped handkerchief and halfhearted
anonymity of the necklace's return? I was angry. Who was
I to you that you should be so personal? What right had
you to shadow me and pry into my affairs?

I had said very little to Weiner. He assumed all valu-
ables brought to his door were because of bad luck in the
Kursaal. Perhaps you told him you were my guardian.
But you knew nothing of me; we had not even spoken.
You knew nothing of the letter from my mother. It was
my necklace to dispose of as I wished. I might have been
instructed to pawn it. Why did you assume it was of any
importance to me? Why your assumption that I had an
obligation to keep it? You knew nothing of its provenance.
You bought it back for what was to you small change.

In my room I wept from tiredness, anger, frustration, confusion. So many damning things had already happened. I needed to believe in my own worth. Yet behind my anger I dared feel flattered, dared hope your concern was an invitation to intimacy and that you were as drawn to me as I to you. Your intrusion wounded my pride, but when you wrote of your hope of my not again risking the necklace's loss, perhaps you were offering to save me from future risk and keep me safe. I packed the necklace wrapped in your note and handkerchief and my own confusion. Your words were a reproach, like your critical gaze as I gambled. But my youthful hope was not immoderate. You were young, handsome, seemingly unattached. In the cool of early morning why should you leave your hotel, track the path of a beautiful girl to a shop, ask about her transaction there, try to put right her suspected hardship, find the address of her lodgings . . . ? Why should you bother to do all that unless you were smitten.

I had no choice but to leave Homburg immediately. I could not risk seeing you again in the Kursaal or the street. A servant called me to breakfast. I dried my eyes and joined the von Langens. "Mama has written," I told them. "She urgently needs my help and has summoned me to return home at once."

My hosts protested at my traveling alone. I assured them I would travel in the ladies' compartment, rest on the train, and be safe. They took me in their carriage to Homburg station, instructed the porters, and waved me farewell. I arrived at Offendene on the following Saturday morning.

Offendene—set amid tranquil pastures and the leafy lanes of Pennicote village. It is the only house I have ever viewed as home. We had lived there scarcely a year when news of this financial calamity came.

Mama, my half sisters—Alice, Bertha, Fanny, and Isabel—and Miss Merry, the housekeeper, all were grouped on the porch when I stepped down from my carriage. "Well, dear, what will become of us?" was Mama's bleak greeting. I observed her faded beauty and shabby black dress. Her despondency cut me. My sisters looked at me with subdued concern. I was the eldest. I was responsible. Before my luggage was lifted down, I resolved to safeguard the roof over all their heads.

PERSEVERE WITH MY story, and you will learn how a welter of humiliation led me to sell my soul to achieve this. I did what I knew to be wrong, then paid heavily as the wheel of my misfortune kept spinning.

THE HOUSE, A sprawling redbrick mansion, was serene: the smell of applewood fires in the hearths, the flickering shadows of candlelight. Oil paintings hung above the staircase that led from the large stone hallway: a huntsman on a bay surrounded by hounds, a poacher, and a gamekeeper; sheep and goats in a barn; girls on a riverbank. The dining room's oak paneling smelled of beeswax; the rosewood chairs were covered with worn red satin. Over the mantelpiece dogs snarled at each other in two dark paintings, and Christ worked his wonders with loaves and fishes. The wainscot carved with garlands in the drawing room, the organ built by Henry Willis, all the familiar detail seemed impervious to bad news.

WE HAD NOT seen Offendene before we moved in. Uncle Henry—the Reverend Gascoigne—arranged matters for us after Captain Davilow, my stepfather, died. On moving day Mama and my sisters gathered on the porch and looked questioningly at me. "Well, dear, what do you think of the place?" Mama asked, and I made my rapid and abiding judgment: "I think it charming, a romantic place; anything delightful may happen in it; no one need be ashamed of living here; it would be a good background for anything." Offendene gave ample room for me, Mama, my half sisters, Mrs. Startin (their governess), Miss Merry, and Jocasta Bugle (the maid). Though the house lacked the splendor Mama thought my due, I truly believed we might be happy in it and that I might shut out the apprehension that the dark comes however bright the day. I have always been afraid to hear about the indifference of the universe, my own insignificance, the casual inevitability of death, and the caprice of chance. Even at school I trembled when astronomy was taught.

On the day we moved in I found that under Offendene's protective roof was hidden a prescient warning. I and my sisters excitedly explored the house. In the drawing room Isabel tapped a hinged panel in the wainscot. A painted image of a dead upturned face sprang out, with a panicked figure fleeing from it. The effect on me was extreme. I froze with fear and trembled but could not scream. Mama and Miss Merry wrapped me in a blanket. When revived, I shouted at Isabel, "How dare you open things that were meant to be shut." I ordered Miss Merry to fetch the key, lock the panel, and give the key to me. No one, I instructed, was ever, ever to open it again. The device, we later learned, was a practical joke by the Earl of Cork, who first owned the house. The eccentric earl wore knee breeches and costumes of his own invention. Another of his jokes, long removed, was a suit of armor that drew a sword when a key was turned.

Mama tried to shield me from the terror within me and assuage my fear of the dark and of being alone. I tried to assuage her loneliness and disappointment. She looked to me for comfort when my stepfather was often away. At Offendene I did not want a room of my own; Mama and I shared the large bedroom, decorated black and yellow with a view of the garden. My small white bed was made up beside hers.

On the night I returned from Homburg, in bed and overtired, behind my closed eyes I again saw Mama in her shabby clothes and heard her supplicating words, "Well, dear, what will become of us?" and then came a hallucinatory image of the dead face in the wainscot and the figure in flight. I cried out. Mama lit a candle, I crawled in with her, she called me her darling, and I slept with her arms around me. To others I seemed beautiful, daring, and rash. To her I was a child.

IF ONLY WE could have stayed at Offendene a few years before misfortune struck! There was society enough to make life pleasant. Mama accompanied me to parties and dinners: the Arrowpoints at Quetcham Hall; our landlords, Lord and Lady Brackenshaw, at Brackenshaw Castle; Mr. Quallon, the banker, at the Firs. Sometimes in summer Mama, my sisters, and I, along with my cousins Rex and Anna, picnicked on the grounds of Diplow Hall. Though the house, owned by Sir Hugo Mallinger, for most of the year was unoccupied and shuttered, its acres of secluded grounds, forested with elms and beeches, were open. Deer grazed on the grassland. We spread ourselves under the trees or by the lilied pool.

I was petulant and hard to please. I viewed myself as superior to provincial Society, voiced discontent with what was around me, and expressed little gratitude for such good fortune as I had. Though unable to define what I wanted or was capable of achieving, I could not view the Archery Club, dances at Brackenshaw Castle, and dinner with the Arrowpoints as the zenith of my ambition. Being so much admired and so often told I was beautiful set me apart. I liked to be the center of attention, in control, and to have the last word. I came to see my beauty as a kind of genius, an accomplishment of my own doing. It was like a magnet. In hotels waiters fawned, smoothed my napkin, brushed crumbs from the cloth in front of me. If the laundress ironed a crease into a sleeve, the maid would say, "This will never do for Miss Harleth." If the wood smoked in the bedroom fireplace, though Mama's eyes watered, she apologized to me. If, after a long and tiring journey, I was last at the breakfast table, the main concern would be, Was Gwendolen's coffee hot, was Gwendolen's toast crisp? "Gwendolen will not rest without having the world at her feet," Miss Merry said. And it was true. Forgive me. I was young.

I did not hide my exasperation with my half sisters. I assured them they were lesser creatures—deserving of their back to the highway in the carriage, entitled only to the smaller piece of cake.

I was incredulous that you, though you saw my charm, resisted it and even criticized me.

ON OUR SECOND day at Offendene, as I brushed my hair in front of the tall mirror in our bedroom, Mama said, "Gwendolen, dear, if you had a wreath of white roses in

your hair, you'd pass as Saint Cecilia." (Mama, I have to
tell you, thought my singing voice divine.)

"Except for my nose," I joked. "Saints' noses never in
the least turn up. I wish you had given me your perfectly
straight nose. It would have done for any sort of character—
a nose of all work. Mine is only a happy nose. It would not
do for tragedy."

"Oh, my dear, any nose will do to be miserable with in
this world," Mama replied. It was typical of her to imbue
a jest with gloom. I wanted her to be enthusiastic. I believed
her melancholy made gloomy things happen. It was as if
all my hope and joy could never counterbalance her pes-
simism, and yet she looked for and found her happiness
through me.

I told Mama her dullness made me feel nothing was of
use. Was it marriage, I asked, that left her disaffected? "You
must have been more beautiful than I when you were young."
She protested at this, of course, and in my secret heart I
doubted it. "Marriage is the only happy state for a woman,
as I trust you will prove," she said, and although I did not
want that to be the case, I supposed it had to be true.

"I would not put up with it if it was not a happy state,"
I said, then told her I was not going to muddle away my life
in service to a man and do nothing remarkable for myself.

I did not want to believe in the imperative of marriage.
It held no appeal. I knew little about men beyond what I
had read in books. I grew up with women. Mama's marriages had sapped her wealth and twice left her widowed

then penniless. Family life I viewed as curtailing and petty. I had no wish for children, I found them irritating. Yet I supposed I *would* marry—someone of distinction and rank—I neither doubted it nor dwelled on it. I was resolved, though, that I was not going to let a man have power over me; lovemaking appalled me; when propositioned, I felt obliged to tease. I felt no attraction to any man until I met you. Marriage was not the focus of my ambition. I wanted fame but thought no further than that my life should be pleasant, that I should star at parties, be victorious at the Archery Club, applauded at the piano, and admired on horseback.

I read novels, poems, and plays, had views on Mr. Rochester in *Jane Eyre*, Becky Sharp in *Vanity Fair*, the silliness of Lydia in *Pride and Prejudice*, the awfulness of Casaubon in *Middlemarch*, the piety of Eva in *Uncle Tom's Cabin*. I was praised for my soprano voice, the skill with which I played the piano, my graceful dancing. I could read music. I spoke passable French. But my power, my gift, was to be the most captivating person in the room. My wit sparkled.

HOW PUNISHED I was for such hubris. But through the torment I endured, I did not fall victim to Mama's dulled acceptance of misfortune. Beyond my suffering I kept alive a longing for a life that was free and a love that linked me to your wisdom; or was it to your kind dark eyes and beautiful voice?

Mama and I do not quarrel. Our love is deep. She is magnanimous, as was her mother, I believe. I was her favored child, her princess, best friend, and source of pride. She coiled my hair, fastened my dresses, advised me which gloves and what jewelry to wear. She would do anything for me, make any sacrifice, and readily forgive me any misdemeanor. In her eyes I never truly could do wrong.

But I was rash, impulsive, consumed by my emotion of the moment, and at times cruel. I recall with shame a cold night when in our beds Mama felt unwell but had forgotten to take her medicine. She asked me to fetch it. I was warm and sleepy, and I refused. "She would have done that for you whatever the discomfort, whatever the cost" was the rebuke that went through my head as I heard her stumble to the cabinet.

I was short-tempered with my sisters too. Remembered incidents of wrongdoing added to a sense that I deserved my punishment when it came . . . One afternoon while I was playing Chopin's "Minute Waltz," Alice's canary kept up a shrill whistle, which I found intolerable. It was as if the wretched creature mocked me. I exploded in temper and crushed it in my fist. I killed it. Alice wept. I was shocked at myself. That I could so lose control and be provoked into rage and violence. *I am capable of murder,* I thought. To compensate, I bought her a white mouse, but she said she hated mice and was scared of them. I think she became afraid of me and what I might do next, and it was true I was unpredictable. To myself most of all.

———

THE DEATH OF Captain Davilow, my stepfather, accorded
me no grief. I always hated him to come home. His attention to me was leery and unwanted. I tried never to be alone
in a room with him. I could not admit my aversion to
Mama. To do so would have destroyed her fragile world.
But I came to resent my four half sisters and the life Mama's
marriage to him compelled me to live. He squandered her
money and stole her jewelry and sold it.

I think of your childhood, Deronda. Sir Hugo told me
of it: how you grew up knowing nothing about your parents or even your true name. How you thought Sir Hugo
was your father and on the one occasion when you met your
mother she told you she could not love you.

We were both outsiders, you and I. More united by
uncertainty than ever you allowed. But you plucked cer-
tainties for yourself from the fictions of the past: a prescrip-
tive, demanding religion, a directional quest, a constant
wife, whereas I . . . I blew with the wind and hoped to arrive
at a perfect destination.

Davilow inflicted a bewildering lifestyle on us. We
moved from hired Paris apartments to hired villas in Lau-
sanne, Baden, Amsterdam. We stayed nowhere long enough
to settle, make friends, or feel part of any place. It was a
lifestyle that made me restless, rootless. Mama gave birth
to Davilow's tedious daughters: Alice, to whom I was asked
to give lessons, was slow, pulled silly faces, and had no ear

for music or languages. Bertha was always sketching flowers and leaves but covered the sketches if I asked to see them. She and Fanny whispered and giggled a great deal. Isabel was clumsy. That was how I viewed them then.

Davilow disappeared for weeks at a time without saying where he was. I do not know if Mama ever asked. I was her anchor, her link to my father, the eldest daughter, the one apart, the one in charge. I was contrary and demanding, but looking back to the days before the calamity of our loss of money, the impending loss of Offendene, my terrible marriage, I believe what formed my character, shaped my courage, was the haven of Mama's love for me. She protected me from my fears: of the dark, of loss of control, of failure, or of someone bending my brittle will to theirs.

I knew almost as little about my forebears as you of yours. Mama's father had owned sugar plantations in Trinidad, so when the American Civil War began I think she was ashamed of her family's links to the Confederates and slavery. My father's family, apparently titled, cultured, and certain of themselves, viewed Mama as inferior and an unsatisfactory wife for one of their kind. When I was twelve Mama showed me a miniature of my father, a colored portrait in a silver frame. I saw little beyond eyes shaped like mine, but I offended her by asking, "Why did you marry again, Mama? It would have been better if you had not." She blushed and said I had no feeling.

I had not then learned what she perhaps knew: that it is not only love that binds people in wedlock. Circumstance,

sudden impulse, misguided optimism, and fear of loneliness and penury shape our decision making and our lives
and, when we are unlucky, herald our despair.

I did not want to be shaped by Mama's melancholy, but
I was. I think her marriage to Davilow began as a social and
economic necessity, then became an endurance about which
it was difficult for her to speak. I think her melancholy
grew in the gap between the reality of life with him and
the love she knew she could feel and had felt for my father.

THAT SPACE BETWEEN you and me, across the tables in the
ornate salon of the Kursaal, I see and feel it now. How I
longed to bridge it. As my passion for you grew, I became
acquainted with the ache that life without you brought.

From the start you resisted your attraction to me. I
appeared to you spoiled and impulsive. You looked for the
madonna, an unswerving virtue of a sort I lacked, a purity
of heart. You sensed your mother in me: your beautiful,
ambitious, unavailable mother; the wicked princess who
turned you from her throne. But I was not like that. I was
not like that. And why did you focus on me and encourage
me toward you only to reject me? You chose Mirah Lapidoth, compliant, dependent. She was the better singer and
had the sweeter nature, but—and I only dare write this
because I will never say it to you—she was the lesser woman.

———

AFTER CAPTAIN DAVILOW died, leaving Mama penniless, she, my sisters, and I managed on what Uncle Henry gave us. How I resented living under his obligation! He was excessively clear about his own importance and had strong views that he stated as facts. He sat at the head of the table, said grace as if privy to the ear of God, and his word was law. His tedious sermons made no sense to me. In his church my mind drifted, and I heard only the authority in his voice. Before taking holy orders he had been an army captain. His own expenses were great, as he was ever at pains to remind us: six sons whose education much stretched him to finance, two daughters for whom husbands must be found. The rectory came rent free, but he was obliged to entertain with formal dinners and to pay the groom, gardener, and cook.

Mama, to him and my aunt, was "poor dear Fanny," victim of not one but two unfortunate marriages. My aunt looked like Mama and was concerned for her, but her own contentment and security made her behave as if she was superior: a condescending manner accompanied her comfort and good fortune.

Uncle weighed the worth in money of my beauty. He was intent for me to be seen to advantage in Society, so that I should marry well. His thinking was that then the burden of caring for Mama and her brood would shift to my husband. He was paternal toward me, felt that as a child I had missed out on family life, and at heart found it hard to resist me. He encouraged friendship between me and his elder daughter, Anna. She was tiny, admiring of me, less aggravating and rambunctious than my half sisters, and I liked her well enough but could not view her as an equal.

Uncle frequently reminded Mama of his cleverness at finding Offendene for us, how the house was more than she might expect for the low rent she paid, its running costs no greater than an ordinary house, and how the landlord, his friend Lord Brackenshaw of Brackenshaw Castle—Uncle cultivated influential friends—owned the Brackenshaw Archery Club as well as much of Wessex.

I loathed the way I had to weasel and cajole Uncle for anything I wanted. I loved riding. There was nothing I liked more than to gallop across fields or ride with the hunt, and I very much wanted a saddle horse of my own. I put it to him, but he balked at the expense. I persisted, and when he next called for tea with my aunt and Anna, I flattered him, played the piano to his liking, induced him to join me in a duet, then urged Mama to speak up for me. "Gwendolen desires above all things to have a horse to ride—a pretty, light, lady's horse," Mama said. "Do you think we can manage it?"

Aunt looked disapproving and suggested I borrow Anna's Shetland pony. I protested I could not endure ponies and was willing to give up all other indulgence if I might have a horse. Uncle lamented the expense of his carriage horses, how a horse for me would cost a good sixty pounds, and then there was its keep, and how he only afforded a pony for Anna. As ever, he reminded Mama of the cost to him of her and her fatherless brood.

My pride wilted as Mama demeaned herself and said she wore nothing but two black dresses. I winced to hear her tell Uncle how I was prepared to tutor my sisters when Mrs. Startin left. It was as if she was begging. I wanted Mama to have diamonds, furs, whatever she wanted and not need to ask anything of anyone. Aunt went on about how Anna rode only the wretched donkey and how no horse was afforded her. But Uncle's indulgence was calculating: if I was to acquire an expensive husband—an aristocrat and landowner, with a fortune to benefit them all—a degree of finery and show was essential. "Gwendolen has," he said, "the figure for a horse."

I got my horse. I called her Twilight. Anna, content with her pony, did not begrudge me. And before long Uncle saw his worldly ambitions for me realized.

Apparently, on their way home Aunt rebuked Uncle for his indulgence toward me, but he spoke again of his duty to help me "make a first-rate marriage to a man more than equal to himself." Aunt feared one of her boys, Rex or Warham, might fall in love with me, but Uncle assured her that would not occur. First cousins, he said, must not fall in love. If it happened, marriage would not be allowed and, more to the point, the boy would have nothing. "At worst," he said, "there would only be a little crying. You can't save boys and girls from that." And crying there was, for Rex did fall in love with me, though not I with him. My crying was for you, Deronda. No one saved me from that.

Such were life's problems even before the catastrophe.

It is hard to be proud when you have no money and are dependent on a pompous uncle. I had little freedom to do as I chose, nor did I know how or what to seek. I strongly felt the confinement of home, and I dreamed of breaking free, of being more than the chattel of my uncle or the elusive ambition of Mama. I wanted my own achievement, my own expression, but what did I have beyond my beauty and high spirits? Yes, I got my horse, but what I longed for were the wild plains where the horse might take me.

HERR KLESMER. LOOKING back, I realize the chain of my humiliation began with him. He was famed as a composer, pianist, and teacher. I met him at Quetcham Hall, in our first spring at Pennicote, at a dinner party given by the Arrowpoints. They had hired him as music tutor to their clever, gifted daughter, Catherine, who played the piano, violin, and harp. Mrs. Arrowpoint declared him a genius, and he looked the part, with his large head, long brown hair, flowing cape, gold spectacles, and flamboyant gestures. I did not at first know he was a Jew like you. I had never before met a Jew socially. I did not know Jews could be geniuses. I thought they were all moneylenders and pawnbrokers.

Mrs. Arrowpoint had written extensively on the sixteenth-century Italian poet Torquato Tasso. She had a voice like a parrot, wore startling headdresses, and was provoked by my beauty and its effect on men. I have often observed that unappealing women resent me. I told her, at this party, how I adored Tasso and that I too would like to be an authoress. She offered to loan me her unpublished manuscript, in which, she said, she corrected popular misconceptions about his insanity, explained his complex feelings for Duke Alfonso's sister Leonora, and gave the real reasons for his imprisonment. Such was the lure of creative excitement in the district of Wancester.

After dinner Klesmer and Catherine played a four-handed piece on two pianos. It was a more accomplished performance than I could ever aspire to, but it was very long. Mr. Arrowpoint then asked me to sing and led me to the piano. Klesmer stood a few feet away and smiled at me. I had no nervousness. Mama told me my voice was like Jenny Lind's, and I believed this to be so. I sang the aria "Casta Diva" from Bellini's *Norma*.

> *Ah! bello a me ritorna.*
> *Ah, riedi a me.*
> Ah return to me my beautiful
> Ah, come back to me.

Jenny Lind, though ordinary and uneducated, succeeded in the world as I hoped to do.

Klesmer stared at me as I sang. I was aware of his gaze. It seemed to bore into me, a prelude to yours at the Kursaal. "Ah, riedi a me," I sang. There was such applause. "Bravo!" Mr. Arrowpoint shouted with tears in his eyes.

"Bravo, encore, encore!" Herr Klesmer stood mute. I prepared to sing again but first said to him, expecting contradiction, "It would be too cruel, don't you think, Herr Klesmer? You cannot like to hear poor amateur singing."

In his German accent he replied, "That does not matter. It is always acceptable to *see* you sing." The insult took away my breath. I felt myself blush with anger. Why did he need to say that? I had been asked to sing. It was a dinner party. The guests were thrilled by me, far more so than by his virtuosity. His was the first in a series of blows that tore at my pride and culminated, months later, in your return to me of my turquoise necklace.

Catherine Arrowpoint compounded my humiliation by commiserating: "See what I have to go through with this professor," she said. "He can hardly tolerate anything we English do in music. He tells us the worst that can be said of us. It is only bearable because everyone else is so admiring."

I tried to regain my poise, said I supposed I had been ill-taught and had no talent, and would be obliged to Herr Klesmer were he to tell me the worst.

"Yes, it is true you have not been well taught," he said to me and all who wished to hear. "Still you are not quite without gifts. You sing in tune and have a pretty fair voice." He told me I produced my notes badly and the music I sang was "dawdly canting seesaw kind of stuff. Music for people with no breadth of vision. It makes men small as they listen to it. Sing something larger and I shall see."

So much for Bellini and so much for me. Klesmer was God, I the unworthy earthling, trapped by superficiality. "Oh, not now," I said. "By and by."

"Yes, by and by," Catherine Arrowpoint agreed, then joked it always took her half an hour to recover from the maestro's criticism. After such pretense of allegiance with me, she invited him to play, "to show us what good music truly is." Which he did. A composition of his own called "Freudvoll Leidvoll Gedankenvoll." And I am sure his talent was huge, so much more huge than his manners. I tried not to cry.

Clintock, the archdeacon's son, came up to me and asked what *Freudvoll* meant, but I did not know. He said he wished I would sing again, for though he could listen to me all night he got nowhere with this sort of tip-top playing. I told him if he wanted to hear me sing, he was in a puerile state of culture, for I had just learned how bad my taste was, which gave me growing pains. He smiled politely and asked how I liked the neighborhood. I replied I liked it exceedingly, for it had a little of everything, and not much of anything, and most people in it were an utter bore.

Clintock then talked of croquet and told me it was the game of the future. I hear my voice now as I cut him down: "I shall study croquet tomorrow. I shall take to it instead of singing."

That was how stung I was. I viewed myself as superior to Wancester Society, yet I was judged by it and found wanting. You might have rescued me and shown me a path. But all this was before I met you.

Clintock informed me of a friend of his who had written a poem in four cantos about croquet that was as good as anything by Alexander Pope. He offered to send me a manuscript copy. I said he must first promise not to test me on it, or ask which part I liked best, "because it is not so easy to know a poem without reading it, as to know a sermon without listening."

He did not care to find barb or insult in my remark, he was staring at my breasts and legs, but Mrs. Arrowpoint overheard, made a judgment, and did not share her Tasso with me.

CATHERINE ARROWPOINT, PITIFUL of the smallness of my talent yet assured of Klesmer's regard for hers, continued to invite me to dinners and soirées, but I could not see her again without a wave of jealousy and self-doubt, though her looks were unremarkable, her complexion was sallow, and her features were small. She was an heiress with unshaken confidence in her own talent, secure enough to disregard her plainness as an irrelevance, whereas I who was poor had only my looks and my dreams.

After that evening at the Arrowpoints, though at Brackenshaw Castle, the Firs, and Quetcham Hall my singing had hitherto given such pleasure, I vowed never again to sing before an audience; I was as obstinate as I was offended. My admirers viewed me as exceptional. I was determined my detractors should see that too. I was not going to condemn myself to giving lessons to Alice like an impoverished governess or to help in the village school with Anna. If I could not be a singer, I would have a stage career. Mama told me I was more beautiful and alluring than the actress Rachel had been in *Phèdre.*

CHRISTMAS EVE BROUGHT my next humiliation. To show my theatrical talent, I decided to stage a *tableau vivant* from *A Winter's Tale* before invited neighbors in the drawing room at Offendene. My intention was to let Herr Klesmer know that though my musical gifts might be unequal to Catherine Arrowpoint's, my acting skills were another matter. I was director and principal player—Hermione, the beautiful, virtuous, vilified queen, shut away from the world for sixteen years. My cousin Rex, home for the holidays from his law studies, was King Leontes, my husband crazed with jealousy. Mama, in a white burnous, was my friend Paulina. Anna, Miss Merry, and Mr. Middleton—Uncle's assistant clergyman, who had pale whiskers, wore buttoned-up clothes, and seldom laughed—were to have small parts. George Jarrett, the village carpenter, built the stage.

The charade's climax was the miraculous animation when I, the statue, came to life and Leontes kneeled to kiss the hem of my dress.

Herr Klesmer was to strike the chord of animation. He sat at the piano. I stood immobile, elevated on a sort of plinth. Leontes gave permission for Paulina to make the statue speak and move. "Music awake her, strike!" Mama declared. Klesmer crashed the piano keys. As he did so, the panel in the wainscot opposite the stage flew open. There again, illumined by candlelight, was the dead face and fleeing figure. I screamed, collapsed to my knees, and covered my face. Mama and Rex rushed to help me from the room.

The perplexed guests conjectured whether or not the scene was intended and wondered about the provenance of the panel. I was mortified. I forced myself to reappear quickly as if nothing was amiss. "We have to thank you for devising a perfect climax," Klesmer said, and I flushed with relief and embarrassment and half took him to mean he recognized my acting talent. Later I learned he and everyone else concluded it was an unplanned mishap. His newfound tact was prompted by pity. As witness to my frailty, not my talent, he chose to spare me further mortification. Rex, who already loved me, saw proof of my sensibility and loved me the more. Other guests let the matter drop.

I did not understand my eruptions of madness, and I was disturbed that the helpless fear which beset me in private could show itself in such a public way. Apparently Isabel, curious about the image that caused me acute distress, had taken the key and unlocked the panel. She trembled as she asked my forgiveness, which I granted out of a wish not to mention any of it ever again.

In sport I was reckless in the face of danger, but the terror in my heart I could neither contain nor understand: of the dark, of being alone in confined spaces, of abandonment and death, of any sort of lovemaking. Mama called it my sensitiveness, but it was something else, a spiritual dread, a sense of isolation, a fear of being consumed or of loss of control. None of Uncle's exhortations in church helped me. I came to think you might reconcile me to this inner darkness and guide me to a place of peace with myself. "Safeguard your fear," you were to say to me. Down the years I have so often said that to myself: "Safeguard your fear, Gwendolen. Safeguard your fear." I might have managed that with your arms around me.

REX WAS ONE of the men I spurned. Oh, and poor Mr. Middleton. And poor Mr. Clintock. Rex and Anna were devoted siblings. He was the light of her life, her guide and mentor. I liked his company and found him handsome and clever. The three of us would sing and play the piano, go riding, walking, and on picnics.

Anna observed his love for me and rightly feared I would reject him. The simplicity of his devotion made me cruel. Though I loved him as if he was my brother, I could not return his passion. He was so upright, so defined by Pennicote: the dutiful son, loyal to his family, ambitious to serve as a lawyer, respectful of polite Society. Anyway Uncle would never have countenanced our marrying—young as we were, first cousins, and without money.

Rex loved my frailty, strength, and beauty. He laughed at my jokes and respected my moods. Had we married, he would have been my attentive husband and wise, judicious friend. He would have encouraged my ambition, adored our children, provided a smart house and secure income. He was so opposite to Mama's feckless husbands. But his virtues were a problem to me.

I recall with shame the morning I inveigled him to ride with the hounds. I chose to ride despite forbiddance from Uncle and dissuasion from Mama, who was conscious of how my father had died in a riding accident. Uncle said no lady rode with the hounds except Mrs. Gadsby, who until she married the yeomanry captain had been a kitchen maid and still spoke like one. I scorned their concerns and lightly disobeyed. Lord Brackenshaw, who owned the hunt, had invited me. (His pink coat was always stained, and from his appearance it was hard to believe him a man of fabulous wealth.)

His daughters, Beatrix and Maria, were to ride with him, so I urged Rex to ride with me. Uncle was away. Rex reluctantly agreed and, without asking, took the old horse Primrose. It was a beautiful January morning, the branches of the elm trees were bare, the air was fresh, and the hedges were sprinkled with red berries. As we trotted along, Rex asked what I hoped to do in my life. I feared a forthcoming hint at marriage. I was amused by his adoration but alarmed lest he, or anyone else, might overtly make love to me. I did not want to hear the words or sense a desire to embrace me. The idea made me shrink. I told him I should like to go to the North Pole, compete in steeplechases, dress like a man, and be queen of the East like Hester Stanhope.

"You don't mean you'd never be married?" Rex asked. I said if I married, I should not do as other women did, nor be like them. He then made some silly speech about a man who loved me more dearly than anything else in the world and would let me do just as I liked. I asked if he meant Mr. Middleton, then cantered away after the hounds.

I soon was far ahead. Primrose, stiff and slow, was not a hunting horse, and Rex struggled to catch up. In the effort Primrose caught her hoof in a hole, fell, broke her knees, and threw Rex over her head. He was stunned, his shoulder dislocated. Joel Dagge, the blacksmith's son, found him lying alone on Mill Lane, wrenched his shoulder back into its socket, and helped him home.

I knew nothing of all this. I supposed Rex to have given up and gone home. I enjoyed the chase and thought no more of him. All those taking part commended my spirited riding. At the end of a triumphant day, escorted by Lord Brackenshaw, I rode home with the fox's tail fastened to my saddle.

At the rectory Uncle chastised Rex for taking Primrose without asking, using her as a hunter, and allowing me to ride with the hounds. He ordered him to leave Pennicote the next day, spend the rest of his vacation in Southampton, then go back to Cambridge.

Rex cried and said he could not leave without first telling me he loved me. Uncle told him it was impossible: he was too young, first cousins should not marry, and I must ally myself to rank and wealth. Rex, he said, would soon recover; life was full of such brief disappointments. Uncle sent Rex to his room and told him they would talk again in the morning.

He then came to Offendene to tell Mama and me of Rex's fall. Rex had suffered no great damage, so I could not care about it. I thought the incident absurd: I had a picture of Rex, ridiculous on Primrose, stumbling in the lane, his cheeks puffed and red. Uncle saw I was not the least in love, but he forbade me to hunt again. "When you are married, it will be different," he said. "You may do whatever your husband sanctions. But if you intend to hunt, you must marry a man who can keep horses."

I made some pert retort and left the room. The exchange wiped away my elation of the morning. I abhorred the idea of the wife as a chattel. I intended to hunt without a husband's sanction. The previous evening I had told Mama men were too ridiculous and I could never fall in love. Of the men who wooed me, Rex was an adoring boy, Clintock wrote risible poems about croquet, and Middleton, the assistant clergyman, had watery blue eyes, pale whiskers, and yellow teeth.

Uncle, satisfied by my lack of concern, gave Rex permission to walk over and see me the next day.

Offendene was two miles from the rectory. Rex, his arm in a sling, arrived in the early morning. I, tired from the previous day, was not yet down from my room.

He waited in the drawing room. I did not want to see him. I suspected he intended to inflict embarrassment on me. I wore a black silk dress and a black band in my hair. I stood by the fire, viewed him coldly, then said formally, "I hope you are not much hurt, Rex. I deserve that you should reproach me for your accident." He responded with some gracious remark about the small price of paying for the pleasure of my company with a tumble.

He talked about going to Southampton, said it was an empty place without me, and that all the happiness of his life depended on my loving him more than anyone else. I loathed such drivel. It felt like an invasion. He tried to take my hand, and I backed away. "Pray don't make love to me," I scolded. "I hate it." He went pale, and his mortification compounded my contempt. I glared. He was twenty like me. "Is that the last word you have to say to me, Gwendolen?" he asked. "Will it always be so?"

I observed his wretchedness, felt anger toward him for subjecting me and himself to this, and regret for the companionship I knew we now would lose. "About making love? Yes," I said. "But I don't dislike you for anything else." I resented being forced to say such things.

He looked entirely crushed. There was a pause. He said

good-bye and left the room. I heard the hall door bang
behind him.

The whole scene had been intolerable. I sat on the couch
by the fire and sobbed. Mama came in, circled her arms
around me, pressed her cheek against my head, and tried
to tilt my chin to see my face. I crumpled in her arms. "Oh,
Mama, what can become of my life?" I sobbed. "There's
nothing worth living for. I shall never love anybody. I can't
love people. I hate them."

"The time will come, dear, the time will come," Mama
said. I put my arms around her neck, clung to her, and said,
"I can't bear anyone but you to be very near me."

And it was true. It was as if a key was needed to unlock
my heart and turn me from a child into a woman so that
I might love someone else besides Mama. That key I came
to believe was held by you.

Of course Aunt and Anna blamed me for Rex's distress.
It must ever be the woman's fault. Anna remained courteous but became wary and distant. My aunt believed if Rex
adored me I must have behaved like a coquette and led him
on. She thought Mama spoiled me. But if I could not say
yes to Rex, what could I say but no.

Rex became depressed and unreasonable and announced
a wild plan to give up studying law, go to Canada as a for-
ester, and live as a peasant in a hut. Anna vowed to go with
him to cook and mend his clothes. She said it would be an
escape from crinolines, feathered hats, gloves, and after-
dinner small talk. Uncle allowed Rex a term out from

Cambridge, forbade any further mention of his feelings for me and "the whole business," and said the less it was mentioned the sooner it would blow over.

TIME PASSED. THERE was the Italian question, the Polish question, the Schleswig-Holstein question. Gladstone resigned as prime minister, in Chipping Norton rioters tried to free the sixteen women known as the Ascott Martyrs, and in London Alexandra Palace was destroyed by fire only a fortnight after opening. But Wancester was peaceful and unchanging. Horse dealers and saddlers plied their trade. Farmers sold their hay. The most exciting news in Pennicote was that Sir Hugo Mallinger's nephew, Henleigh Mallinger Grandcourt, was to visit and stay at Diplow Hall for the hunting season.

We had heard rumor of Sir Hugo's dislike of this nephew; how poor Lady Mallinger was afflicted with a sense of failure for having borne four daughters and no son to inherit the Mallinger estates; how this Henleigh Grandcourt, already rich beyond the dreams of most, stood to inherit, because of the law of primogeniture, Topping Abbey, Ryelands, Diplow, and the rest.

There was much anticipation about the arrival in Pennicote of such a wealthy bachelor. He was thirty-six, his mother also owned land, and there was some hereditary title, so given a couple of other judicious deaths, more riches and status would be his. Provided he was not too gross in appearance or irredeemably venial, any shortcomings of character were as nothing in the light of such virtues.

Mama told me you were commonly supposed to be Sir Hugo's beloved son, the result of a passionate romance with a foreign princess, but as you were illegitimate you could not inherit from him. I thought you sounded mysterious, the victim of an injustice on a par with those directed at women.

Mr. and Mrs. Arrowpoint hoped their Catherine would win Henleigh Grandcourt's hand. Quetcham Hall was magnificent and Catherine already worth half a million pounds, but the rich like to become richer. To their chagrin, she had recently turned down Lord Slogan, who owned much of County Cork. Uncle and Mama, seduced by the prospect of country estates, a London town house, and hunters and racers, hoped for Grandcourt to be smitten with me. Uncle chose not to hear gossip from male acquaintances about Grandcourt's personal life. Mama saw no solution to my ambition except through marriage and hoped, even if Grandcourt did not win my heart, I would find him suitable or at least acceptable. I was aware that after the fuss with Rex, I would provoke harsh criticism if Grandcourt evinced interest in me and I then spurned him.

Grandcourt was expected to appear on the twenty-fifth of June at the Brackenshaw Archery Club competition, to be followed by a dinner and dance at the Castle. Tickets were for the privileged; I was invited as a new member on Uncle's recommendation for he and I shared an enthusiasm for archery. He was one of the best bowmen in Wessex, and I thought it an elegant, artful sport—my namesake, Gwendolen, was the Lady of the Bow.

THIS WAS OUR first summer at Offendene, we had been there eight months, the hours of daylight were long, and the weather was warm after months of rain. On the day of the meeting I chose to wear white cashmere with a pale green feather in my hat. I sensed Mama's anticipation as I dressed. I teased her: "You and Uncle and Aunt all intend me to fall in love with this Grandcourt," and I made a gesture as if drawing my bow. I assured her that with me in the fray no other girl had a chance of piercing his heart.

Brackenshaw Castle, built of limestone, was set high on a hill among beech and fir trees, and its park spread far into the valley. On that June day some of Lord Bracken-shaw's tenants and their families were allowed into the white arcaded archery hall to watch the competition.

Klesmer was in the Arrowpoints' party. Gesticulating, animated, out of place in this most English of gatherings, with his mane of hair and chimney-pot hat, bowing at the ladies, his hand on his heart, he looked like Genius in an allegory. Catherine, in a gold dress, looked like Wealth. "What extreme guys these artistic fellows are," Clintock said to me.

I was the most beautiful woman there. In perfect surroundings, with admiring eyes on me, I felt exhilarated, less in awe of Klesmer, less wounded. I loved sport and I excelled at this. Luck came into it but it required skill. Though I was a newcomer, my prowess astounded participants and guests. I promised to get one of the best scores. Among those superior people with their money, titles, and airs, I so wanted to win the golden arrow—to be better than them or at least on a par. Catherine Arrowpoint had won it the previous year.

Brackenshaw took out his watch and said Henleigh Mallinger Grandcourt was late. He added that he was always late and quite probably would not appear at all because he cared nothing for archery.

I did not want to hear that. Whatever Mr. Grandcourt's failings, I wanted him to appear and admire and desire me over and above Miss Arrowpoint. That was part of the competition, part of the day.

I assiduously avoided looking toward him when he arrived. I concentrated on the shooting, and, unlike when I subsequently met you, consciousness of his presence spurred me to win. Your presence made me vulnerable; his, at first, made me bold. There was applause when I scored three hits running in the gold contest. I was awash with compliments. Lady Brackenshaw pinned the gold arrow to the shoulder of my dress. I needed such triumph and for Klesmer to see it.

Then Lord Brackenshaw came up to me and said, "Miss Harleth, here is a gentleman who is not willing to wait any

longer. Will you allow me to introduce Mr. Mallinger
Grandcourt?"

It was as if my fate was decided; a smooth beginning
to what would change my life from hopefulness to despair.

Mama had given permission for the introduction. I
knew in her mind she was farther along than that. We all
were: Mama, Uncle, Grandcourt, and, I have to admit,
myself. Our momentous decisions are made on impulse.
We decide in seconds and repent with our lives.

Face-to-face with Grandcourt, I was flustered, I blushed,
resented my confusion, and struggled to correct it. He was
unlike my expectation, though I had no clear preconceived
image. He was handsome in the English manner; his complexion was fair; his features were proportioned and chis-
eled. He was bald with a fringe of reddish hair. His hands
were elegant, his fingers tapered. He was an inch or so taller
than I. Our eyes were on a level; his, long, narrow, and gray,
expressed . . . I don't know what, indifference perhaps or
calculation. There was no hint of self-consciousness or
unease in his bearing. He raised his hat and scrutinized
me, a confident appraisal, but he did not smile.

That was how I perceived him. Before every bit of him
became hideous to me. Before I hated him with a force
stronger than my love for you.

He told me, with a smooth compliment that seemed
bleached of intention, that he thought archery a bore until
he saw me shooting. He drawled when he spoke, with a
pause between each utterance. His gestures were as lan-

guid as his voice. He intrigued me. He gave nothing away. He asked if I liked danger. Such a non sequitur startled and thrilled me, though now I see I should have viewed it as the threat it undoubtedly was. I told him I was never happier than when on horseback, galloping, thinking of nothing, and that then I felt myself strong and free. (I wondered if he might give me a faster horse than Twilight.)

He said I might like tiger hunting and pig sticking, that he had done such things but now they bored him. His manner and demeanor suggested that all there was to do he had done, all there was to be killed he had killed, and that anything he wanted he might have, including me, but that at heart he wanted nothing. He affected boredom with everything. I told him I was bored with this neighborhood, for there was so little to do in it. "You have clearly made yourself queen of it," he said, and I protested that if so, I was queen of an insignificant kingdom.

When the contest was over, Mama asked him if we might meet again in the ballroom. Yes, he replied in his bored, laconic way.

"You can't find anything ridiculous about Mr. Grandcourt's appearance and manner," Mama said as a coachman drove her and me the short distance to the Castle. I replied I was sure I could if I tried but that as yet I did not want to.

AT THE CASTLE, at Lord Brackenshaw's ruling, women dined separately. He liked to quote Byron's opinion that a woman should never be seen eating, unless the meal was of lobster salad and champagne, the only acceptable feminine viands. I was scornful of this segregation: the lesser room, the smaller chairs, and the assumption of lesser conversation.

I told the assembled women Lord Byron was mad, and in order to be thin ate only hard biscuits, or potatoes drenched in vinegar, and drank only soda water. The women thought me sharp-tongued. Only Catherine Arrowpoint talked to me in a friendly way as if she understood my predicament and was herself in rebellion at a woman's lot.

We moved to the ballroom. The chandeliers glittered; the perfume of jasmine and lilies wafted from the conservatory. I loudly informed Mama I would dance only the quadrille and not waltz or polka with anyone. The ladies viewed this as attention seeking, and the dancing men, who all wanted me as their partner, thought me deliberately cruel. But the truth was I could not bear being held close by any man; I hated their breath on my face, the feel of their rough clothing against me, the proprietorial sense of being led in a dance.

Grandcourt, I noticed, positioned himself so he could see me. Klesmer commented on it: "Mr. Grandcourt is a man of taste," he said to me. "He likes to see you dancing."

"Perhaps he likes to look at what is against his taste," I said, mindful of Klesmer's insult about liking to *see* me sing. "He may be so tired of admiring that he chooses disgust by way of variety."

Klesmer chastised me for impertinence, which he said ill-fitted my beauty. I explained it was a joke, but Klesmer was worse than ponderous over the weighty business of jokes.

My attention was then caught by a fat man with a florid face and bulbous eyes staring at me with an expression that made me recoil as if a slimy reptile had crawled all over my skin. I asked Klesmer if he was a friend of his; he told me no, but that he had met him socially. He was Grandcourt's factotum, and his name was Lush. He dismissed him as an amateur, "too fond of the mechanical-dramatic, too fond of Meyerbeer and Eugène Scribe." I did not understand the reference, but it was clear that as Klesmer thought him unworthy, he must be so.

I took refuge with dear Mama. Suddenly, Grandcourt was at my side. He asked me to dance the next or another quadrille. I looked at my card. Every quadrille was booked. I was glad to be obliged to refuse. "I am unfortunate in being too late," he said without a smile. I said I thought he did not care for dancing, that it was one more thing to bore him.

"Yes, but I have not begun to dance with you," he drawled. "You make dancing a new thing. As you make archery." It was another of his considered utterances— between pauses as if in parenthesis, a cool compliment.

I asked if novelty was always agreeable to him.

"No, not always."

"Then I don't know whether to feel flattered or not.

When you once had danced with me, there would be no more novelty in it."

"On the contrary," Grandcourt said. "There would probably be much more."

"That is deep."

"It is difficult to make Miss Harleth understand her power," he said to Mama, who smiled at me and replied, "She does not generally strike people as slow to understand."

"Mama," I said with self-deprecating delight, "I am adorably stupid and want everything explained to me when the meaning is pleasant."

"If you are stupid, I admit stupidity is adorable," Grandcourt rejoindered.

SUCH WAS OUR pretty exchange. What a light flirtation. Interest shown, conquest achieved. Grandcourt's stamp of purchase was put upon me. I saw delight in Mama's face. And then, in one of those chance happenings we view at least as serendipity, at most as fate, I had space on my card for the next quadrille. Lady Brackenshaw came up to say Clintock was *au désespoir*, but his father, the archdeacon, had called him home on some all-important matter.

Grandcourt walked the quadrille, eyed me gravely, and did not touch me. His seeming reticence so suited me. I did not know, I could not read, that his cool charm and flattery were as false and dangerous as the bright flies fishermen use to deceive their catch.

Grandcourt was my crowning triumph on that winning day. Among all the contenders, I was prized to walk on his arm. He promised wide horizons, good fortune, jewels, luxury, and servants. But there was a shadow: Lush lurked nearby, like Iago, watching, listening, scheming.

Catherine Arrowpoint approached Grandcourt and me to give us details of the next archery meeting, a roving outdoor affair in three weeks' time, followed by a picnic at sunset *en plein air* at Cardell Chase, a pretty place of glades and elms which, Miss Arrowpoint said, would feel more poetic than a formal dinner under chandeliers. Lush interrupted her to inform Grandcourt that Diplow was more suitable for such a gathering: "between the oaks toward the north gate," he said, and I realized with revulsion that he was entirely familiar with Grandcourt and his residences, and in his confidence. While Grandcourt provided me with pleasant anticipation, Lush, fat, bulging-eyed Lush, with his oily voice and scheming manner, seemed to forebode harm.

To be freed from Lush's proximity, I told Grandcourt I should like to view the conservatory. The grounds were lit by Chinese lamps, the scent of flowers was in the evening air, and we walked in silence. Grandcourt asked if I liked "this kind of thing." I replied yes, not knowing quite to what he referred.

When we returned, Mama was talking to the slimy Lush. "Gwendolen, dear," she said. "Let me present Mr. Lush to you." I turned my back, moved to my seat, and said I wanted to put on my cape. Lush swept it up and held it out. "No thank you," I said. Grandcourt took it, slipped it over my shoulders and asked permission from Mama to call at Offendene the next day.

AND SO IT began: life-changing decisions made by sudden inclinations, vanity, and rash daring. Had Grandcourt vanished at that point, I would have forgotten him within a week. I did not stop to consider what it meant truly to know another person or myself. I knew nothing of the world beyond the drawing rooms of Pennicote and the bewildering nowhere places of my childhood travels: nothing of the war in America, the struggles of the suffragists, the suffering of the workhouse, the customs and mores of other societies. And nothing whatsoever of the motivations of men or of qualities that might matter, beyond chandeliers, paddocks, and diamonds, when choosing a husband.

Within a minute of seeing me Grandcourt decided I should be his wife. I believe he thought, *I shall have that. Or I shall break that.*

Even his name, and certainly his manner, suggested stately homes, servants, fine carriages, and Mediterranean yachts. I saw his coolness as a haven. He implied boundaries, reserve, and distance from intimacy. I could not face my own terror of intimacy, its roots and implications. I had not so much as kissed a man or held a man's hand. Over the next fortnight, by some arrangement or other I saw him almost every day. Mama and Uncle viewed the marriage as made.

We looked splendid together; both tall, I beautiful, he haughty and understated. He had a habit—how I grew to loathe it—of lightly stroking his mustache. He said little and exuded self-importance. I anticipated that he would make few demands on me, allow me anything I wanted, indulge my caprices, love my follies, grant me freedom. I thought he would be proud to be seen with me on his arm in high Society: in London, Paris, and Cannes. I would sparkle and be impulsive, witty, and independent. I would take singing lessons, enroll in classes to study acting and dance.

Grandcourt arranged a lunch party for Mama and me at Diplow. His cousin Mrs. Torrington, a steel-eyed woman with a slight limp, was in charge of preparations. Before lunch we all toured the grounds. By the lake Grandcourt's spaniel, Fetch, amused us by plunging into the water, bringing a waterlily to the bank, and dropping it at his master's feet, like the spaniel Beau in William Cowper's poem "The Dog and the Water Lily."

Grandcourt then invited me to walk with him to a hilly part of the garden. When we were alone together, he said he thought Offendene too somber for me and asked what sort of place I liked. I told him of my restless resentment that I could not go up in a hot-air balloon, meet unusual people, or travel to Africa or in search of the Nile. I swept my hand toward the herbaceous borders. "Women must stay where we grow," I said, "or where the gardeners like to transplant us. We are brought up like the flowers to look as pretty as we can, and to be dull without complaining. My notion about the plants is they are often bored and that is the reason why some of them have got poisonous."

He looked inscrutable and asked if I was as uncertain about myself as I made others be about me. "I am quite uncertain about myself," I said. "I don't know how uncertain others may be."

"And you wish them to understand that you don't care," he asked.

"I did not say that," I replied, and ran off, back to Mama.

WHAT DID I feel? Anxious, exhilarated, flattered, hopeful, confused? All of those things. I hoped I had not been so capricious as to deter Grandcourt from this courtship. He appeared in thrall to me: he fixed on me and sought me out. I wanted the dignity and luxury I thought marriage to him would bring: the power to do as I liked, hats and finery and outings to the opera with Mama. I thought I could manage such a cool, undemanding husband, a husband restrained and free from absurdities. Rex was a boy, Grandcourt a man. I did not wonder about Grandcourt's life of thirty-six years, I had no curiosity about him beyond his interest in me. He told me he had traveled and hunted the tiger. I did not consider whether he had ever been romantically involved.

After lunch he suggested he and I go for a ride. He offered me a horse, Criterion, a beautiful chestnut. Mama followed in a carriage. It was a quintessential English land-scape of peace and permanence: midharvest time—a light breeze rippled through the corn, the fields were bordered by poppies, and in green pastures cattle rested under wide oak trees. I felt happy. I had almost made up my mind to say yes when he proposed.

We passed a wide brook, and I said I would like to gal-lop and jump it. He encouraged my daring and suggested we both take it. I told him Mama would be ill with worry if she saw me take such a leap.

"But Mrs. Davilow knows I shall take care of you," he said.

"Yes, but she would think of you as having to take care of my broken neck."

Then he said, "I should like to have the right always to take care of you." I felt myself blush then go cold. I heard myself say, "Oh, I am not sure that I want to be taken care of; if I choose to risk breaking my neck, I should like to be at liberty to do it." I did not intend to be flippant. I was nervous. I did not want to lose him. He was an enigma to me. His manners concealed, he gave nothing away.

I WAS TO learn how he controlled his responses: when to withhold, when to unleash. But at first I saw no trace of that. While courting, he treated me with attentive restraint. I was undisturbed by the cool graze of his lips on my hand as he greeted me or bade me farewell. I did not dwell on vows to be made at the altar about bodily worship, or let my thoughts travel to what might happen when the ceremony was done, the confetti thrown, the guests dispersed, and he and I alone in the marital bed. My hatred of being made love to; I did not stop to think of the manner in which it might be breached.

That evening Mama quizzed me anxiously: Had Grandcourt proposed? Did I approve of him? Would I accept him when he did? I teased and evaded. I told her he was quiet and *distingué* and had all the qualities that would make a husband tolerable: "battlement, veranda, stables, et cetera, and no grins and no glass eye."

Mama, used to my mischief, was untroubled by it. Uncle, who was visiting Offendene, asked to see me alone in the drawing room; he wanted to speak to me as if he were my father on a subject "more momentous than any" as far as my welfare was concerned. His concern amused and pleased me; it almost gave me a sense of a family wherein I belonged.

We sat facing each other on the rosewood chairs. "Had I discouraged Mr. Grandcourt's advances?" Uncle asked.

I admitted that when Grandcourt began to make advances I turned the conversation.

"Will you confide in me so far as to tell me your reasons?" Uncle asked.

"I am not sure I had reasons, Uncle," I said.

He became stern and lectured me on my duty to myself and to my family. This, he said, was an opportunity that

would probably not occur again. Had I heard anything disagreeable about Henleigh Mallinger Grandcourt? he asked.
I said I had heard nothing about him other than that he
was a great match, which affected me very agreeably. I did
not at that point know of the worse than disagreeable
rumors about this potential husband, which Uncle had
heard but chose not to impart to me.

Uncle reiterated my responsibility to my family and told
me he would regard me with "severe disapprobation" if, as
he phrased it, through coquetry and folly I put Grandcourt
off. Men, he informed me, did not like their attachments
trifled with, and such good fortune as this rarely happened
to a girl in my circumstances. I must stop being capricious.
His advice, he said, was meant in kindness.

I did not doubt that Uncle cared for me and wanted
my happiness. I told him I knew I must be married and
did not see how I could do better than Grandcourt, so I
intended to accept him. What I could not say, to Mama,
to him, or to myself, was that I loved Grandcourt, for I
did not. I had known him a fortnight. I did not know if
he took sugar with his coffee, if he could swim, if he had
brothers and sisters, or a mother who drank gin. Uncle
hoped I would find "a fountain of duty and affection" in
the marriage. "Marriage is the only true and satisfactory
sphere of a woman," he said. "And if your marriage with
Mr. Grandcourt should be happily decided upon, you will
have probably an increasing power both of rank and wealth,
which may be used for the benefit of others. You are fitted

by natural gifts for a position which, considering your birth and early prospects, could hardly be looked forward to as in the ordinary course of things; and I trust that you will grace it not only by those personal gifts but by a good and consistent life."

"I hope Mama will be the happier" was all I could say. For there it was spelled out for me: marriage was the only way. My "natural gifts" were the length of my legs, the curve of my breasts, the whiteness of my teeth, the wave of my hair, and the slant of my eyes. Given the misfortune of my social position, such gifts raised me above the "ordinary course of things."

Later I came to forgive Mama's enthusiasm for she was even more naive than I. But Uncle knew more. In the gentlemen's dining rooms he had heard of profound irregularities in Grandcourt's life. Alarming rumors which he ought to have investigated. Perhaps he chose not to remember what he heard. Money was what mattered, money and rank. Uncle pressed me into this union as if it was a moral imperative. And he a man of God.

I FELT RADIANT, confident, on the day of the roving archery match in Cardell Chase. I wore white, as on the previous shoot. I anticipated Grandcourt's reserved proposal and my unequivocal but equally reserved acceptance. We congregated at Green Arbor, a grassy spot ringed by fir trees. The sun shone. A coachful of servants organized our picnics.

The archery targets were positioned within a wide curve, landmarked by the Double Oak, the Whispering Stones, the High Cross. The agenda was to explore the course with the warden in the morning, have lunch, make the roving expedition in the afternoon, then picnic again as the sun set.

Grandcourt was beside me as, lagging behind the other guests, we toured the course. He asked, "Do you know how long it is since I first saw you in that dress?"

"The archery meeting was on the twenty-fifth of June; this is the thirteenth of July. I'm not good at calculating, but I venture to say it must be nearly three weeks."

"That is a great loss of time," he said in his considered monotone.

"That knowing me has caused you? Pray don't be uncomplimentary. I don't like it."

Another careful pause. "It is because of the gain that I feel the loss."

I was silent. I thought his conversation ingenious, clever, courteous, stylish, and oh so flattering. "The gain of knowing you makes me feel the time I lose in uncertainty," he said. "Do *you* like uncertainty?"

Uncertainty, it seemed, was a state he wished to overcome. "I think I do," I truthfully replied. "There is more in it."

He did not raise his voice or seem eager to please. He looked into my eyes with his translucent, unblinking gaze. "Do you mean more torment for me?" he said.

I supposed him to be sincere. I thought he voiced vulnerability. "That would make me sorry," I said.

His declaration was so unlike poor Rex's earnest and blushing outburst. I did not reflect on how ludicrously short a span three weeks is, or how I knew nothing of this man and he knew nothing of me beyond my appearances on summer days in a white dress. I intended to marry him; to do well for myself and Mama and to please Uncle, though it was as hard for me to say an unqualified yes to the prospect as to leap to my death from the high chalk cliffs at Bat's Head.

COMPLETING THE TOUR, we rejoined the group. The tables were loaded with food and champagne. The men smoked cigars; the women looked as if they had stepped from a painting by Tissot. Lush smarmed and pandered, but even he could not spoil my perfect day. Or so I thought.

To avoid his help or attention, I went to collect my own bow from the carriage. Lord Brackenshaw's valet saw me approaching and brought it to me together with a letter. The handwriting was a woman's, smaller than a man's, and not from anyone I knew. I felt no apprehension, but I moved behind a tree to read unobserved.

If Miss Harleth is in doubt whether she should accept Mr. Grandcourt, let her break from her party after they have passed the Whispering Stones and return to that spot. She will then

hear something to decide her, but she can only hear it by keep-
ing this letter a strict secret from everyone. If she does not act
according to this letter, she will repent, as the woman who writes
it has repented.

The secrecy Miss Harleth will feel herself bound in honor
to guard.

I felt shocked excitement but not fear. *It has come in time*, I
thought. *As You Like It* was perhaps now the play. I was
Rosalind and Grandcourt my Orlando. There were to be
diversions in the Forest of Arden before our marriage was
made. Yet the intrigue of this letter seemed intrinsic to the
drama of the afternoon and did not diminish my self-
assurance.

We picnicked on cold salmon, pigeon pie, jellies, straw-
berries, grapes, cheese. But when we were ready to set off
for the match, Grandcourt said he preferred to stay at Green
Arbor and smoke a cigar, and Mama said she preferred a
quiet stroll.

The archery was spirited; I was elated; the landscape
shifted from forest to open glade. It took an hour for us to
reach the Whispering Stones: two granite blocks that leaned
toward each other as if imparting a secret. That afternoon
they were dappled by sunlight, though I had heard on starlit
nights they turned into ghosts. Behind them was a grove of
beech trees.

There were a couple of miles more for the party to
circle before the return to Green Arbor. I held back. The

others, under Lush's guidance, moved forward toward High
Cross. This felt like adventure. I wanted something to
happen, I anticipated revelation and feared no one would
be there. But then I was startled when a woman appeared
from behind one of the stones. I supposed her to be about
forty. She had intense dark eyes and black hair and must
once have been very handsome. Her demeanor was poised
and determined. A few yards from her, two children sat
playing on the grass, a dark-haired girl of about six and a
small boy of five with light brown curls.

"Miss Harleth?"

"Yes."

"Have you accepted Mr. Grandcourt?"

"No."

"I have something to tell you. And you will promise
to keep my secret. However you may decide, promise me
you will not tell Mr. Grandcourt or anyone else that you
have seen me."

"I promise."

"My name is Lydia Glasher. Mr. Grandcourt ought not
to marry any one but me. I left my husband and child for
him nine years ago. Those two children are his, and we have
two others—girls who are older. My husband is dead now,
and Mr. Grandcourt ought to marry me. He ought to make
that boy his heir."

The small boy was pretending to play a toy trumpet;
he looked cherubic. "You are very attractive, Miss Harleth."

The woman's voice was cold, angry, and controlled. "When Mr. Grandcourt first knew me, I too was young. Since then my life has been broken up and embittered. It is not fair that he should be happy and I miserable and my boy thrust out of sight for another."

She stared into my eyes. My sense of adventure died; my courage drained; I felt icy tentacles around me. Here was the specter of death from the wainscot. Here was my fear. I sensed she was desperate enough to do anything. A voice in my head said, *I am a woman's life.* I struggled to breathe. I told the woman I would not interfere with her wishes. There was silence. I asked if she had more to say. "Nothing," she replied. "I have told you what I wished you to know. Inquire about me if you like. My husband was Colonel Glasher."

Within a minute I was back in the beech grove. The day had become unreal. The party had moved from sight. I did not try to catch up with them. I took a short route back to Green Arbor. Mama was astonished to see me return alone. My excuse was that I had lingered to look at the Whispering Stones and grown tired of walking. Mrs. Arrowpoint probingly asked the whereabouts of Grandcourt. "Where *can* he be?" I said. "I should think he has fallen into the pool or had an apoplectic fit."

My tone was worse than sarcastic. Mama looked troubled by my distress. I told her I was tired and needed to go home. I ordered the carriage. Then Grandcourt appeared with the rest of the party. He supposed my *froideur* was because I felt neglected by him on the shoot. He asked if he might call at Offendene tomorrow.

"Oh yes, if you like," I said. I hurried into the carriage to avoid the sight of him. He raised his hat and walked away.

Journeying back to Offendene, I told Mama I intended to telegraph our friends the von Langens, whom I knew to be in Homburg, to say I would join them on their trip. I would pack as soon as I got home and set off for Dover on the early morning train.

Mama made no sense of it. She too thought I was offended by Grandcourt not accompanying me on the shoot. She protested that my response was extreme. I said it was useless to quiz me; I was not going to marry Grandcourt.

"Gwendolen, what can I say to your uncle? Consider the position you place me in," Mama pleaded. "Only last night you led him to believe you had made up your mind in favor of Mr. Grandcourt."

I told Mama I would not alter my resolve or give reasons, other than that I hated all men and believed them evil and did not care were I never to marry anyone. I apologized for causing confusion. The woman at the Whispering Stones had made my situation invidious: She exacted from me a promise to tell no one of our meeting. To break that promise would rebound on her and her children and achieve nothing for me. I could confide in no one. I was alone with my misery and the cause of upset to Mama and Uncle.

Mama sat in speechless misery in the carriage. She wept. I chastised her for her tears and told her to remember the troubles in her own life and leave me to be miserable if that was what I chose.

Back home I packed. Nothing had prepared me for this reversal. I felt locked out of my own life. I hated causing Mama pain. At dawn she accompanied me to the railway station. I was running away, not running to anything or anyone. At the station I watched the carriage turn back to Offendene with Mama in it. When Mr. Grandcourt called, no one was at home.

I SAT ALONE in the ladies' carriage on the train to Dover. My thoughts raced as the landscape slipped by, taking with it my plans and expectations. Lush, I suspected, had schemed for Mrs. Glasher to lie in wait for me at the Whispering Stones. Later I learned I was right. I sensed his loathing of me.

I pondered Mrs. Glasher's letter, her threats and hatred. She was chasing me away, and I was resentful. Perhaps Grandcourt ought to have married her, but how could it be my fault that he had not? She said she was young, lovely, and happy when she met him, but what of Colonel Glasher and their son? Where were they when she was young and happy with Grandcourt? She implied I held her happiness and that of her children's fortune in my power. But arrangements and matters of the heart between her and Grandcourt ought not have involved me. Why should the onus of correct behavior be mine? Grandcourt pursued me. In Society's terms she was his mistress, and he wanted me as his wife. She was urging me to put her wishes above his choice and my own self-interest. She implied that were I to refuse Grandcourt, he would marry her, but there was no certainty of that. They had had nine years to establish their feelings for each other and make plans. Colonel Glasher was now dead, so there was no obstruction to legitimizing their union other than Grandcourt's reluctance. I had hardly pushed my way into his view. She did not speak well of him or want good for him. It seemed she hated him for robbing her of her youth. She wanted his money and status for their son.

I was not in love with Henleigh Mallinger Grandcourt, though if, as seemed inevitable, I had to marry, I wanted to marry well, please Uncle, and above all provide for Mama. But I again realized, as I sat alone on my desperate journey of escape, that I knew almost nothing about him. Why had he not told me of Mrs. Glasher and their four children? What else might there be about his past and present to alarm me? He was vain about how he appeared in Society; he would sooner marry me than a woman no longer beautiful, but perhaps his concern was for himself alone. Would he act as he pleased whatever vows he made, whatever contract he signed? How, I wondered, would he treat me when I showed signs of wear?

The countryside flattened, the dividing sea approached. I did not know what choice to make, where to turn for help, or whom to trust. I would be damned if I married Grandcourt, damned if I did not. I wanted to make this journey to escape the muddle that troubled and tormented me, and take me to a resolution.

That was how, on that September afternoon, I found myself at the mercy of the roulette wheel, hoping for luck to bring me wealth and set me free. Such was the turmoil of my life when I met your gaze. Your gaze that seared into me and that I see now.

Mama knew only of my distress and reversal of plan; she did not know my confusion's cause. Uncle interpreted my flurried departure as a coquettish flounce, designed to tease the interest of my admirer. Grandcourt saw my leaving as a challenge. Had events not followed in the way they did, he would probably have forgotten me before autumn was through and pursued an alternative quarry. But accompanied by Lush, he set off for Homburg in slow pursuit of me. In his bored, languid manner he stopped for a few days yachting in the Baltic, then to gamble in Baden-Baden, and reached Homburg five days after I had left. There he met with Sir Hugo, the Mallinger family, and you. From you he learned I had received disturbing news, you did not know what, and gone home to Pennicote. From Lush you learned that Grandcourt had been on the point of marrying me, but I had run off without explanation. I do not know what you made of all you saw and heard.

I HAD LURCHED from one disaster to the next. No one was at Wancester station to meet me when I returned from Homburg to face our bankrupt future. Alone in the waiting room I felt defined by the dirty paint, the dusty decanter of water, the poster calling on us all to repent and find Jesus, and the melancholy lanes and fields outside. A sullen porter with a squint in one eye ignored me. I was a woman without status or prospect. I, Mama, and my sisters had no money and no home. I could not think what we would do; wander abroad perhaps—out of view from social scorn.

A dirty old barouche eventually was brought from the railway inn. Squashed in the back of it, with my two large trunks, I felt hatred for Grandcourt, his deceit that had led me to this impasse, and for men in general, including you. Had you not watched me with such disapproval, I might again have won at the tables.

At Offendene, Mama and my sisters waited on the porch to greet me. Mama wept as I kissed her. Fresh lines of sorrow had etched into her face. I tried to console her and lift her mood, conscious that any strength she might have must be drawn from me. I assured her I would make things right. "I will be something, I will do something," I promised, for

in my heart I thought my charm or luck, or some benevolent spirit, would shape our destiny.

Mama and I spent the day alone together, our food
brought to us on trays. Misfortune did not seem so evident
in the large friendly house and in each other's loving company. In our black and yellow bedroom I did not mention Grandcourt, and she dared not ask. We did not mention
our problems until evening came. I then said I felt sure
Lord Brackenshaw would let us stay on for a while rent free
at Offendene.

Mama countered he was in Scotland and knew nothing about us, and anyway neither she nor my uncle would
ask favors of him. Moreover, even if he agreed, we had no
money to pay bills or the servants, nor did we have money
to travel abroad. Uncle intended to adapt to penury: keep
no carriage, buy no new clothes, eat no meat for breakfast,
subscribe to no periodicals, and tutor his sons himself. It
all sounded utterly dismal. As for Mama and me, Alice,
Bertha, Fanny, Isabel, we were all to move to Sawyer's Cottage and make do with basic furnishings gleaned from the
rectory.

I knew Sawyer's Cottage. Mr. Partridge, an exciseman,
had died there. I knew its scrubby cabbage patch, steep narrow staircase, four tiny bedrooms, two cramped parlors with
green and yellow wallpaper. Mama said she and the girls
might earn a pittance wage by sewing. "Sewing what?" I
asked. "A tablecloth border for the ladies' charity at Wancester? A communion cloth for Pennicote church?"

I could not bear her choked-back tears. We must go to law, I said, to recover our fortune such as it had been. This man Lassman, the land agent who so carelessly speculated with and lost our money by investing in mines and risky dealings, must be held accountable. Mama said we had no money to go to law, and anyway there was no law for people who are ruined.

She had discussed my fate with Uncle. I was to be a governess or teacher. Uncle knew of two possible openings: I could live with a bishop's family, a Dr. Mompert, and teach French and music to his three dismal daughters, or teach the dull narrow curriculum for girls in a school for a wage of eighty pounds a year.

I vowed to Mama I would not see her cooped in Sawyer's Cottage, be dictated to by Uncle or anyone else, or sink so low as to be a governess. I would sooner emigrate. I assured her my determination would prevail; I would devise a rescue plan; I had talent I could employ that had not yet been tapped or recognized. And to provide in the short term, I had pieces of jewelry to sell.

I went to my desk and without reflection wrote a note to Herr Klesmer. I urgently requested him to call the next day. I said unfortunate family circumstances of a very serious nature obliged me to turn for advice to his great knowledge and judgment.

I dispatched this note to Quetcham Hall. I wince even now at the thought of its arrival. I was not good at anticipating how my actions affected others or at considering their point of view. It did not occur to me Herr Klesmer might be in an agitated state, immersed in problems of his own.

The night my note arrived, Catherine Arrowpoint, in a heated exchange with her parents, had declared to them that she loved Klesmer and intended to marry him. Her parents forbade it. They expected her, their only child, to marry in accordance with their wealth and status. The husband must be a man connected to the institutions of England, of good family, and in line for a peerage. Grandcourt would suit. Klesmer, the music teacher in their paid employ, a foreigner, and, worse, a Jew, though perhaps a first-rate musician, was not the right sort.

Catherine's parents summoned Klesmer and told him Catherine would be disinherited were he to marry her. Neither he nor she viewed that as much of a threat. He told them that notwithstanding their power and money they could not confer on him anything he valued. He had earned success as a musician, would change his career for no other, had enough money to support Catherine, and sought no alteration to his life but her lifelong companionship.

Mr. Arrowpoint threatened him with a duel and ordered him to leave the house. My note arrived in the middle of all this.

Apparently, so as not to disappoint me, he stayed on at Quetcham as a most unwelcome guest for another day. At Offendene I set the scene for his arrival. I coiled my hair and, to look demure, dressed in black with no jewelry. I strewed music sheets on top of the piano and instructed Mama I wished to receive Herr Klesmer alone.

He was shown into the drawing room. I was direct. I told him of our loss and my need to provide for Mama to save her from true hardship. I informed him of my plan to study acting and go on the stage. I asked for his help. I said I accepted my voice alone was not good enough for me to succeed professionally, but if I combined it with acting I could perhaps perform like the dramatic soprano Giulia Grisi, for whom both Rossini and Donizetti had written.

I am embarrassed to remember. I was twenty, and I aspired to stardom and to save Mama, who looked to me for sunlight. I was her best-loved daughter. I did not know the meaning of talent, how exceptional it is, how it cannot be plucked from the air. I did not know of the gulf between aspiration and achievement, or of the essential of hard work.

Klesmer put his hat and gloves on the piano and folded his arms. He spoke in a deliberate manner. He again told me I was beautiful. I had, he said, been brought up in ease. I knew nothing of the demands of an artist's life, of inward vocation, subduing mind and body to unbroken discipline, and of thinking not of celebrity but of excellence, of the work required to achieve any sort of recognition, the disappointments that needed to be endured, the uncertainty of any chance of praise. He said for a long while I should expect to earn nothing and get no engagements.

All of which was merely a gentle preamble. Was I too old, I asked, to set out on such a path, too wanting in talent? Yes, he replied. My voice would never have counted for much, but had I been trained years previously, I might have found some minor outlet as a public singer. Seeing me blanch with pain, he then compounded his insults by commending my personal charm.

Only because my plight was desperate did I persist. Might I find engagement at a theater and study singing at the same time? I asked. No, Klesmer said. It could not be done. "Glaring insignificance" was one of his phrases. I could not pitch my voice; I did not know how to move about a stage. However hard I tried, whatever efforts and sacrifices I made, I would never achieve more than mediocrity. I would have to pay a manager to employ me. My beauty, he said, would surely find me a husband, but such beauty had nothing to do with art; it was a substitute when nothing more commanding was to be found.

I had sought Herr Klesmer's help. I received an exercise in humiliation. I had no money, family connections, or friends to help me. I wanted to achieve independence and recognition. I had been encouraged to view my beauty as a gift, a work of art in itself, and my singing voice as its accompaniment. Klesmer made both seem meretricious.

He then told me of his intended marriage to Catherine Arrowpoint and of how exceptional she was. If I still wanted, after hearing these truths about myself, to try my luck in London, they would support me financially. That was the final laceration. I vowed never again to ask anyone in authority for their opinion of me.

I congratulated him on his engagement to marry, said "If I take the wrong road, it will not be because of your flattery," then thanked him for his kindness, his offer of hospitality, and his time. He gave me his card, said "God forbid that you should take any road but one where you will find happiness," kissed my hand, and left.

My hopes receded with the sound of coach wheels on the gravel. I had wanted King Klesmer, messenger from the god of Art, to admire something in me, but I was too old, mediocre, and vainglorious. I was a fantasist, a spoiled girl with a beautiful face and no talent who would earn no money and merit no applause. The acclaim accorded me thus far was from people who knew nothing of quality.

Sawyer's Cottage, the bleak railway waiting room, the governess's room at the top of the bishop's house, the death's head in the wainscot, the woman at the Whispering Stones—their curse was upon me.

Mama came into the room when she saw Klesmer had gone and observed my tears and brittle mood. I told her I accepted Sawyer's Cottage and being governess to the bishop's daughters. I resolved to try not to care, to try to bear it all. I thought I had reached the depth of my own misery. I was wrong.

THE NEXT ORDEAL was with Uncle and my aunt. They and my cousins faced financial devastation with a fortitude to shame me. They took to penury with Christian zeal and embraced sacrifice and austerity. Aunt sorted depressing window coverings for Sawyer's Cottage from the rectory storeroom. Uncle endlessly boasted of no meat for breakfast. Rex, even while working for a fellowship, arranged both to tutor his brothers and to take pupils.

Mrs. Mompert, Uncle told me, wished to interview me before confirming my appointment as governess. Why? I asked. I had done myself the violence of accepting the humiliation of her employing me. Was that not enough? Did I need to be vetted like a horse for the stable?

Mrs. Mompert needed to be sure of me, Uncle said. A woman of strict principle, she presided over her daughters' religious and moral education. She would not, for example, have a French person in the house. She needed to assess my character and likely influence on her daughters.

He went on to extol the bishop's ecclesiastical credentials. He talked of the Bible Society, private strictures, and Lord Grampian, and conveyed a sense of oppression more stifling than embroidering table napkins for Pennicote church. I became awash with anxiety. I felt like a trapped and drowning bird. The pompous bishop was to inform me on church matters of infinite dullness. His prim wife would have me hide my hair under a maid's cap. Their wretched unmet girls already irritated me far more than my own sisters. I wanted to fly to the open sea, jump to freedom from any high window. I inquired desperately about the alternative: the position in a school.

The teaching post was not good enough, Uncle said,

nor did I have an equal chance of securing it. "Oh dear, no," Aunt added. "It would be much harder for you. You might not have a bedroom to yourself." They apprised me of the character-building benefits of self-abnegation and how, from Mrs. Mompert, ghastly Mrs. Mompert, I would learn to conduct myself from a woman who was my superior.

Life was hateful. Mama watched me in distress. I evinced no interest in dreary furnishings for the horrible cottage; I refused to go to the rectory and face Uncle's stoicism; I dreaded being subjected to Mrs. Mompert's scrutiny.

The interview with her was fixed for a week away, but I could not rouse myself. I had known since I was little that Mama was unhappy. Now it seemed I was to be even more unhappy than she. I do not think I suffered from over-weening arrogance, only naive optimism. You had given me insubstantial hope; Grandcourt concealed a nest of iniquities; Klesmer apprised me I had no talent; Uncle insisted I resign myself to a gray flannel costume and a straw poke hat; Aunt derided me for rejecting Grandcourt; Anna viewed me as shameful for not being in love with Rex. I had failed them all, but especially Mama. She was so used, abused, and hard done by, and I could not rescue her, only become like her. She would have to stitch her fingers to the bone. The best I could do was to give her the eighty pounds a year I might earn as a governess. I saw Mama as old and white haired and I no longer young but faded. I felt her grief that she could not contrive my happiness. "Poor Gwen too is sad and faded now," I seemed to hear her say.

ONE EARLY MORNING I got out my jewelry box thinking
its contents might buy us a month's respite. I told Mama to
sell everything but the necklace from my father's chain. In
my barren world you were my consolation and the chain
my talisman link to you. Mama was doubtful that the sale
of a few pearls and clasps would mitigate our problems. She
asked about the handkerchief, from which you had torn
your initials, in which it was wrapped. I was vague in my
explanation, but, as I held both necklace and handkerchief,
I yearned for your advice, your soft voice, and your kind eyes.

A few days later I, who viewed tears as a weakness and
seldom cried, was in bed weeping with disappointment
when Mama came in, put her arms around me, and when
I was calm gave me a letter delivered by a Diplow servant.
In it Grandcourt announced he had returned from Homburg, where he had gone in the hope of finding me, and
asked if he might call at Offendene the following day to
see me alone.

I was torn between guilt and hope: I saw the dark-eyed
woman and beautiful boy and heard her warning voice. I
thought of Grandcourt's cold allure and life of such high
style. I felt a rush of obstinate determination: here was the
only way for me to recapture authority and steer my life.
Marrying Grandcourt would at one stroke resolve so much:
Mama need not go to Sawyer's Cottage and stitch for
sixpences; I need not defer to Bishop Mompert and his

catechisms, pretend piety, feign respect for his self-important wife or concern for their prim and pampered daughters. You? Where were you? Grandcourt was the armored knight who came to rescue me from the undoubted trouble I was in.

I read the note to Mama. If Grandcourt had heard about Sawyer's Cottage, she said, it was proof of his strong and generous attachment to me. Why else would he choose a wife from a family reduced to beggary? She urged me to reply while the Diplow messenger waited. I did not wish to reflect. I told her to fetch pen and paper.

Grandcourt had declared his paramount reason for not marrying Mrs. Glasher: the insuperable obstacle was that he did not love her. He loved me.

But that night I could not sleep. Grandcourt's promise buoyed my hopes but enhanced my fear. I had been rendered powerless, brought savagely to heel. I wanted, needed, to find control and command. I neither loved nor trusted Grandcourt. I was muddled and uncertain, and in my troubled heart I loved and trusted you.

The next afternoon Mama coiled my hair; and I dressed in black silk. Grandcourt arrived on Yarico, his beautiful black horse, accompanied by his groom, who rode the chestnut Criterion. The groom waited outside. Miss Merry announced that Grandcourt was in the drawing room. I went down alone. I see and feel the day so clearly: the view that beckoned from the window, the horses that symbolized freedom, the scent of rose attar.

Grandcourt and I sat facing each other. He held his hat in his left hand and gazed at me with his long, narrow, light-colored eyes. It occurred to me he had the stillness of a snake. The atmosphere was intense. He asked if I was well. "I was disappointed not to find you at Homburg," he drawled in a voice that admitted no disappointment at all. "The place was intolerable without you. A kennel of a place, don't you think so?"

"I can't judge what it would be without myself," I said, relieved to be reacquainted with my sparring wit. "With myself I liked it well enough to have stayed longer if I could. But I was obliged to come home on account of family troubles."

He had no need to ask what those troubles were; he knew from his repulsive scout. "It was cruel of you to go to Homburg," he said, then told me I was "the heart and soul of things" and must have known my going would spoil everything.

"Are you quite reckless about me?" he asked. The question made me blush.

Was there another man who stood between us?

I wanted to say, No, but there is a woman. You were only half formed in my mind as my guide and hope.

He persisted: "Am I to understand that someone else is preferred?"

"No," I said. We were both guilty of concealment, but a preference of mine for someone else was not the obstacle to this wooing.

"The last thing I would do is to importune you," Grand-court said. "I should not hope to win you by making myself a bore. If there were no hope for me, I would ask you to tell me so at once, that I might just ride away to—no mat-ter where."

I felt a rush of alarm at the thought of him riding away. Were he to do so, nothing was left for me. His lack of ref-erence to Mrs. Glasher made it seem she did not exist. There was just him and me, the sunlight of the morning, the beautiful horses waiting outside the window, the coolness of his wooing to soothe my hurt and quieten my fear. I wanted no other reality to intrude and break this fragile spell of make-believe.

I spoke briefly of Mama's troubles and our dismal pros-pects. The money needed to spare her from Sawyer's Cot-tage and me from Bishop Mompert was as nothing to Grandcourt but everything to us. He looked at me with his pale eyes. I thought I held him in my thrall. I did not know how much it mattered to him that I had not so much as held a man's hand. I did not know he liked my inso-lence not because it amused him but because he intended to subdue it.

He was impassive, his timing perfect; his manners were faultless. He drawled, "You will tell me now, I hope, that Mrs. Davilow's loss of fortune will not trouble you further. You will trust me to prevent it from weighing upon her. You will give me the claim to provide against that."

I felt I had quaffed wine. Momentarily I loved this man.

He was my savior and the woman at Cardell Chase no more than an unsettling hallucination. My fears were needless, my pain gone. I told Grandcourt he was very generous. I meant it.

"You accept what will make such things a matter of course?" he asked without urgency, eagerness, allusion, or caveat that might frighten me away. "You consent to become my wife?"

A word was needed, but I could not utter it.

Was it shame at my moral recklessness that froze my voice, or did I again perceive the fly fisherman who entices with perfectly crafted bait, who knows the necessity for concealment and stillness if his prey is to be deceived?

I walked to the mantelpiece, folded my hands, and turned to him. He too rose, held his hat, but did not move toward me. My hesitation fired him. Here was the moment of my renunciation. "Do you command me to go?" he asked. He let me believe, for oh so brief a time, my word was his command. I feared his going more than I feared the consequence of his staying. I could not steer; I could only yield to the tide I hoped might carry me to a safe shore.

"You accept my devotion?" The question was a command. It had all gone too far. There was to be no explanation, no straying from intention.

"Yes," I said, as if answering to my name in a court of law. He savored my fear, which his authority forbade me to express. My frozen voice and nervous posture made conquest the more thrilling. He let the silence linger, put down his hat, came toward me, took my hand lightly, pressed his lips to it, then let it go. Such manners were perfect for me in their cool restraint. I felt the air of liberation. The sparring was over, his victory a nonchalance. Yes to Grandcourt meant no to Sawyer's Cottage and the wretched bishop. I said with glittering brightness that I would fetch Mama.

"Let us wait a little," Grandcourt said. He stood in his favorite pose, the perfect gentleman, the perfect stranger, left forefinger and thumb in his waistcoat pocket, his right forefinger stroking his blond mustache. Such was my naïveté, my self-delusion, I almost imagined "Reader, I married him" to be the answer to my problems, almost imagined that the drama which within a little month had taken such twists, such turns, was destined for a happy ending.

You, Deronda, were lodged in my heart; I had nothing of yours but a penetrating gaze and a handkerchief with your initials cut away. Your one assertion had been to return to me my father's turquoise chain, which for unexamined reasons I now knew I would not part with again.

To my relief Grandcourt made no move to kiss me. "Have you anything else to say to me?" I asked, my shattered charm restored.

"Yes, though I know having things said to you is a great bore," my compliant lover said.

"Not when they are things I like to hear."

"Will it bother you to be asked how soon we can be married?"

"I think the question will bother me today." I was the coquettish, happy bride-to-be.

"Then tomorrow. Decide before I come tomorrow. Let it be in a fortnight or three weeks. As soon as possible."

"You fear you will tire of my company." I had heard, I added, that the husband, when married, did not feel the need to be so much with his wife as when engaged. "Perhaps I shall like that better too."

Such was my hour of confidence, my brief taste of triumph and control. Outside the window Criterion and Yarico waited, so much more elegant than Twilight, so other than Anna's pony or Primrose or the old barouche at the railway inn. They heralded an end to scrimping and Mama's sad resignation. Grandcourt asked if I should like to ride Criterion tomorrow. I felt a burst of joy. I would gallop free and fast. "You shall have whatever you like," he said. Was ever there a greater lie than that?

"And nothing that I don't like? Please say that. I think I dislike what I don't like more than I like what I like."

He repeated the lie. Whatever I liked I should have. Boldly, I said I disliked Lush's company and asked him to spare me from it. To please me, he said he would dispense with Lush, who was foisted on him in his youth, and whom he called a cross between a hog and a dilettante. Lush would be got rid of. I laughed with satisfaction.

"Take my arm," Grandcourt said. I did so, we left the room, he waited in the hall; I hurried to the bedroom, kissed Mama on both cheeks, announced there would be no Sawyer's Cottage, no scrutiny by Mrs. Mompert, and everything from now on would be as I chose and as I liked. "Come down, Mama, and see Mr. Grandcourt," I said. "I am engaged to him."

I WAS THE heroine of the fairy tale. The turning wheel of my fortune in three weeks had spun from hope to fear to loss and now to resolution. Here was my husband-to-be, who would do everything for me, take nothing from me, who was courteous, solicitous, protective. Mrs. Glasher was locked away like the death's head in the wainscot to which I held the key. You were out of sight.

Mama, Alice, Bertha, Fanny, Isabel, Miss Merry, and Jocasta Bugle viewed me as their savior. That same evening Uncle, Aunt, and Anna came to Offendene. Uncle commended Grandcourt's generosity, my aunt warned me there was now no room for caprice and that I had a debt of gratitude to a man who persevered with such an offer, Anna, who hoped the troubles might have softened my heart toward Rex, was quiet and tearful, but the evening and all glory were mine.

Mama wanted to know about the estates to which I would eventually be chatelaine: Ryelands, Diplow, the London town house. Ryelands, Uncle said, was one of the finest seats in the land, the house designed by Inigo Jones, its ceilings painted in Italian style, its parkland and woods extensive, the income from it twelve thousand pounds a year. He spoke of a baronetcy, a peerage. Grandcourt would become Lord Stannery and I Lady of It All.

"You must lose no time in writing to Mrs. Mompert, Henry," my aunt told him. "It's a good thing you have an engagement of marriage to offer as an excuse, or she might have felt offended. She is rather a high woman."

Again that night I slept feverishly. I had closed my ears to the lion's roar, but in the dark I heard it nearby. Grandcourt smoothly made vows and promises to me, but what vows and promises had he given Lydia Glasher? He had rendered her miserable; might he do the same with me? And might Lush still snake in the undergrowth of this affluent paradise? All I thought I longed for: fine houses, dresses, diamonds, heads turned in admiration, release from Mama's low expectations—all were now waiting for me, but with them came the taint of wrongdoing and the taste of poison.

In a dream the door of the wainscot again snapped open, then the death's head and fleeing figure leaped out. The head was that of the woman at Cardell Chase; it hovered in front of me, emaciated, the eyes large and angry. Her words coiled in my thoughts: *My life has been broken up and embittered . . . not fair that he should be happy and I miserable and my boy thrust out of sight for another.* I cried out to Mama, she lit a candle, I joined her, and in the comfort of her arms I dreamed of dancing.

———

LATE NEXT MORNING Mama woke me. Grandcourt's groom
had brought Criterion with a message that he was to be
my horse. He had also delivered a small packet. In it, within
a jewelry box, a diamond ring glittered. The accompany-
ing note was on colored paper.

> *Pray wear this ring when I come at twelve in sign of*
> *our betrothal. I enclose a check drawn in the name of Mr.*
> *Gascoigne for immediate expenses. Of course Mrs. Davilow*
> *will remain at Offendene at least for some time. I hope when*
> *I come you will have granted me an early day for when you*
> *may begin to command me at a shorter distance.*
>
> > *Yours devotedly,*
> > *H. M. Grandcourt*

The check was for five hundred pounds. Mama evinced
pleasure and relief but irked me by saying she did not want
to be dependent on a son-in-law and hoped I was not marrying for her sake. I was marrying for many reasons, most
of them understandable, though not many of them good.
Yes, Mama's security was one, but so was my own deliverance and saving of face. And there was a private matter:
my acceptance of Grandcourt had much to do with the fact
that he did not touch me. I was reassured by his restraint,
cool flattery, and lack of any physical move toward me. I
was spared the horror of expressed desire. Because I shunned
this, I thought he would not impose it on me.

I was carried along by the whirlwind of events that

swirled around me. Had I searched my heart, the only person whom I might have loved was you. It was the seedling of love, but all it might grow into was coded there. My feelings for Grandcourt were unformed. Perhaps I ignored intimation of his viciousness. Perhaps I sought punishment for the betrayal of a promise.

It was for me to put the ring on my own finger. This marriage was to be managed by me. Grandcourt was not going to kneel. I should have despised him had he done so. Here was a man whom I would rule. Married, I would urge him to be generous to Mrs. Glasher and the children. I did not want children of my own; my needs were not excessive. Grandcourt could leave his estates to the boy. There was enough money, enough property, to provide for all.

I was triumphant for Mama and exalted in our new-found wealth. On the first day of my engagement, in anticipation of Grandcourt's arrival, I told her to dress like a duchess with her point lace over her head. When he came, he raised my hand to his lips and kissed the diamond. I graciously thanked him for thinking of everything.

"You will tell me if there is anything I forget," he said.

"I am unreasonable in my wishes" was my pert response.

"I expect that. Women always are." His voice had an edge, which I noticed but thought nothing of. I did not imbue the remark with the misogyny I was to find it held; I was more intent on my pretty reply. "Then I will not be unreasonable," I said. "I will not be told that I am what women always are."

"I did not say that," Grandcourt said in his careful manner. "You are what no other woman is."

"And what is that, pray?" I asked, safe in this realm of teasing banter, so much in command, my heart so uninvolved.

"You are the woman I love," he said, and I smiled, for he must have said that to another woman or with her fathered four children out of wedlock using language of another sort.

"What nice speeches," I said, wondering about the others.

"Give me a nice speech in return," he said. "Say when we are to be married."

"Not till we have had a gallop over the downs," I said, with Criterion in mind. "I can think of nothing else. I long for the hunting to begin. It will begin in ten days' time."

"Let us be married in ten days then," said Grandcourt. "So we won't be bored hanging around the stables."

"What do women always say in answer to that?"

"They agree to it."

"Then I will not."

Oh, we were both so carefully clever and insincere. He portrayed himself as the complaisant husband: obliging, devoted, and deferential. I was the pert girl-wife. Galloping across the downs was splendid and glorious. On my wonderful horse I felt so free. I agreed for the marriage to be three weeks away.

———

I WAS TO repent for my haste. Grandcourt only pretended to bend to my wishes. He had no taste for a woman who was all tenderness and willing obedience. It thrilled him for me to shrink from his advances. He wanted to master a woman who would have liked to have mastered him and was capable of mastering a different man. He anticipated the pleasure it would give him to cause me to kneel, against my inclination but at his command, like a horse trained for the circus arena. He did not believe I was in love with him. He supposed, accurately, that had penury not subdued my family, I should have refused him.

What a tainted equation it was.

ENGAGEMENT TO GRANDCOURT was a formal exchange of niceties. He spoke of yachting in European ports; I pretended to do needlework. We rode most days. He said it was not in his power to protect me from *all* harm and that if I chose to hunt on Criterion, he could not prevent my having a fall. He advised me that when married I was to have a parure of diamonds, which his mother had requested should go to his bride.

Once he kissed not my cheek but my neck a little below the ear, and I shuddered and recoiled as if from a snakebite. He said, "I beg your pardon—did I annoy you?"

"Oh, it was nothing," I replied. "Only I cannot bear to be kissed under my ear."

I did not read his expression, but he spoke of my

unkindness to "us poor devils of men." "Are you as kind to me as I am to you?" he asked, and I felt guilt and in his debt. I had sold the right to be candid. I could not tell him how repellent it was to me—the sensation of his mouth on my neck. I could not speak of the fear that dredged through me as I realized I was not at liberty to flout him as I had Rex. I replied archly, "If I was as kind to you as you are to me, that would spoil your generosity; it would no longer be as great as it could be—and it is that now."

"Then I am not to ask for one kiss?" Grandcourt asked. "Not one," I replied, so he lifted my hand and brushed it with his lips, which I found acceptable. I again blocked my mind as to what might follow when we were married. I chose to believe in his reticence, chose to believe he respected and matched my resistance.

We were silent about much that needed to be said. Grandcourt pretended to defer to my will while imposing his own. I half knew that but closed my eyes to the abyss where I was heading. A week before the marriage he nonchalantly said he would be going away for a couple of days. He did not say where, but I knew it was to visit Mrs. Glasher. As if conceding to my unspoken vexation, he said he would travel at night so as to be gone only one day.

Before that visit he invited me and Mama to luncheon at Diplow to say how I might want the rooms to be arranged. His cousins Captain and Mrs. Torrington would be there, and her sister and a gentleman whom I had met at Homburg: "Young Deronda, a young fellow with the

Mallingers." I embroidered my cloth, my heart leaped, my
fingers froze. "I never spoke to him," I said. "Is he disagreeable?"

"Not particularly" was Grandcourt's reply. "He thinks
a little too much of himself. I thought he had been introduced to you."

"No. Someone told me his name the evening before I
came away. That was all. What is he?"

"A sort of ward of Sir Hugo Mallinger's. Nothing of consequence."

"How very unpleasant for him." I turned to the window. "I wonder if it has left off raining."

I LATER LEARNED that your visit to Diplow was as Sir
Hugo's envoy. Vexed that Grandcourt was heir to all he
owned, to safeguard a home for his wife and daughters, Sir
Hugo wanted to buy Diplow in perpetuity for fifty thousand pounds. Grandcourt welcomed ready cash to maintain his existing properties, dependents, and lifestyle. Sir
Hugo had asked you to put the proposition to him.

I rode to Diplow on Criterion. Mama followed in a carriage. I had a superstitious dread of meeting you, as if that
first encounter determined all that would ensue. I feared
you were the moon to my tide and that it was not in my
power to turn from you.

Mrs. Torrington, Mama, and I viewed the rooms. I
found I could not care about the house or its furnishings.

I resolved to greet you with formal distance, but as we assembled for lunch my heart beat hard and I noticed you and no one else.

"Deronda, Miss Harleth tells me you were not introduced at Homburg," Grandcourt said.

"Miss Harleth hardly remembers me, I imagine," you replied, and bowed. "She was intensely occupied when I saw her."

I controlled my nerves. "On the contrary, I remember you very well," I said. "You did not approve of my playing roulette."

"How did you come to that conclusion?" you asked.

"Oh, you cast an evil eye on my play. I began to lose as soon as you looked at me. I had been winning until then."

"Roulette in a kennel like Homburg is a horrid bore," said Grandcourt.

"I found it a bore when I began to lose," I said, my face turned to him, my attention fixed on you, your clear deep voice, your attentive gaze, the disturbing sense you gave of infallible judgment.

At lunch I was so conscious of you I could not eat. The talk was of rinderpest and Jamaica. Grandcourt called the Jamaican Negro a beastly sort of Caliban; you said you had always sympathized with Caliban, who had his own point of view and could sing a good song; Mama spoke of her father's sugar plantation, which she had never seen, in the West Indies. Mrs. Torrington said she was sure she would never sleep in her bed if she lived among blacks; Captain

Torrington said the blacks would be manageable were it
not for the half-breeds; you said the whites had themselves
to blame for the half-breeds; I trifled with my jelly and
looked at each speaker in turn so as not to be conspicuous
for looking only at you.

I had never seen a black person or thought about one.
I was familiar only with the Wessex assumption of superiority. I had not, like you, been brought up in an atmosphere
of splendor, diverse cultures, and liberal thinking, though
Mama had always made sure I had nice gowns and pretty
jewels.

Grandcourt dismissed you as "a man of no consequence,"
but no one was more consequential to me than you. I so
minded what you thought of me, so wanted your approval,
admiration, and advice on my impending marriage. I hoped
you admired me in my riding gear. I wondered why you
were solemn and apart. In the drawing room, when Grandcourt was distracted, I approached you and asked if you
would hunt tomorrow. My heart thrilled when you said,
"Yes, I believe so."

"You don't object to hunting then?" I asked.

"I find excuses for it," you said. "It is a sin I am inclined
to when I can't go boating or play cricket."

"Do you object to my hunting?"

"I have no right to object to anything you choose to do."

"You thought you had a right to object to my gambling."

"I was sorry for it. I did not speak of objection."

"You hindered me from gambling again," I said, and blushed. You blushed too.

I turned away to a window, fearing I had gone too far. Your eyes were grave. I wanted to confide my impulsiveness, doubts, and muddle and for you to tell me what being good must be. I was awkward yet aware of a transparency between us, a lien of truth-telling, whatever that truth might be. I hoped you would not resist me. You had become so quickly my hero. My Deronda. My engagement to Grandcourt was two days old.

THAT EVENING, AT home at Offendene, Mama asked if it was true you had made me lose at the casino. I joked that it was simply I noticed you looking at me, which unnerved me, so I began to lose. Mama said she could understood why: you were striking to look at and put her in mind of Italian paintings. She had heard from Mrs. Torrington that your mother was some foreigner of high rank and that Sir Hugo, who was probably your father, would like to have left his estates to you as he had no legitimate son. Mama said she was unsurprised to hear there was foreign blood in you.

I imagined a beautiful, dark-eyed princess who might be your mother. And then I thought of another once beautiful dark-eyed woman and was ashamed to think that you too, like Mrs. Glasher, might one day resent me for being the mistress of Topping Abbey. In a fairer world Sir Hugo's estate would pass to you and his daughters, not to

Grandcourt or Mrs. Glasher's son and least of all to me. Were you to know of the existence of Mrs. Glasher and, even worse, know that I knew of her, I thought you would be compelled to despise me. I felt mired. I was betraying myself and my belief that for women marriage was a renunciation. That night in bed I quizzed Mama about my stepfather and spoke of my resentment at her marriage to him.

IT WAS NOT my way to mope or dwell on obstacles. Morning brought the prospect of the hunt. We started at dawn, the master sounded his horn, the hounds picked up the scent, Criterion was perfect, and we went so fast and far through brush, undergrowth, and meadows, jumping brooks and logs, I had no moments to doubt or fret. But as dusk came, on that gray November afternoon and the setting sun drew a streak of yellow in the west, I felt crushed by disappointment, for the day was gone, and you and I had not talked at all.

The Diplow party were escorting me home to Offendene. Grandcourt rode beside me, Mrs. Torrington and her husband were just in front, I heard your horse behind me, and the desire to speak with you overwhelmed me. We passed through a wood of pines and beeches, I reined Criterion, Grandcourt also paused, I waved my whip, and affecting playful imperiousness, I said, "Go on. I want to speak to Mr. Deronda." He could not deny me. We were not married.

He rode on slowly. I waited for you. You came up alongside me. There was tacit acceptance now that it was you who sent the necklace. I asked, "Why did you think it wrong of me to gamble? Is it because I am a woman?"

It was not only that, you said, though you regretted it the more because I was a woman, but you thought gambling an unhealthy thing, and to rake in a heap of money at someone else's cost and loss revolted you. I pleaded we could not always help profiting at someone else's expense. You agreed and said that consequently we should help it where we could.

Self-reproach and doubt about my impending marriage washed through me. I resorted to flippancy. Why, I asked, should you the more regret my gambling because I was a woman?

You said, "Perhaps because men need that you should be better than we are."

"But suppose *women* need that men should be better than *we* are?" I countered.

"That is a difficulty," you said. "Perhaps I should have said we each of us think it would be better for the other to be good."

"There. You see?" I said. "I needed you to be better than I was, and you thought the same."

I urged Criterion on to join Grandcourt. Who was worse than piqued. His silence and stillness warned. "Don't you want to know what I had to say to Mr. Deronda?" I asked.

"No" was his laconic reply. I chided him for his first

impoliteness, but I was not yet cowed by him. "I wish to hear what you say to me, not to other men," Grandcourt said.

I should have heeded this warning.

"Then you will wish to hear this: I wanted to make him tell me why he objected to my gambling, and he gave me a little sermon."

"Excuse me the sermon," Grandcourt said. *I should have taken careful note of the ice in his voice.* He cared about my speaking to you, and he very much cared at my telling him to ride on. I was not to be allowed such impertinence again.

Grandcourt delivered me to Offendene, bade me farewell, then left that evening for his unspecified journey—to see Mrs. Glasher and his four children at Gadsmere.

IN THE BRIEF days of my engagement there was much to arrange: the dress, my trousseau, the wedding invitations. Only in the silence of night did doubt overwhelm me: your disapproval at the gambling tables, my broken promise to Lydia Glasher, self-disgust that I had agreed to a mendacious contract, alarm at the life in store for me as Grandcourt's wife. I feared I had lost hold of the direction of my life and was falling, an endless fall.

Thought of your wise words and still demeanor calmed me. And thoughts of the lavish life I soon would lead: maids winding my watches, servants lighting the candles, my horses in the best of stables, my gowns pressed, my every whim indulged. I blocked my apprehension that marriage would entail more than Grandcourt's hated kissing of my neck below my ear. I closed my mind to what might happen when I went through the bedroom door.

THE DAY OF my wedding was bright, clear, and cold. Half of Pennicote lined the pathway to the church to watch me walk from my carriage. Mine was a rags-to-riches tale: Grandcourt, the romantic hero, must be hopelessly in love to save a penniless girl from a governess's fate and her mother from Sawyer's Cottage. I was the princess bride, my dress of silk and satin, trimmed with Honiton appliqué lace, my coronet of jasmine and stephanotis. Mama's eyes were pink from crying, Anna was a bridesmaid, and she too cried, though perhaps on behalf of Rex. I was exultant, defiant, but my ecstasy was unreal, as if I had taken an opiate, and my cheeks as white as my bridegroom's hands. I made the vows in a steady voice. Grandcourt slipped the gold ring onto my finger.

"Thank God you take it so well, my darling," Mama said when, back at Offendene in our room, she helped me from my bridal gown and into my traveling clothes. She made it sound like a tooth-pulling. I teased her tearful face. "I am Mrs. Grandcourt," I said, and spread my arms wide. "You might have said that if I'd been going to Mrs. Mompert. Remember, you were ready to die with vexation when you thought I would *not* be Mrs. Grandcourt? Now

I shall have everything: splendid houses, horses, diamonds . . . I shall be Lady Certainly and Lady This and
That and very grand, and always loving you better than
anybody else in the world."

"My dearest Gwen," Mama said, "I shall not be jealous
if you love your husband better, and he will expect to be
first." I told her that was a ridiculous expectation but that
I would not treat him ill unless he deserved it.

I jested with the optimism of ignorance, of a playful
creature who supposes the dark to be just a tunnel with
light at its end. But then I wept, for I so wished Mama was
coming with me into this new uncertain life.

In the porch Uncle consoled her, and they waved good-
bye as Grandcourt led me from Offendene to the waiting
carriage.

We were to go to Ryelands. A train journey of some
fifty miles took us to the nearest railway station, where a
carriage waited. It was twilight when we at last arrived at
the gates. I was aware of a long winding drive, shadowy
vistas of parkland, woodland, lakes, and formal gardens,
then a large white house, an imposing entrance porch, a
pavilion tower, oriel windows. Even in the gloaming and
my febrile state, I knew this was all as far from the Momperts as are diamonds from coal dust.

I chatted incessantly, excitedly. Grandcourt held my
hand and squeezed it. I grasped his hand with both mine
to stop this. "Here we are at home," he said, and for the
first time kissed me on the lips, but I scarcely noticed; it

was simply a gesture; a piece of theater, part of the absorb-
ing show.

Uniformed lackeys opened doors. I was shown long
corridors, stately rooms with Corinthian columns, high
ceilings, gilded zephyrs blowing trumpets, painted garlands, glittering chandeliers, formal portraits, Olympian
statues. We ascended the tulip staircase like a king and
queen.

"These are our dens," Grandcourt said, showing me into
rooms three times the size of Sawyer's Cottage. "You will
like to be quiet here until dinner. We shall dine early." He
pressed my hand to his lips, then left.

Hudson, my maid, trained by the housekeeper, took my
hat and cloak, curtsied, then left. I threw myself into a chair
by a glowing hearth. The room was decorated in pale green
satin, and I and it were reflected infinitely in mirrored pan-
els. I wanted to be alone to absorb the warmth and luxury
and get some grasp of who and where I was. The housekeeper
knocked and entered. She was holding something. I asked
her to tell Hudson to put my dress out, then leave me until
I rang for her. She said, "Here is a packet, madam, which
I was ordered to give into nobody's hands but yours when
you were alone. The person who brought it said it was a
present ordered by Mr. Grandcourt but that he was not to
know of its arrival until he saw you wear it."

I had already guessed that here was the parure of
diamonds Grandcourt said I was to have. I had not worn
diamonds before. In the packet was a box containing a

jewel case within which, as I opened it, the diamonds sparkled. Lying on them was a letter. I knew the handwriting. It was as if an adder was lying there. My hands trembled as I unfolded the thin paper.

> *These diamonds, which were once given with ardent love to Lydia Glasher, she passes on to you.*
>
> *You have broken your word to her that you might possess what was hers.*
>
> *Perhaps you think of being happy as she once was and of having beautiful children such as hers who will thrust hers aside. God is too just for that. The man you have married has a withered heart . . .*

My eyes skimmed the letter. I read it fast and once only. Its words etched into me. To this day I remember them: *broken your word . . . The man you have married has a withered heart . . . You had your warning . . . I am the grave in which your chance of happiness is buried . . . You will have your punishment . . . You took him with your eyes open . . . The willing wrong you have done me will be your curse . . .*

I trembled and gasped for air, then turned and threw the letter into the fire. As I did so the jewel case fell to the floor and the diamonds scattered. *You had your warning . . . His best young love was mine . . . He would have married me . . . You chose to injure me and my children . . . You will have your punishment. I desire it with all my soul . . .* I collapsed back into the chair, I do not know for how long. Grandcourt tapped at the door and entered dressed for dinner. My breathing turned to screams.

So began my husband's tyranny. He closed the door but made no move toward me. He said, "Stop screaming." It was a command. He did not, he said, want his servants thinking he had married some harpy from the gutter. "You are," he said, "Mrs. Grandcourt now."

I became silent, though I trembled still. "Pick up the diamonds," he said, "and put them into their case." I crawled the floor. "There is another under the chair," he said. "Pick it up." I picked it up.

"I shall tell you when I wish you to wear them," he said. His voice was uninflectioned, quiet, controlled, but oh so different from the morning and brief yesterdays of courtship. He was, he said, going down to dinner and would wait for me at the table. I was to dress; he would send a servant for me in fifteen minutes. "You are tired," he said, "after the journey. You are overwrought. We will retire early." At the door he turned and added with what seemed like vitriol, "Mrs. Grandcourt." I cannot tell you how absolute my sense of isolation was.

The door closed. My explosion of terror was replaced by more vigilant fear. I wanted to run from this terrible place. I willed myself to be calm, breathe evenly, and stop trembling. I longed for Mama to comfort me, longed for our black and gold bedroom and my annoying sisters. I longed for you.

I put on my trousseau clothes. Hudson knocked at the

door to say the master was waiting in the blue room. Under a sparkling chandelier a small table was set for two. Grandcourt behaved as if nothing had happened and nothing was amiss, but his voice now had authority unlaced with compliment and when I looked at him, which I tried not to do, I felt revulsion: the thin mustache, white skin, bald head, and ice-cold eyes. The death's head and figure in flight were now incarnate.

A butler stood with silver dishes: shellfish, poultry, cheese. My plight was more terrible in this luxurious setting. I could not eat, but I drank my wine. When the servant made to refill my glass, Grandcourt waved him away. The terms of the relationship were thus defined. Grandcourt's slanting gray eyes fixed on me and saw what they chose. I was his prey. His voice drawled. He talked of where we would go and when.

An eternity passed. I said I was tired after the events of the day. I wanted, needed, to sit alone in my room by the fire. Eventually, he told me I might go. As I rose to leave, he said he would join me in an hour. I froze with apprehension at what might ensue.

In my room the windows were now shuttered, the cover turned down on the large bed, the organza drawn back between its posts. Candles flickered. I dared not look at the shadows of their flames on the walls lest they transform into the death's head, the snake coiled on the diamonds.

In the dressing table mirror I looked into my frightened eyes. I would not again kiss my own image. There was now, I knew, no way out. I tried to empty my mind and stifle my fear. I sat by the fire unaware of the passing of time until the door handle turned.

He wore a nightshirt, his face was impassive, his movements were unhurried. He asked why I was not in my nightclothes, why I was not in bed. I did not know if there was derision in his voice. I said I felt homesick. There was no expression in his eyes. He held out his hand, I did not take it. I was to learn that any gesture from him, however small, was a command. He took my arm and raised me from the chair. I was wraithlike, a condemned soul.

OH, DERONDA, PLEASE remember I had not so much as kissed a man or been caressed. My revulsion was absolute. Any suggestion of lovemaking felt like an invasion. I had never felt desire for a man; I knew nothing of them beyond their admiration for me and my flirtation with them, which was laced with scorn. I grew up without them. I hated my stepfather to come home, the way he took Mama from me, his unwanted attention toward me. I had no father of my own, no brother. The only closeness I had had was when dancing the quadrille, the waltz, or polka, with Rex or Clintock or Mr. Middleton. Grandcourt had reassured me with his languid distance. I could not have known he sensed my profound terror, which fed his desire, that he had a torturer's mind.

What happened next I have down the years hinted at

but told no one. I tried to excise it from my mind. It took me not from being a girl into a woman but from bright hope to deep despair. Grandcourt led me to the bed, then gestured with a sweep of his arm for me to lie down. I trembled like a condemned creature, the lamb that smells the abattoir. I saw the writing of those terrible words: *The man you have married has a withered heart.* It was not that Grandcourt loved me more than Lydia Glasher; he wished to violate us equally.

He was entirely in control, though more angered than he chose to say. He took off his nightshirt. He had no awkwardness. I had never seen a naked man. I hated him clothed; naked, he was my executioner. He tore my dress and dropped it to the floor. I tried to check myself so I would not scream. To punish my screams would be his triumph. He said again, "Mrs. Grandcourt." To myself I whispered my name, *Gwendolen Harleth.* I tried to think of Mama, to think of you. He pinioned my hands above my head, held me down on the bed, told me twice to open my eyes, stared at me, moved his body against mine, then lunged into me. He was silent, did not seem to breathe, and stank of cigars. I felt a sear of pain, then nothing. I tried to scream but no sound came. I tried to block my senses, not to listen, smell, or feel. He said it again, "Mrs. Grandcourt," then stabbed into me again and again until I bled. When I tried to free myself, he became more vicious. I do not know how long the attack went on. Until he made a strange guttural sound, and I did not know if it was my

blood or his seed that seeped over me. I wanted to die. He
was silent. I thought he might hit me or spit. Then he said,
"That's what women are," threw the covers over me, put
on his nightshirt, said, "Now you can be alone," and closed
the door quietly as he left the room.

I felt myself pulled backward as if into a black tunnel.
I think I fainted. I do not know how long it was before I
rose to stem the bleeding and wash my body, rinse my
mouth. My legs buckled under me. There were bruises on
my neck. I was not beyond fear; I was at its silent core. I
thought, *There is no one I can tell of this, there are no words for
this, this has no voice.* I could not run into the night to Mama,
call for a doctor, inform the police. What Grandcourt had
done to me, would do to me, was not illegal. I was his wife.
I had no right or power to refuse him. Consent was imma-
terial. I was, as he told me, Mrs. Grandcourt.

AND SO IT crashed upon me, the punishment Lydia Glasher
desired with all her soul. For days I kept to my room. I
believe Grandcourt went away, I supposed to her. I was
feverish. The housekeeper, Hudson, the maids, replaced the
bedding, brought hot water, light soups, and custards but
made no comment. I did not read or look at other rooms.
I lay in bed and ceased to be. *Tu sera heureuse, ma chère? Oui,
maman, comme toi.*

What options were there for me? If I ran away, where
might I go or to whom? My husband would command

my return. If I sought divorce, all calumny would fall on me; I would be seen as an ingrate, a hysteric, deserving of the gutter. No Momperts would hire me as their governess, no school as their teacher. Poor Mama would have nothing.

Hatred bred evil in my heart. I wanted Grandcourt dead. I had a knife, a thin blade like a long willow leaf, encased in a silver sheath. I imagined driving it into his throat, stabbing it into his withered heart. I wanted always to keep it near. I wanted to keep it under my pillow, but I never did. Had I done so, I would have used it. I remembered how, with scarce provocation, I killed Alice's caged bird. I locked the knife in the drawer of my dressing case.

FOR FIVE DAYS I stayed in my room. On the sixth afternoon I was summoned to the conservatory. The day was unusually mild, and a door was open to the lawn. Grandcourt languished, smoking a cigar and sipping coffee. Half a dozen dogs of various kinds grouped around him. Hitherto I had supposed him to be a dog lover. Fetch, the spaniel, as ever sat at his feet and watched him constantly, her head on her forepaws.

Grandcourt asked me nothing about myself. He talked as if nothing had happened. He told me of visits, dinner parties, and tours we were to make: the Brackenshaws, the Mallingers, Paris, Basel, Homburg, Venice.

On his lap he fondled Fluff, a tiny Maltese, a sweet puff of white fur with a silver collar and bell. Fetch, jealous, put her paw on Grandcourt's leg. Grandcourt stared at her, put down his cigar, lifted Fluff to his face, and looked at me. Fetch whimpered, tried to restrain her anguish, then rested her head on his leg. Grandcourt continued to caress the Maltese while shifting his stare between Fetch and me. After a minute Fetch, unable to bear the torment, howled. Grandcourt dumped the miniature dog on a table, called to a servant, and, referring to Fetch, ordered him to "turn that brute out."

The mocking look my husband then gave me defined his perverse control. I, the woman at the Whispering Stones, his horses, his dogs—he observed what a creature wanted, needed, then administered the opposite. Cruelty dispelled his boredom; without it he had no interest. My youth, vulnerability, chastity, and reluctance ignited his desire.

Thus my marriage. Each night seemed prelude to murder. I dreaded the turn of the door handle. I learned in those nightly assaults to make no move of resistance. He waited for an excuse to be ever more vicious. I thought he would kill me. I tried never to look at him, but I imagined his white slender fingers closing around my throat. I closed my eyes and thought of the knife in the drawer.

I vowed never to wear the rancid diamonds, emblems of my wrongdoing, my signature to this nightmare, to the face in the wainscot, and to Mrs. Glasher at the Whispering Stones. But a week or so later, on an evening when we were to dine at Brackenshaw Castle, I came downstairs dressed in white, a pendant of emeralds Grandcourt had given me around my neck, emerald stars in my ears. He smoked a cigar, lounged in a chair, scrutinized me, then told me I was not altogether as he liked.

"Oh mercy," I said. "How am I to alter myself?"

"Put on the diamonds."

I tried not to show revulsion and fear, but I suppose they were in my eyes. "Oh please, no. I don't think diamonds suit me."

"What you think has nothing to do with it," he said, and stroked his mustache. He never raised his voice. "I wish you to wear the diamonds."

"Pray excuse me, I like these emeralds."

"Oblige me by telling me your reason for not wearing the diamonds when I desire it."

I turned and went to my dressing room; he followed me. "You will want someone to fasten them," he said. He took them from their case. His hands crawled at my neck, my hair, ears, breasts. I sat with my eyes closed. *What a privilege this is to have robbed another woman of,* I thought.

"What makes you so cold?" asked Grandcourt as he fastened the last earring. "Put plenty of furs on. I hate to see a woman come into a room looking frozen. If you are to appear as a bride at all, appear decently." He kissed my neck below my ear.

Until this marriage I knew nothing of scathing domination. No one had ever spoken to me in a brutal way.

Grandcourt made Klesmer seem like a flatterer. *The man you have married has a withered heart.* I put on the furs.

MAMA. HOW I missed and yearned for her and Offendene. Severance happened within weeks of the wedding. I ventured to ask Grandcourt if she and Uncle might visit Diplow. After a silence he drawled, "We can't be having those people always." That Gascoigne, he said, talked too much and was a bore. I could only infer Mama's unsuitability. I could not tell her she was not wanted, or let her observe the wretchedness of my married life.

Only seldom were she and I allowed to meet. Once Grandcourt arranged for her to be fetched with my uncle and aunt for lunch and dinner. They were driven back next morning soon after breakfast. Twice, I was permitted a brief visit to Offendene while he waited outside on horseback. Mama, bewildered, thought the distance at which she was kept was because of my indifference to her now that I was exalted by this marriage.

My only consolation was that financially she was better off, though I knew that between her penury and my misery she would choose the former. On our wedding day Grandcourt had given her a letter saying the rent on Offendene was paid until the following June and that he would grant her eight hundred pounds a year. That meant Miss Merry could stay and the gardener, Robert Crane, be paid to do the outdoors work.

Grandcourt also suggested that if a cottage on the Ryelands estate became free, Mama and my sisters might like to live there. Mama anticipated this move, but I dissuaded her. I said Ryelands was splendid but we were not much there; she would feel adrift and alone and would miss my aunt and uncle. Nonetheless, I thanked Grandcourt for providing for her. I did not want him to punish her too. "You took a great deal on yourself in marrying a girl who had nothing but relations belonging to her," I said.

"Of course I was not going to let Mrs. Davilow live like a gamekeeper's mother" was his reply.

And so I appeared on the social scene as Mrs. Grandcourt and did not reveal to the world my revulsion and despair at the role. My bleeding was stemmed, my bruises were covered with lace and velvet. Grandcourt's choices of compliance became mine: riding, hunting, visiting, entertaining. I told Mama I was happy.

II · Deronda

So Grandcourt broke me and isolated me. In Society I appeared as his bride, his wife. At night I endured the quiet opening of the door, the brutal commands and savage attack. Then he would leave and go to his room. What I felt went beyond hate. Hate was my daylight emotion. I longed for the time of my menses, for then he kept away. Before marriage, I felt enervated by my monthly cycle; when I married, it became a remission. I waited for signs of my blood. My terror was that I might become pregnant and give birth to a Frankenstein monster in his image.

I dreamed of ways to avoid my life. I thought gambling might divert me, but I feared it would increase my self-contempt. I yearned for your wise counsel. I wanted you to know I was not contemptible but in trouble.

Of course I knew nothing of your life. Only later did I learn of your absorption into Jewish identity, your Jewish parents, the Jewish girl you saved from drowning, how you roamed the East End of London, worshipped in synagogues, read weighty books about Hebrew matters, and planned for a life about which I knew nothing and which excluded me.

At the end of December we met again at Topping Abbey, your home with the Mallingers. I had been married six weeks, though time had ceased to have a dimension. Sir Hugo decreed the seasonal party he gave that year be in honor of the marriage of Grandcourt, heir to the Abbey, and me, his new and beautiful bride.

The Abbey was a place of romantic enchantment, far superior to the boastful affluence of Ryelands. I felt shame to suppose I might one day become the false chatelaine and this historic home turn to my prison with Grandcourt my jailer.

Snow was falling when our carriage turned into the drive. I looked out at white meadowland and frosted trees. As we entered the house my heart beat hard at the thought of seeing you. Liveried footmen guided us past full-length portraits set in cedar paneling, oak boughs burning in huge fires under ceilings painted with coats of arms. I came into the Great Hall on Grandcourt's arm. I was wearing white and at his command the poisoned infestation of diamonds around my neck, in my ears, my hair.

I saw you instantly. I did not look in your direction.

You were talking to Mr. Vandernoodt. I heard him say sotto voce, "By George, I think she's handsomer if anything." A short time previously I might have preened. Now what was I but an adornment, a badge of triumph for an evil man whom I loathed. I again felt your gaze on me. I thought if I met your eyes, my degradation would flood out, the diamonds shatter, and I would sink to my knees. Yet through your eyes was the only place where I longed to be seen.

Plump Lady Mallinger, with protruding blue eyes and red hair, clad in black velvet, and carrying a tiny white dog on her arm, moved graciously among her guests. I was introduced and exchanged courtesies with her four daughters, her brother Mr. Raymond and his wife, the Vandernoodts, Lord Pentreath (white-haired and patrician) and his wife, Mr. Fenn (a cider manufacturer and member of Parliament for West Orchards) and his two daughters, the lawyer Mr. Sinker, and Mr. and Mrs. George Lewes (who were authors—both very ugly, he vivacious, she intense, her voice low, her eyes observant). I had read and quite enjoyed two of Mrs. Lewes's books: *Silas Marner* and *The Mill on the Floss*. She published under the name George Eliot, which had made me wonder if she was a man. She seemed to appraise me with disapproval. Mama had not been invited.

We were called to dinner. The dining room's arches and pillars were now shadowed in candlelight, and long tables glittered with silver and glass. I sat as guest of honor beside Sir Hugo. You sat diagonally opposite me. Grandcourt was at the far end of the table with Lady Mallinger seated to his left and Mrs. Lewes to his right. His concentration, like a predatory mantis, was set on me alone.

I was assiduous in not acknowledging you. My eyes would have said too much. Sir Hugo was attentive and kindly, for I was his special guest. He talked of Klesmer and Catherine and gave his view that the Arrowpoints showed sense in accepting the marriage after all the fuss in the papers. When I told him Klesmer was spending Christmas at Quetcham Hall, he said to you, "Deronda, you will like to hear what Mrs. Grandcourt tells me about your favorite, Klesmer," and I was obliged to raise my eyes to meet your bow, your smile, and your questioning eyes. I blushed and could not speak.

"For the Arrowpoints to disown their only child because of a misalliance would be like disowning their one eye," Sir Hugo said. You rejoindered if there was a misalliance, it was on Klesmer's part. "Ah," Sir Hugo said to you, "you think it a case of the immortal marrying the mortal," then asked my opinion. I failed to check my bitterness. I said, "I have no doubt Herr Klesmer thinks himself immortal, but I daresay his wife will burn as much incense before him as he requires."

"Klesmer is no favorite of yours, I see." Sir Hugo looked at me in a questioning way.

"I think very highly of him, I assure you. His genius is quite above my judgment, and I know him to be exceedingly generous."

Klesmer had contributed to my belittlement. I was in

no mood to hear of his own wonderful union of talent, love, and wealth.

Sir Hugo talked of the Abbey. Grandcourt and I, he said, must tour it in the morning with you, who knew and loved every detail, as our guide. At this mention of a strand of my guilt—that the Abbey would one day go to my unworthy husband—I glanced awkwardly at you, then to cover my discomfort said to Sir Hugo, "You don't know how much I am afraid of Mr. Deronda."

"Because you think him too learned?" Sir Hugo asked.

Not that, I said, then told him how at Homburg you watched and disapproved as I played roulette, how then I began to lose, and how now I feared lest any word or action of mine caused your opprobrium.

I seemed compelled to return again and again to that first encounter, as if it had shaped my destiny and as if, were I now to find a way to escape from my devastating mistake, help must come from you.

Sir Hugo confessed he too was rather afraid of you if he felt you did not approve, but then he facetiously said, "I don't think ladies generally object to having Mr. Deronda's eyes upon them." I disliked his flippancy and innuendo, or perhaps I was jealous.

"I object to any eyes that are critical," I said.

The conversation turned to the Abbey. Sir Hugo confessed he had overreached himself with extensive, costly renovations; particularly to the long gallery above the cloistered court and to the stables. "You must go and see for yourself," he said. I told him I should like to see the horses as much as the building. Sir Hugo said he had given up riding and hunting and that Grandcourt would look with contempt on his horses.

"Do you like Diplow?" he then asked.

"Not particularly," I replied. How could I say I hated the place and that it held more torment for me than Sawyer's Cottage?

Sir Hugo observed my discontent, looked quizzical, but chose not to question me more. "It will not do after Ryelands," he said. "Grandcourt only likes it for the hunting. But he found something so much better there that he might well prefer it to any other place in the world."

I smiled politely to conceal my loathing of the mere mention of my husband's name.

"It has one attraction for me," I said. "It is within reach of Offendene."

"I understand that," Sir Hugo said, and let the matter drop. Neither he nor anyone else could know how homesick I was, how I yearned for the old imperfect rented house, my small bed in the gold and black bedroom.

We moved to another room. I stood with my back to everyone, looking at a carved ivory head. You stood nearby. I looked into your eyes, and with that look I confessed, admitted my suffering, fear, remorse, and love of and need for you. Your eyes showed sympathy and alarm. You said nothing. It was an exchange more intense than your first gaze of consternation in Homburg. Even now I feel and see it, as if we had been captured in a painting, your soul and mine fused into one. I was too fearful to speak of my plight, but I needed you to know how wretched I was. Did I appear full of airs: tall, elegant, my clothes silk and satin, diamonds in my ears and hair? Did you find me superficial: an avaricious creature who cared too much for possession and rank?

Someone requested you should sing.

"Will you join in the music?" you asked. I roused myself to say, "I join in by listening. I gave time to music, but I have not enough talent to make it worthwhile."

You said if I was fond of music, I should play and sing for my own delight. For yourself, you saw it as a virtue to be content with your own middlingness and not expect others to want more of you.

I recovered my sparring manner: "To be middling in my thinking is another phrase for being dull," I said. "And the worst fault I have to find with the world is that it is dull. The best thing about gambling is that it provides a refuge from dullness."

You did not admit the justification. Your view was that when we called life dull, it was because of our own shortcomings. I was again reprimanded. You had no quarrel with middlingness. You were convinced about what was right and what was wrong.

"Oh dear," I said. "So the fault I find with the world is my own fault. Do you never find fault with the world or with others?"

"When I am in a grumbling mood," you said.

"And hate people?" I asked. "Confess you hate them when they stand in your way—when their gain is your loss? That is your own phrase, you know."

"We often stand in each other's way when we can't help it. It is stupid to hate people on that ground."

"But if they injure you and could have helped it?" The injury I had done, my broken promise, my sense of punishment deserved—all plagued my mind.

"Why then, after all, I would prefer my place to theirs."

"There I believe you are right," I said. I had my answer. Lydia Glasher's curse had found its home. The assault I endured nightly from Grandcourt was just. I deserved my punishment.

Or so I believed in that dark time. Now I am kinder to myself. I think on impulse I acted foolishly and events took a course. My mistakes were naïveté, rashness, and bad advice. Grandcourt had no worthy regard for Lydia Glasher. They were complicit in evil. He knew of her showing at Cardell Chase and that on my wedding day she would send a note with the diamonds. Too late I turned to you, the kindest of men. You would have urged me not to marry Grandcourt. Yet unintentionally you hurt me in the most enduring way. Unwittingly, you began something with which you could not follow through. On that New Year's night I realized that the feelings and thoughts I had for you were of love but that time with you must always be stolen.

You moved to the piano. Grandcourt of course had

observed our exchange. Slumped in an easy chair, smoking, and half listening to Mr. Vandernoodt, he appeared bored but missed nothing in relation to me. Out of the corners of his narrow eyes he kept me under his rule. Seeing my desire and need for you, he would bide his time, then punish me.

BY THE NEXT afternoon the snow had mostly thawed. Sir Hugo recommended we meet in the library at three and tour the stables before dark. Longing to see you alone, I hurried down early in my sables, plumed hat, and little thick boots. You were reading a paper, and I dared not disturb you. You did not hear me come into the room. I waited by the door, dreading the arrival of the others. At last you saw me. "Oh, there you are already," you said. "I must go and put on my coat," and you left the room as Grandcourt and Sir Hugo came in. I felt a rush of disappointment. I had so wanted time with you.

"You look rather ill," Grandcourt said to me. "Do you feel equal to the walk?"

"Yes, I shall like it," I replied. I always now tried to avoid his eyes.

Sir Hugo suggested we put off the excursion if I wished. "Oh dear, no," I said, "let us put off nothing. I want a long walk."

We were joined by Miss Juliet Fenn, Mr. and Mrs. Lewes, and others. You walked beside me. As we toured, you gave us the history of what once had been the sacristy, the chapter house, the dormitory. You told us when and why the bells were sold and where the monks were buried. I thought how perfect life would be were you and I to reside in such an ancient romantic English setting. You explained the significance of architectural fragments and embellishments and of niches in the stone walls. In the old kitchen, shadows from a huge fire flickered on polished tin, brass, and copper. Sir Hugo gave his reasons for mixing the modern and antique. He said we should be flexible about restoring old fashions. You agreed and said to delight in doing things because our fathers did them was good if it shut out nothing better, but that new things enlarge the range of affection and that affection was the basis of good in life.

I expressed surprise. I said I thought you cared more about ideas and wisdom than affection. "But to care about *them* is a sort of affection, and an indivisible mix of people and ideas forms the deepest affections," you said.

I only half understood what you were saying. I told you I was not very affectionate. Was that, I asked, the reason why I did not see much good in life? You replied that if I sincerely believed that of myself, you should think it true.

Sir Hugo and Grandcourt joined us. "I never can get Mr. Deronda to pay me a compliment," I told them. "I have quite a curiosity to see whether a little flattery can be extracted from him."

"Ah," Sir Hugo said, "the fact is, it is hopeless to flatter a bride. She has been so fed on sweet speeches that everything we say seems tasteless."

"Quite true," I said. "Mr. Grandcourt won me by neatly turned compliments. If there had been one word out of place, it would have been fatal."

"Do you hear that?" Sir Hugo asked him, cautiously encouraging the banter.

"Yes," said Grandcourt, with a warning look to me. "It is a deucedly hard thing to keep up, though."

Sir Hugo only half thought it a tease, and I did not want to hear the truth spoken. I made light of my bitterness and contempt, but you had more than glimpsed into the casket where the serpent writhed over my diamonds. You turned your attention to the other ladies and kept out of my way.

We walked the gravel paths; snow had massed on the boughs of a great cedar. The stables were formed from what once was the Abbey's beautiful choir. The exterior brick wall was covered with ivy, but inside each finely arched chapel had been turned into a stall for beautiful, sleek, brown and gray horses. The original stained-glass windows were crimson, orange, blue, and palest violet; there were four carved angels below the grand pointed roof; for the rest the choir was leveled, paved, and drained in modern fashion. Hay hung from racks where saints once looked down from altarpieces. A little white-and-liver-colored spaniel had made his bed in the back of an old hackney carriage.

I cried out, "Why, this is glorious! I wish there were a

horse in every box. I would ten times rather have these stables than those at Diplow," then blushed with shame at such
a blunder.

"Now we are going to see the cloister," Sir Hugo said.
"It's the finest bit of all, in perfect preservation. The monks
might have been walking there yesterday."

My odious husband came to my side. "You had better
take my arm," he commanded. I took it. I did not now
speak to him unless he addressed me or some practicality
needed to be arranged. "It's a great bore being dragged
about in this way and with no cigar," he said.

"I thought you'd like it."

"Like it? Eternal chatter. And these ugly girls—inviting
one to meet such monsters. That hideous Mrs. Lewes,
and how that fat Deronda can bear looking at that Miss
Fenn . . ."

"Why do you call him fat? Do you object to him so
much?"

"Object? No. What do I care about his being fat? I'll
invite him to Diplow again if you like."

"I don't think he'd come. He's too learned and clever
to care about us."

"That makes no difference. Either he is a gentleman,
or he is not."

In all Grandcourt said I was warned; mild rebuke was
punishment deferred. Irritation with me transmuted to violence against me. We moved to the cloistered court. You
explained the arched and pillared openings, the delicately

wrought foliage on the capitals. You said that when you were a boy, the carving on these capitals taught you to observe and delight in the structure of leaves, which made you wonder whether we learned to love real things through their representations or the other way around.

Mrs. Lewes stood beside me. She remarked on the particular intricacy of the carving of the willow branches. Without looking at me, she said, "You have a knife, shaped and carved like a willow leaf." I was breathless. I did not answer. How did she know? Had Grandcourt told her? Was my every move surveilled and known to her as well as to him? Did she know of my temptation, my hatred?

"You must love this place very much," Juliet Fenn said to you. She had inquisitive eyes and was making notes. "So many homes are alike, but yours is unique and you seem to know every cranny of it. I daresay you could never love another home as much."

"I carry it with me," you said. "There's no disappointment in memory. And one's exaggerations are always on the good side."

Your words seemed to relinquish the Abbey and acknowledge your loss and my unwanted triumph. They implied loneliness and severance from all that appeared to be yours but at root was not. I wondered about your mysterious foreign mother.

I was prevented from talking to you. Sir Hugo showed us the portraits in the gallery above the cloisters: rows of Mallinger descendants, males from the female line, females from the male line, painted by Lely, Kneller, Reynolds, Romney, men in armor with pointed beards, ladies lost in hoops, ruffs, and coiffures, men in black velvet and wigs, politicians in powdered perruques. Their resemblance to each other recurred in the family aquiline nose, the ladies' rosebud lips, the alabaster skin. I searched every one for likeness to you but could find no resemblance to your dark curls, dark eyes, and light brown skin.

At the tour's end Grandcourt went to the billiard room and I to the boudoir assigned me. I shut myself away and in despair looked at my image in the glass. In seven weeks my past life was crushed and belief in my own power gone. My will had been imperious but girlish. Grandcourt had rendered my body and spirit helpless and gained a mastery like that of a boa constrictor that goes on pinching and crushing without alarm at thunder. I dreaded hearing from him that, before our marriage, he already knew I had broken my promise to Mrs. Glasher. Were that admitted aloud, his hold over me would be complete.

ON NEW YEAR'S Eve at the Abbey Sir Hugo and Lady Mallinger held a grand ball in the picture gallery above the cloisters. As a signal to you of our secret allegiance, I wanted to wear the turquoise necklace as my sole ornament. Knowing Grandcourt would not allow it, I put on his hated diamonds, wound the turquoise three times round my wrist, then concealed it with the lace frill of my glove.

Half the gallery was to be used for dancing, the other
for the huge supper table. The red carpet was down; hot-
house plants and flowers filled every recess. Sir Hugo opened
the ball dancing with me, Lady Pentreath danced with you,
and Lady Mallinger was obliged to dance with Grandcourt;
it was hard not to see her as the mother who produced nothing better than daughters and so let her husband's land and
mansions slip into the pocket of this arrogant man.

To my surprise, you then boldly asked if I wished to
dance. Grandcourt was beside me grumbling he was bored
and wanted to leave. My hopes lifted; here was my chance
to show you the necklace. I said I had danced enough but
asked you to fetch me a glass of water. As you brought it,
I drew off my glove. You noticed the necklace. Grandcourt
noticed you noticing. "What is that hideous thing you have
on your wrist?" he asked.

With you there I was fearless. "It is an old necklace I
like to wear," I said, looking at you. "I lost it once, and
someone found it for me." I drank the water and handed
you the glass. When you returned you spoke of a fine view
from the side windows of moonlight on the stone pillars.
I said I should like to see it and asked Grandcourt if he
wished to. "Deronda will take you," he said, and walked
away.

You offered your arm. I felt proud to hold it. I looked
out at the moon, the light and shadows, and they soothed
me. I felt I must talk to you but had so little time. You
knew I was unhappy, needed you, and could not speak

directly. "Suppose I had gambled again, and lost the necklace again, what would you have thought of me?" I asked.

"Worse than I do now," you said.

I whispered I had done much worse, a great deal worse, and because of this felt wrong, miserable, and deserving of the punishment that had come. I asked you what I should do, what you would do. I wanted to tell you what was happening to me, but I could not utter the words. You were so honest and pure minded. You did not encourage me to be candid. I could not tell you I was nightly ravaged by a man whom I had voluntarily married, that I asked him not to come to my bed but that made him more vicious, that I wanted to kill him and feared I would do so. You said pure thoughts and good habits helped us bear inevitable sorrow and that wrongdoing could not be amended by one thing only. I wanted to say, Yes, that is all very well, but help me, please.

"Why," I asked, "did you make me doubt what I was doing and stop me gambling at the Kursaal? I might have won again. Why shouldn't I do as I like and not mind? Other people do."

"I don't believe you would ever get not to mind," you said. "I don't believe you could ever lead an injurious life without feeling remorse. If it were true that baseness and cruelty made some escape from pain, what difference would that make to you if you can't be quite base or cruel?"

"Tell me what better I can do," I pleaded to you, knowing I must return to my jailer.

"Many things. Look on other lives besides your own. See what their troubles are and how they are borne. Try to care for something in this vast world besides the gratification of small selfish desires. Try to care for what is best in thought and action. Something that is good, apart from the accidents of your own lot."

Your words scored into my thinking as much as Lydia Glasher's curse. They gave me hope that even though I was trapped, I might one day be free. I was the chattel of an evil man who intended to tame me, bring me to heel, make me respond to the rein; but he could not take my resistance from me, he knew nothing of my soul. It was not that I thought I might become a missionary, suffragist, nun, or teacher, but rather that were I to find a path to freedom I would go down it, were I to find a place of kindness and courage I might live again. My sorrow was that I wanted that place to be you.

You returned me to Grandcourt. We passed Mrs. Lewes, who looked intently at us. I told my wretched husband I was ready to go, I asked you to excuse us to Lady Mallinger, then thanked you, and we left.

Unpleasantness, I knew, would follow. Grandcourt came to my boudoir, sprawled in a chair, and said, "Sit down." I sat. "Oblige me in the future by not showing whims like a madwoman in a play," he said.

"What do you mean?"

"I suppose there is some understanding between you and Deronda about that thing on your wrist. If you have

anything to say to him, say it, but don't carry on a tele-
graphing that other people are supposed not to see. It's dam-
nably vulgar."

"You can know all about the necklace," I said, pride
overcoming my fear.

"I don't want to know. Keep to yourself what you like.
What I care to know I shall know without your telling me.
Only you will please to behave as becomes my wife and
not make a spectacle of yourself."

It gave him no discomfort to chide me in this way. After
our marriage he only ever addressed me by way of command and punishment.

"Do you object to my talking to Mr. Deronda?" I asked.

"I don't care two straws about him or any other con-
ceited hanger-on. You may talk to him as much as you
like. But you are my wife, and either you will fill your place
properly—to the world and to me—or you will go to the
devil."

"I never intended anything but to fill my place properly," I said. I did not say that in taking my place with him
I had gone to the devil and beyond.

"You put that thing on your wrist and hid it from me
till you wanted him to see it. You will understand that you
are not to compromise yourself. Behave with dignity. That's
all I have to say."

He stood with his back to the fire and looked at me
with derision. It was futile for me to try to explain, coun-
terproductive to argue or show emotion. There was much

I might have said about compromise and dignity. Grand-court pursued argument only to regard subduing me as winning it. He was not jealous but contemptuous and vicious. He would punish every independent move I made; I would do as he said, endure all he did, or be damned. I was his wife.

"Please leave me to myself tonight," I whispered. He left the room and returned within an hour.

MISERY FED MY defiance. The next day I determined to make use of Grandcourt's scornful permission for me to talk to you. I encountered you in the drawing room at tea-time. You were in conversation with Mrs. Lewes, whom I again thought ugly, with her jutting chin and big nose. I approached. "Mrs. Grandcourt," she said, and I was dis-comfited by her appraisal of me with her thoughtful blue eyes. I feared she was critical and considered me shal-low because I cared about my appearance and was young and not learned. I told her I had enjoyed *Silas Marner* and wished that I, like Eppie, had had a loving adoptive father such as Silas. "Yes," she said. "It was a pity you were so young when your father died, and that Captain Davilow proved unsatisfactory."

How strange I again felt. I could not fathom how she knew about my father and Davilow, or who in the room might have told her of them. She seemed to scrutinize you, too, as if to measure the effect of my presence on you.

I attempted with scant success to follow your conversation. The topic was synagogues and Jewish customs and how you both were studying Hebrew with Emmanuel Deutsch. From her bag Mrs. Lewes gave you a list of eighteen books about the Jews and their history, which she thought would interest you. I could only ponder why.

I gathered she was working on a novel in which she hoped to overcome English attitudes of narrow-minded arrogance toward the Jews. You mentioned Mirah Lapidoth, "a little Jewess" known to you both. Mrs. Lewes had invited her to dinner to hear her sing Hebrew hymns. Miss Lapidoth, she said, was equally accomplished singing in Italian or German. Herr Klesmer had called at the house where she lodged and been impressed by her rendition of Leopardi's "Ode to Italy" and Faust's "Songs to Gretchen." So taken were you with her enchanting voice, you suggested Lady Pentreath and Lady Mallinger arrange singing lessons with her for their daughters, or hire her for private concerts. Were I to hear her, you assured me, I might revoke my resolution to give up singing. It would more likely confirm it, I said, for I would plainly see my own middlingness. On the contrary, you said, Miss Lapidoth would inspire me to try.

Your praise of Miss Lapidoth's talent made me jealous. Nonetheless, since you so admired her, I decided I should like to hear her and have lessons from her when in town. "I mean lessons in rejoicing at her excellence and my own deficiency," I could not resist saying.

Was she, I then asked, as perfect in everything else as in her music? You replied you had seen nothing in her you would wish to be different. She had had an unhappy life and childhood, but no advantages could have given her more grace or truer refinement. Mrs. Lewes concurred.

I asked about her unhappiness. I was well versed in my own. You said she had been abandoned and ill-used by her father and in despair was on the brink of drowning herself. "What stopped her?" Mrs. Lewes asked, and you spoke in your oblique way of a ray of light, piety, and submission to duty. I became impatient. "I have no sympathy with women who are always doing right," I said. "I cannot believe in their great suffering."

I was stung to compare myself in ill light with this Miss Lapidoth. There was much in me you would wish to be different. Unhappiness had spawned in me not grace and refinement but bitterness and hate. Klesmer lauded her playing and singing with the same authority as he dismissed mine. No doubt you and Mrs. Lewes would do likewise.

You did not endear me to Miss Lapidoth. Nonetheless, beyond the catalog of my inferiority, I felt you were as drawn to me as I to you, although it seemed there was a barrier, even beyond my marriage, to your making any move toward me.

ON THE LAST day Grandcourt and I were to leave at three in the afternoon. In the morning he went with Sir Hugo

to King's Topping to see the old manor house. Other gentlemen went shooting. I strolled with the ladies, looked at
the waterfowl and shrubs, endured Lord Pentreath's anec-
dotes about the Crimean War and Mr. Vandernoodt's compliments on my complexion and figure.

Hoping to find you, I slipped away, ran back to the
house and through a side door into the library. You were
sitting at a writing table, your back to the door. There was
a huge log fire, and the room was like a sequestered private chapel, which I scarcely dared enter. When you seemed
to pause, I said your name. You rose in surprise. "Am I
wrong to come in?" I asked.

"I thought you were out on your walk," you said.

"I turned back."

You offered to accompany me, if I wished, to join the
others. I said no, that I needed to say something to you
and could not stay long. I had so little time. I needed your
guidance. I rested my arms and muff on the back of the
chair and spoke quickly. I had planned to confess and tell
all, but my words, when they came, were evasive and cir-
cumventory. Vandernoodt, I believe, had hinted to you
about Grandcourt's establishment at Gadsmere. But I found
I could not mention Lydia Glasher by name or directly say
what I had done.

I told you I had deliberately thrust others out and made
my gain out of their loss. I could not alter that, but what
should I do, I asked, as recompense for the injury caused?
"What would *you* do, what would *you* feel in my place?"

Your reply was guarded. In my place, you said, you would feel the sorrow I was feeling. That, I understood as a tautology. It was not enough. I persisted, "What would you try to *do?*"

"Order my life so as to make any possible amends," you said, "and keep away from doing any sort of injury again." I said I could not make amends; I had to continue on the path I was on.

I wanted to be taken to a safe harbor, to be shown what to do today and tomorrow. Instead, in a circumlocutory exchange of hints and suggestions, you gave me advice more lofty than Uncle's sermons. You talked of "the yoke of my own wrongdoing," said I must submit to it as if to an incurable disease, and, to counterbalance evil, use this unalterable wrong I had done as a reason for effort toward good. "Be spurred into higher conduct," you said, "and save other lives from being spoiled."

How might I do that? I wondered. I did not love "other lives" and never thought much of anyone's life except my own and Mama's. "But what can I do? I must get up in the morning and do what everyone else does. It is all like a dance set beforehand. The world is all confusion to me, and I am tired and sick of it."

You became severe and said again that life would be worth more if I had an interest beyond the drama of my small personal desires. "Is there any single occupation of mind that you care about with passionate delight or even independent interest?" you asked.

I had no answer. Grandcourt insisted I be what he commanded. You suggested I be someone in my own right. It was hard for any woman to have passionate independent delights and interests, least of all a woman in my circumstances, young, disastrously married, and weakly educated. I wanted to cry to you, "Don't you see I am in a trap? Can't you see that I need help to escape?"

I felt like a child shaken and told to wake up, get up, but into an empty house with locked doors. I said I would try, but that I was living without affection around me. I so wanted to be with Mama and that was impossible, everything had changed in such a short time, and the old things now gone, which I used not to like, I now longed for with all my heart.

"Take your present suffering as a painful letting in of light," you said. "You cannot escape that painful process."

I wanted to tell you of the cruel form of suffering given to me, but I could not. I said, "I am frightened of everything. When my blood is fired, I dare do anything, take any leap, and that makes me frightened of myself."

I wanted to tell you of my battle with anger and hatred, of the knife with the willow-shaped blade, my fear of what I might do if the moment came when I could bear my affliction no longer. But, you see, you could not know what it was to be used by Grandcourt in the way I was used.

"Turn your fear into a safeguard," you said. How often would I cling to those words. *Turn your fear into a safeguard.* "It is like quickness of hearing," you said. "When calm, we can change the bias of our fear. Take hold of your sensibility and use it as if it were a faculty, like vision."

You looked at me as if I was drowning, which indeed I was, and as if you could not save me. I believe you wanted to help me but could do no more than share with me thoughts that had consoled you. Perhaps all I heard was your soft voice and all I sensed was your concern. I reassured you I would think of what you told me. I said you had helped me, that my life would be better because I had known you. I could not tell you that you were my only lifeline and that I loved you.

Deronda, I struggled with your advice. My rejection of it was not willful, but I did not know how to apply it. I wanted redemption and to be guided toward virtue, but you were telling me to bear the unbearable.

With silence, space, and the passing of time, I see my situation differently. What had happened to me was not like an incurable disease. I had married a cruel and deceitful man. It should have been possible for me to leave him, gain my freedom, expose his wrongdoing, and turn the spotlight of wrongdoing on him.

I LONGED FOR you to respect me. I wanted to improve and change. I wondered what books you might advise me to read. When Grandcourt and I returned to Ryelands, from the library I took to my room *Discourse on the Method of Rightly Conducting One's Reason and of Seeking Truth in the*

Sciences by René Descartes and *The History of Civilization in Europe* by François Guizot, but I could not get far with either. I read some pages, then was deterred by their impenetrability, and my thoughts strayed.

Grandcourt's visits to Gadsmere were frequent and not to be discussed. He never said when he was going, or where, or for how long, but I knew and was resentful, though glad to be free of his presence. Usually he was away a day and a night.

As soon as he was gone, I would take Criterion and ride fiercely across the fields and through the woods. I instructed the groom and servants never to mention this to my husband. I galloped fast, jumped brooks and streams, and hardly cared if I fell. Those were my times of escape, my means of defiance. Riding fast and recklessly, I dared hope that one day my captivity and suffering might end.

On one occasion, soon after Grandcourt left the house, on impulse and unannounced, I rode to Offendene to see Mama. My aunt and uncle were there, the four girls, and Miss Merry. I was warmed by seven family kisses.

They all urged me to join them for lunch. Impatience with any of my family had vanished. I had no hunger, but, determined not to show unhappiness, I agreed to a drink of chocolate. I said I wanted to say good-bye, for I was soon to go to our house in Grosvenor Square for the spring months. Uncle said that at Easter both he and Anna would also be in London, staying at Lord Brackenshaw's house, to meet with Rex, who was excelling in his law studies and one day would be a great lawyer. I missed Rex's friendship with the same sense of bereavement as I missed my sisters. I formally invited Uncle, with Anna and Rex, to visit me in Grosvenor Square, but in truth I hoped they would not come near the place for I did not want my misery seen.

Lord Brackenshaw had assured Mama she could remain at Offendene, whatever her circumstances, but the White House, smaller, at a lower rent, and only a mile from the rectory, had become available. Mama liked the house and the views of trees and was saving for new furniture. I felt I would cry at her moving from Offendene and how less than generous, despite his promises, my husband was to her.

Uncle spoke of the great influence of wives in better-ing their husbands' careers and advised me to urge Grand-court to enter Parliament. I might have laughed were I not so bitter. I had gone into this marriage confident of the wife's influence to manage I was not sure what, my own happiness and freedom, I suppose. I was too proud to let Mama and Uncle know I could not influence Grandcourt even to permit me to wear the clothes and jewels I chose. Uncle spoke of the power of MPs and how a suffrage bill was to be debated because of demands by working-class men for the right to vote. (No mention was made of wom-en's demands.) I did not tell him Grandcourt despised the working class and favored dictatorship over democracy; I merely said he would not like making speeches, then praised the chocolate drink Jocasta had brought to me.

I tried to be bright, but when I went upstairs with Mama

to our bedroom I felt weak with homesickness. My made-up bed was there. I gave Mama an envelope containing thirty pounds. It seemed a feeble generosity. I said it was for the girls to spend on things for themselves when they went to the new house.

GRANDCOURT INTENDED TO go to London to make his will and sort financial matters. I was indifferent to where I went with him. My one enthusiasm for the visit was the thought of seeing you.

Three days after we arrived at Grosvenor Square, we attended a music party at Lady Mallinger's. I wore pale green velvet and at Grandcourt's command the poisoned diamonds. The Mallinger drawing rooms on Park Lane were regally decorated in white, gold, and crimson. Gathered in them was London Society. Herr Klesmer, of course, with his now adoring wife, Catherine. You were in a group with Mrs. Lewes, the talented Miss Lapidoth, and your artist friend Hans Meyrick, who had shoulder-length golden curls, was a member of the family with whom Miss Lapidoth was staying, and apparently, from when he first saw me, referred to me as "the van Dyck duchess."

Miss Lapidoth was the evening's star. The little Jewess held this sophisticated audience in her thrall. She sang "O patria mia" from Verdi's *Aida*, with Klesmer accompany-ing her on the piano. I watched you while she sang. You were absorbed and admiring. She was where I aspired to be, but I was merely one of the crowd in silk and gems, whose only worth was to praise or find fault.

The applause was prolonged. I offered my congratulations and told her Herr Klesmer had advised me to take lessons from her. "I sing very badly, as he will tell you," I said. "I have been rebuked for not liking to be middling, since I can be nothing more." Too straightforward to sense my bitterness or troubled mind, she replied she would be glad to teach me if she could. "If I do it well, it must be by remembering how my master taught me," she said.

I asked where she first met you, but all I really wanted to know of course was how much you meant to each other. "Did you meet Mr. Deronda abroad?" I asked. She said she had been in great distress, you helped her, then took her to the Meyrick family, who gave her shelter and protection. She owed everything to you. Though vague, her answer satisfied me. It allowed me to see her relationship to you as gratitude for practical help given, not as a romantic attachment. I placed her in a lower social class than yours. I wondered if it was you who saved her from drowning, or if you had found her destitute and furnished her with money.

She moved to the piano to sing again. I dared not approach you for fear of angering Grandcourt, but my fear turned to scornful determination when I saw him talking with Lush, with whom he had not for a moment dispensed. Lush was just as central to his life, the architect of much of it, and conspired with everything connected to the secrets that made me wretched.

I chose to sit on a small settee with room only for one other person, then looked toward you and smiled encouragement. You sat beside me. Mrs. Lewes, I observed, was watching me as if reading my mind and heart. Lush came and stood nearby, I supposed at Grandcourt's instruction to spy. I told you I thought Miss Lapidoth lovely, not in the least common, and a complete little person who would be a great success.

You looked annoyed. Conscious of having blundered, I felt my heart lurch. I waited for Lush to turn his head away, then asked what had displeased you. What had I done wrong? I asked. You said you couldn't explain, that it was hard to explain niceties of words and manner. I wanted to cry. I suppose jealousy provoked me to speak with condescension.

"Have I shown myself so very dense to everything you have said?" I asked you.

"Not at all," you replied, but with a formality and distance that belied your politeness. I wanted you to focus on me, my heart, my needs. I said I could only become a better person if I had people who inspired good feelings in me, for I did not know how else to set about being wise.

I hated your reply. It left me feeling so alone. You said you seldom did any good by your preaching and perhaps should have kept from meddling. I took you to mean you regretted returning the necklace and saw your action as prelude to a fatal encounter. I said that if you wished you had not meddled, it meant you despaired of me and had forsaken me, and that if you despaired of me, I should despair, for it would mean you had decided for me that I should not be good. "It is you who must decide," I said, "because you might have made me different by keeping as near to me as you could and believing in me."

You looked perturbed. I had gone too far. When Miss Lapidoth began to sing again, I got up and sat elsewhere. I suspected I had driven you away. I tried not to weep in my velvet and gems, my wounds hidden from all but you, and with dread in my heart and fear of the compulsion that made me turn to you in a search for protection and love. Mirah Lapidoth was singing Beethoven's "Per pieta, non dirmi addio" (For pity's sake, do not leave me).

Grandcourt's eyes were on me of course. In the carriage home he said, "Lush will dine with us among the other people tomorrow. You will treat him civilly."

I did not speak the enraged words in my head: *You are breaking your promise. The only promise you made me.* I feared a quarrel might end with his white throttling fingers around my neck. "I thought you did not intend Lush to frequent the house again," I said. Grandcourt retorted he wanted his presence and found him useful.

Why was I angered? Grandcourt was not a man to whom a promise meant anything. To compound my loathing he said, "Nothing makes a woman more of a gawky than searching out people and showing moods in public. A woman ought to have fine manners. Else it's intolerable to appear with her."

Grandcourt had no cultural or political curiosity. He scanned the newspaper columns only to describe as brutes all Germans, commercial men, and voters liable to use the wrong kind of soap. He assumed a scornful silence if Schleswig-Holstein, the policy of Bismarck, trade unions, or household suffrage were mentioned. But no movement of mine in relation to you escaped him. He had no regrets about marrying me; far from it, the marriage brought purpose to his life, indulged his brutality, and did not impede his visits to Mrs. Glasher. My shoulders, nails, hair, ears, neck, teeth, feet satisfied his fastidious taste. My spirited repartee aroused him. He did not care that I hated him. My hatred fed his cruelty. Nor did it pain him that I preferred your society to his. But he wanted me to know, with as much clarity as if I were handcuffed with the keys dangling from his chain, that my inclination toward you was useless.

My expression of longing for intimacy with you was punished that night in the usual way.

FROM THE GROSVENOR Square house Grandcourt and I attended and gave splendid receptions, went on conspicuous rides and drives, and made fashionable appearances at the opera. In this opulent display of city life, my only ambition was to see you.

One morning at breakfast I said I had a mind to take singing lessons. "Why?" Grandcourt asked, in his disparaging way. "Why?" I replied. "Because I can't eat pâté de foie gras to make me sleepy, and I can't smoke or go to the club to make me want to go away again. I want a variety of ennui." What, I asked him, would be the most convenient time, when he was with his lawyers, for me to take lessons from the little Jewess whose singing was all the rage?

"Whenever you like." He pushed back his chair, gave his lizardlike stare, and fondled the ears of the tiny spaniel on his lap. How I loathed the way he made those dogs fawn on him. Then he said, "I don't see why a lady should sing. Amateurs make fools of themselves. A lady can't risk herself in that way in company, and one doesn't want to hear squalling in private."

"I like frankness," I said. "That seems to me a husband's great charm." I looked at the boiled eyes of the prawns on my plate in preference to looking into his.

"I hope you don't object to Miss Lapidoth's singing at our party on the fourth of May," I said. "I thought of engaging her. Lady Brackenshaw had her, you know, and the Raymonds, who are particular about their music. And Mr. Deronda, who is a musician himself and a first-rate judge, says there is no singing in such good taste as hers for a drawing room. His opinion is an authority."

I dared to sling that small stone. A rock was thrown in return. "It's very indecent of Deronda to go about praising that girl," Grandcourt said in his bored voice.

"Indecent? To go about praising?" I felt trepidation.

"Yes, and especially when she is patronized by Lady

Mallinger. He ought to hold his tongue about her. Men can see what is his relation to her."

"Men who judge of others by themselves," I said, heedless of the repercussions of my daring.

"Of course. And a woman should take their judgment—else she is likely to find herself in the wrong place. I suppose you take Deronda for a saint."

"Oh dear, no," I replied, careless of retribution. "Only a little less of a monster than you."

I HURRIED OUT, locked the door of my dressing room, and tried to calm my racing heart. Were you betraying me and Mirah Lapidoth, setting us against each other, as my poisonous husband betrayed two women? I loathed Grandcourt for imparting such suspicion. It hurt me to consider you might be other than how I imagined you. But I was not entitled to you; the grounds for my faith in you were fragile; I knew little of your life; my opening up to you was impulsive and childish; from our first meeting on you had rebuked me. Might the grave beauty of your face be as much a mask as Grandcourt's aristocratic ease? Did both conceal untrustworthiness?

Suddenly, though the morning was gray, a stream of sunshine poured through the window from the fast-changing skies of April. And although I try not to be guided by signs and auguries, with this flood of warmth and light that bathed me and the room, I dared plant the seedling of hope that one day, one day, I might flourish in a world beyond my fear, dark thoughts, and captivity.

I rang for the housekeeper, ascertained Grandcourt had gone to his lawyers, ordered a carriage, and dressed for the drive. Grandcourt would find out and punish me, but I was punished enough. It would be hard for him to punish me more.

The carriage drew up at a humble, terraced house in Chelsea overlooking the river. Miss Lapidoth was at home. I was shown into a cramped room with folding doors. When I heard your voice behind them, I became agitated and wanted to leave. I buttoned and unbuttoned my gloves and feared I had gone beyond the bounds of acceptable behavior.

Miss Lapidoth came in, smiled, took my outstretched hand, and drew a chair near as if prepared for confidences. Her calmness contrasted with my agitation. I apologized for calling, said perhaps I ought to have written but that I had a particular request. She said she was glad I called. I was aware of the difference between us: my height and pallor, her smallness and fresh complexion; she in her simple clothes, I in my plumed hat. I wanted to tell her I now hated diamonds and was not born with an expectation of finery. I said I would be much obliged if she would sing at our house on the fourth, in the evening, at a party, as at Lady Brackenshaw's.

"At ten?" she asked.

"At ten," I said, then paused. My embarrassment grew.

My impetuosity and impertinence were out of place, but I could not restrain myself: "Mr. Deronda is in the next room?" I whispered.

"Yes, he is reading Hebrew with my brother."

"You have a brother?" I asked, though I had heard this from Lady Mallinger.

"Yes," she said. She told me how dear this brother, Mordecai, was to her and how ill with consumption, and how you were the truest of friends to him and her. I put my hand on hers and whispered, "Tell me the truth: Mr. Deronda—you are sure he is quite good? You know no evil of him? Is any evil people say of him false?"

She drew back, glared at me, then flared with anger. She said she would not believe evil of you if an angel told it to her; you found her when she was so miserable, poor, and forsaken she was about to drown herself; you saved her life, treated her like a princess, searched London for her adored brother, with whom she was now reunited.

I had heard all I needed. You and your life were no more like Grandcourt's conception than southern starlight is like London smog. I was reassured your interest in Mirah Lapidoth came from your Christian kindness and was not amorous. But then I had a sudden dread of the dividing doors opening and you finding me there. I hastily thanked Miss Lapidoth and bowed myself out.

As I arrived at Grosvenor Square, so did Grandcourt. He threw down his cigar, helped me from the carriage, and accompanied me upstairs. I went to my boudoir and tried to ignore him. He followed and sat in front of me, his chair too close. "May I ask where you have been at this extraordinary hour?" he asked.

I felt choked like a tight-leashed dog. Not even the air I breathed belonged to me. I sat by the table, laid my gloves on it, and did not look at him.

"Oh yes, I have been to Miss Lapidoth to ask her to come and sing for us."

"And to ask about her relations with Deronda?" Grandcourt added with the coldest sneer, the deepest threat.

My control broke. I spat out in fury, "Yes, and what you said is false, a low wicked falsehood." Oh, I could have said much more, that his whole life was a low wicked falsehood, that I detested him, saw no good in him, liked nothing about him, and wished him dead.

"She told you so, did she?" he said with calm aggression. He stood, barred me from rising from my chair, looked down at me, and tipped my face upward. I longed for the knife with the silver blade. "It's of no consequence so far as the singing goes," he drawled. "You can have her come to sing if you like. But you will please to observe that you are not to go near that house again. You have married *me* and must be guided by me. As my wife you must take my word about what is proper for you. When you undertook to be Mrs. Grandcourt, you undertook not to make a fool of yourself. You have been making a fool of yourself this morning, and if you were to go on as you have begun, you might get yourself talked of at the clubs in a way I would not like."

It was as if a disinterested physician, going about his workaday job, was explaining how an invasive cancer had so eaten my life there was nothing to be done. As Grand-court left the room I thought of Uncle's wish for him to enter politics. Had he done so, how calmly he would seek to exterminate those of whom he disapproved.

I thought of the casino at Homburg, the anticipation of winning, and the disappointment of loss. I had lost fatally, but I had hardened. Grandcourt could not again make me doubt my faith in you. I believed you to be as generous and kind as he was mean and vicious. I chose to believe I was the woman you loved. A refractoriness settled in me, which Grandcourt sensed, a defiance of mood, a hardness of social manner, a careless insincerity that broke, when I saw you, into such signs of agitation and need.

MAMA AND MY sisters moved to the White House, known as Jodson's, a mile from Offendene and circled by pine trees with windows that opened wide to a garden of roses. But I despaired at the loss of the old home, the red and pink peonies that bloomed on the lawn, the hollyhocks that grew tall by the hedges.

My visits to the new house were few. Anna was our link. She came often to London to visit Rex. Mama said that when he called, to avoid paining him, I was not mentioned. Anna gave her and my sisters news of my London life, the house at Grosvenor Square, comment about me in the Soci-

ety pages. Rex was a friend of Hans Meyrick's; they too
met when students at Cambridge. Hans gave Anna a sketch
of Rex, which showed his strong jaw and wide mouth.

It was my joy and sorrow to manage a visit to Jodson's
alone. Mama's hair was more silvery, my sisters more grown-
up. They wanted to hear firsthand about my city life: the
fashions, scandals, plays, parties, and opera. I told them
about Mirah Lapidoth and her brother, Mordecai. Fanny
could not imagine what Jews believed, Alice was sure she
could not bear them whoever they were, Isabel wondered if
they talked and looked the same as other people, and Miss
Merry suspected that Mirah and her brother lacked education. Mama said Society Jewish families in Paris and London
were quite what they ought to be, but the vulgar uncon-
verted ones were objectionable. I was calm in this female
company, the bright chatter, the murmurs of the garden,
the sound from the lane of hoofs and carriage wheels, but
I yearned for Offendene and the life I had lost.

ONE MORNING GRANDCOURT came to my room, hat and
gloves in hand, and said, "I am going out. I want Lush to
come and explain some business about property to you. He
knows about these things. I suppose you'll not mind."

"You know that I mind," I said. "I shall not see him."
I tried to leave, but he barred my way.

"It's no use making a fuss. There are brutes in the world
one has to talk to. People with *savoir vivre* don't fuss about

such things. Some business must be done. If I employ Lush, the proper thing for you is to take it as a matter of course. Not to make a fuss. Not to toss your head and bite your lips."

I had no *savoir faire*. I tossed my head and chafed like a horse. I moved back from him, he moved toward me. What was the point? I was bored with my hatred, so deadening in its repetitiveness. If I did not hear whatever it was from Lush, I would hear it from this husband, whom I loathed even more.

"I have arranged for him to come up now while I am out," Grandcourt said. "I shall come back in time to ride, if you would like to get ready." He tipped my chin and kissed my neck.

Lush was announced. I noted his fat hands and smarmed hair and nodded toward a chair. I might have thought him risible were he not so repulsive. With his bulging eyes and oily voice, he was like an incidental character from a novel by Charles Dickens. He held a piece of folded paper and began a nasal oration: "I need hardly say I should not have presented myself had not Mr. Grandcourt expressed his strong wish to that effect. My having been in Mr. Grandcourt's confidence for fifteen years or more gives me a peculiar position. He can speak to me of affairs he could not mention to anyone else. But there is something I have to say by way of introduction—which I hope you'll pardon me for, if it's not quite agreeable."

"Get to the point," I chided, my temper tried.

"I have to remind you of something that occurred before

your engagement to Mr. Grandcourt. You met a lady in Cardell Chase who spoke to you of her position with regard to Mr. Grandcourt. She had children with her—one a very fine boy. Mr. Grandcourt is aware that you were acquainted with this unfortunate affair beforehand, and he thinks it only right that his position and intentions should be made quite clear to you. It is an affair of property and prospects. If you have any objections to make, Mr. Grandcourt wishes that you make these to me. It is a subject about which, of course, he would rather not speak himself. If you will be good enough just to read this."

He unfolded the piece of paper he held. I instructed him to leave it on the table and go to the next room; I did not want him to see my trembling hands. Now I had heard it outright: Grandcourt knew all along of my unvoiced collusion with his wrongdoing, knew I had full knowledge of the terms on which I married him. I was as tainted as he. I deserved to be in his power and taunted by him even beyond the grave.

I absorbed the paper at one reading like the wedding day letter: If I had no son in this marriage, the Glasher boy, Henleigh, would be Grandcourt's heir. There was some contingent provision for me, but I did not care to read the particulars. I straightened my back, walked to the door of the next room, said, "Tell Mr. Grandcourt his arrangements are just what I desired," went back to my room, and closed the door. When Grandcourt returned I was ready in my riding clothes.

Lush and the wretched piece of paper freed me. I would collude with the deception of silence. Never again would I let Grandcourt see me hysterical or emotional. I would take exceptional care of my dress and toilette, show no sign that might be interpreted as jealousy, and match his coldness if not his violence. I would safeguard within myself a strength that could not be reached or broken by his abuse and goading. I had atoned. Mrs. Glasher could feel victorious. Her boy was to be his heir.

Of course I was neither free nor consistent in this resolve. I longed to withdraw from a contract I should never have made. My longing to be free from Grandcourt was wild. Over and over again I traveled the same ground: The marriage brought Mama a meager maintenance. If I returned to her as the disgraced Mrs. Grandcourt, she would again be destitute. How would I manage her tears and Uncle's command to return? Mrs. Grandcourt deserting her husband after seven months would be a more pitiable creature than Gwendolen Harleth, condemned to teach the bishop's daughters under the critical inspection of Mrs. Mompert. And Grandcourt had power to compel me to return. There was nothing I could allege against him in law. I knew of his prior commitments. Marital rape was not a crime.

I longed to see you but did not know what you could or would do for me. I suspected, even if you knew everything, you would again tell me to bear what I had brought on myself, unless I was sure I could be a better woman and

lead a better life by taking another course. But I knew of
no other course to take.

I locked Grandcourt's will in my desk. I had no intention
to look at it again. Daily, I schooled myself in suppression
of feeling. Day after day the situation stayed unchanged.
May went into June. I played the part of Grandcourt's wife:
scented, plumed, bejeweled, church at one end of the week,
opera at the other. I wished him dead.

ONE DAY IN July I heard from Lush that Mrs. Glasher was
in town to shop for her children. From him she must have
found the hour at which Grandcourt and I rode on Rotten
Row. She positioned herself conspicuously against a rail-
ing, holding hands with one of her daughters and her son.
As we passed she stared at me with her dark eyes. I returned
the stare. I saw her as Medusa, vindictive and jealous, with
snakes in her hair. Grandcourt rode by as if he noticed nothing. His ignoring her shocked me more than the appari-
tion of her again standing there, as at Cardell Cross. I wanted
to say, "You might at least have raised your hat to her." I
said nothing.

Some days later he and I went to a concert at the Klesmers, now living magnificently in Grosvenor Place. The
party was large. You were there. I could scarcely bear the
irritation of any conversation but yours, but you seemed
unaware of me and talked calmly to others. When I at last

managed to get close to you I asked, though both Sir Hugo and Lady Mallinger could hear, "I wish you would come and see me tomorrow between five and six, Mr. Deronda."

"Certainly," you replied, though with hesitation and alarm in your voice.

I moved away, hoping Grandcourt had not noticed, but defiant if he had. I had resolved to confess to you my loathing of this husband, the sexual humiliation I nightly endured, my fear of his white fingers around my neck, the knife I did not dare take from my traveling case, Cardell Chase and Mrs. Glasher, my longing for the life I had lost.

Between five and six was the hour Grandcourt and I rode in the park. His power to divine my plans, no matter how masked and glacial I appeared, made me superstitious. The next day I waited until the horses were delivered to the door before saying I did not feel well enough to go with him. I was afraid he too would stay at home and was exultant when he left.

I sent down instruction that you and only you were to be admitted. I was wearing black. Repeatedly I paced the two drawing rooms checking my appearance in the long mirror. You were announced. We exchanged a curt "How do you do." You seemed uneasy. We both stood, you holding your hat in one hand. My courage faltered. I had spoken to you many times of how troubled I was, how wrong I felt, but I now determined to tell you the details.

But I could not begin to find the words. I stuttered, then other words spilled out in a torrent: "You will wonder why I begged you to come. I need to ask you . . . You said I was ignorant. That is true, but what can I do but ask you what I should do to alter that. I have become contemptible, wicked, because of hating people. I try to plan how to go away from everybody, but there is too much to hinder me. There's no path I can take."

I said I was always thinking of your advice, but what use was it to me if I could not make myself different? I had to go on. I could alter nothing. It was of no use, but if I went on the way things were, I would get worse. I needed not to get worse, I wanted to be what you wished me to be; I wanted to be good and to enjoy great things. "You think perhaps I don't mind. But I do mind. I am afraid of everything. I am afraid of getting wicked. Tell me what I can do."

I was oblivious to everything except that, for you to give me courage and strength to continue, I must voice the details of my misery. The burden of my isolation was too strong. I was not crying. I was far beyond tears. You were my confessor, my counselor, my only chance of repose. My voice was a rushed whisper. I marked my body with the jewels on my fingers that I pressed so hard against my heart.

You walked to the window, turned to face me, then said, "My only regret is that I can be of so little use to you." Hope leached out of me. You looked at me with deep concern and were going to say more. Perhaps you would have advised me to tell everything to my husband and leave nothing concealed. Perhaps that is what you might have said, or perhaps you might have told me to flee to the

hills. But at that point Grandcourt entered. He nodded
to you, glanced at me, then sat at a little distance and trifled with his handkerchief.

My interview with you was over. You put out your hand,
but I did not take it. I could not say good-bye. You
nodded to Grandcourt and left. I collapsed into a chair.
Grandcourt said nothing. He was satisfied to create and
keep a foreboding silence. He had let me know I had not
deceived him and that once again victory was his. He
went out that evening and accepted my plea of being ill. I
thought I would pay that night with sexual humiliation,
but he did not come to my room.

The next morning at breakfast he said, "I am going
yachting in the Mediterranean." My heart took a leap of
hope. "When?" I asked.

"The day after tomorrow. The yacht is at Marseilles.
Lush has gone to get everything ready."

"Shall I have Mama to stay with me then?" I felt a small
burst of hope, like a shimmer of sunlight, at the chance
for a time of peace and affection, however brief.

"No. You will go with me."

I HAD ALWAYS said I liked the sea. The weather was fine,
the yacht pretty. The cabin, fitted to perfection, was lined
with cedar, hung with silk, and adorned with mirrors. The
bronzed crew were solicitous. To an onlooker such boating
might seem an enviable indulgence of the rich, but by tak-

ing me yachting alone with him in the Mediterranean Grandcourt confined me to the ultimate prison.

The sea was calm and shimmered blue. I reclined on cushions. The idle beauty, luxury, and isolation provoked anguish in me. Grandcourt sauntered up and down the deck, and down and up. I feared he would stop near me, look at me or speak to me. In my purse was the key to the drawer of my dressing case in which was locked the silver willow-shaped blade. I thought so often and hungrily of thrusting it into his neck, stabbing, stabbing it into his heart, that, untrusting of my restraint, I dropped it into the water.

Grandcourt could not know the measure of my hatred, nor would he have cared. Alone together he and I were silent. He made no jokes to elicit a false smile, no chitchat observations to compel me to agree. He was polite in arranging a shawl over me as the evening chilled, or in handing me any object he perceived I might need. His solicitousness was just an aspect of his dominance. I accepted such attentions with apparent courtesy.

He smoked, pointed at a distant sail, sat, or gazed at me as if I was as much his possession as the sea and cliffs. At dinner he might remark that the fruit was bruised and we must put in somewhere for more. If I did not drink the wine, he asked if I would prefer another sort. My replies were civil. At night he ravaged me.

Every movement of his, every remark he made, his contentment with inactivity, the way he fingered his mustache, his drawling voice, the manner in which he addressed the crew or ate his food—all of it repelled me. I hoped for a brutal accident to befall him. I thought I might casually push him from the yacht, then act as if nothing had happened. I read my book and dreamed of you.

With me held captive on his wretched yacht he was satisfied. I was denied all hope of seeing you. Here was his unchallenged kingdom. The crew and I provided what was expected by him; any private resistance added piquancy to his rule.

Each hour that passed I hated him more. I could not accept that this was my life and it would not change. And I hated myself. My life was spoiled, and I could blame no one but myself. My only hope of redemption was in my feeling for you. Tied in this pact to Grandcourt, I thought continually of your words: *Turn your fear into a safeguard. It is like quickness of hearing. Keep your dread fixed on the idea of increasing your remorse. It may make consequences passionately present to you.*

Your advice did not prove useful. Now that time has passed, and I am wiser and more confident, my advice to myself would have been "Leave Leave Leave, whatever the social cost, or price of penury." I could not accept such degradation. But you were to me a force for good. Through you I believed there was a place to go where I might be at peace; you made me unafraid of the dead face in the wainscot, or of the night sky, or of Grandcourt.

On board that yacht my malevolent prayers merged

with the wide ocean, the plash of the waves, the creaking
of the mast, the smoke from my hated husband's cigars.
The days elided. We wafted to the Balearic Isles, Sardinia,
Corsica, I was not sure where. We went ashore at Ajaccio,
and it was some relief to see people, life. We visited the
house where Napoleon was born, aimlessly wandered the
streets, then sat by the harbor. I asked Grandcourt how long
we were to go on with this. For an indefinite time, he
answered. He was not tired of yachting so we would continue. "Where would you rather be," he asked, "Ryelands?"

"Oh no," I said, and did not add that any place in which
he was was odious to me. "I only wondered how long you
would like this." He replied he liked yachting better than
he liked anything else, but he supposed I was bored with
it. "Women are so confoundedly whimsical," he said. "They
expect everything to give way to them."

"Oh dear, no," I said. "I never expect *you* to give way."

"Why should I?" he said, and peeled an orange.

So on we sailed, in his wretched yacht, to Italy and who
knows where, until one day there was a squall, which made
me rather ill, and the skipper told Grandcourt the yacht
was damaged so we should have to stay at Genoa for a week
while repairs were made. "It will be a change," I ventured,
and said a silent prayer of gratitude. Grandcourt wanted
no change and announced he did not intend to broil in
Genoa: the city was intolerable, the roads were crowded,
the hotels stifling, and he would go out in another boat
and manage it himself.

The prospect of hours freed from his company made me more cheerful, which he noticed. I hoped the wind might blow him into the deep. I thought of running away, I had no idea where to. That evening I watched the sunset with less aching loneliness than on previous nights. Asleep, I dreamed I was escaping to France over Mont Cenis and I marveled as I climbed to freedom that I found it warm on the snow even in moonlight, but then I met you, and you told me to go back.

I WOKE TO the sound of the crew casting anchor in Genoa harbor, and within an hour I actually met you—on the staircase of the Italia Hotel as we went up to our rooms. I was wearing a thin woolen dress and straw hat. Grandcourt was by my side. You started, raised your hat, and passed on. It felt like a continuation of my dream. I did not question what had brought you to the city; it seemed meant to be. Months later I learned from Sir Hugo the extraordinary story of why you were there. Grandcourt supposed your presence to have been in some way contrived by me, though how that was possible was hard even for him to fathom. What was certain in his suspicions was that I would seek to meet you if for a moment his back was turned.

In our sitting room he ordered coffee and stared at me. I knew I looked beautiful: the sea air, the prospect of hours of separation from him, the omen of your being in the same city, the same hotel. He observed my anticipation, my hope, told me to order dinner to be served at three, took out a cigar, reached for his hat, and said he was going to instruct Angus, his valet, to find a little sailing boat for us to go out in alone: one he could manage with me at the tiller. My stomach lurched. I said I would rather not go in the boat, I had been unwell, would he please take someone else.

"Very well," he said. "If you don't go, neither shall I. We shall stay suffocating here."

"I can't bear going in a boat," I said.

"Then we shall stay indoors." He smoked and stared from the window. I went into my bedroom, an evil anger rushing through me. After half an hour he followed, sat in front of me, and asked with a drawl if I had come round yet or if I found it agreeable to be out of temper. "You make things uncommonly unpleasant for me," he said.

I began to cry. "Why do *you* want to make them unpleasant for *me?*" I asked.

"What is it you have to complain of?" Grandcourt said. "That I stay indoors when you stay?"

I could not answer. I could neither confirm that truth nor tell him more. He knew I would prefer a minute of your company to an eternity of his. In despair, anger, and humiliation, I cried without control.

He called my tears confoundedly unpleasant, said all women were wretches and that we would remain stifling indoors for an interminable afternoon while we might have been having a pleasant sail. "Let us go then, perhaps we shall be drowned," I said. And cried the more.

He drew his chair close, grasped my hair, pulled back my head, pushed his face close to mine, and said, "Just be quiet and listen. Let us understand each other. I know very well what this nonsense means. But if you suppose I am going to let you make a fool of me, just dismiss that notion from your mind. What are you to look forward to if you can't behave properly as my wife? There is disgrace for you if you choose it. And as for Deronda, you are not to converse with him."

I said he could not in the least imagine what was in my mind, that I had seen enough of the disgrace that came from bad behavior, and that it would be better for him if he left me at liberty to speak with anyone I liked.

"You will allow me to be the judge of that." He tugged at my hair, rose, and walked to the window. I felt such a sense of capture, held by bit and bridle. He would keep on until I ceased to be restive, my spirit broken.

"What decision have you come to?" he asked. "What orders shall I give?"

It was to seem, if not my choice, my consent. His words were thumbscrews, his presence the rack. "Oh, let us go," I said.

THE BOAT WAS ordered. We inspected it at midday and went to the quay at five in the afternoon. A group of onlookers admired the scene: this model couple indulging their monied idle life. A fisherman relayed a warning about the gathering wind, but Grandcourt's manner made it clear he could as easily command a boat as a horse or a platoon.

I was afraid not of the wind or the dangers of the sea but of my violent hatred, which grew ever more keen. I guided the tiller under Grandcourt's eye and did exactly as he commanded. I kept to the thought of you. I was sure you would not leave Genoa. You would know I needed to talk with you, needed your help; you would save me from my murderous desires.

The boat was carried eastward by a gentle breeze, the grand city shimmered, the mountains loomed, the sun was setting, and there were sails near and far.

"Don't you find this pleasant?" he asked.

"Very," I replied.

"You admit now we could not have done anything better."

"No, nothing better. We shall go on always, like the Flying Dutchman."

He gave a warning glance. For as long as I hated him he would desire me. In my mind yet again I took that small sharp knife from its silver sheath.

"If you like, we can go to Spezia in the morning and let the yacht meet us there."

"No, I should like nothing better than this."

"Very well, we'll do the same tomorrow."

I hoped for forked lightning to strike him dead. I sat like a galley slave. To see you at the hotel was such joy and reassurance, but knowing you were near, I felt a terrible disappointment at being denied you. I did not look at my captor, who spoke only to order me to pull the tiller. As a child, when my hated stepfather came home, I used to imagine sailing away to a place where people were not forced to live with anyone they did not like. Now I was sailing with no hope of deliverance. My only avoidance of misery was to think of the life I might have, the woman I might be, were I with you.

I let go of the tiller and heard my voice say aloud, "God help me."

"What's the matter?" Grandcourt asked.

"Oh, nothing." I took the ropes again.

An eternity passed. It grew late. He said, "I shall put about." He turned the sail. I do not know if it was my mind or heart that acted. It was so quick. I think I pulled the tiller the wrong way at the same time as the wind gusted. The boom struck him and he fell from the boat. I saw him sink. My heart gave a lurch of joy. I did not move. I feared he would come up again, and he did, though farther off, for the boat moved fast with the tide. So quick. So quick. Like lightning. Like an arrow from a bow. "The rope!" he called in a voice not his own. I stooped for the rope. I felt sure he could swim and would come back whether I threw it or not. The rope was in my hands. I did not throw it. The words *he will come back* were in my mind.

When he pinned me to the bed in humiliation and assault, I so longed for his death. In the mornings when I woke, often after dreaming of you, to the prison I was in, as I felt hope drain from me, I so longed for this moment of his drowning. But all the while I also longed for you to stop me growing more wicked. You were the vision of love, goodness, and redemption beyond the evil of my life.

He went down again. Then again his face rose above the water. He cried out. I held the rope in my hand and my heart said, *Die.* He sank, and I thought, *It is done. I am wicked. I am lost.* Then I let go of the rope and leaped into the water. I was leaping away from myself, thrashing at the waves not to save him but to save myself. And then there was his dead face close to me. I did not touch him. I could not. The sea churned. I thought I would drown too. He went down. Then there was a fishing boat rowed by two men; one jumped from it, held my chin, dragged me from the sea and into their boat. They wrapped me in pea jackets and a tarpaulin.

AS WE REACHED the shore I saw you standing before me as if by plan. I was always expecting you, always hoping against hope for you and at last had found you. The boatmen supported me. I stretched out my arms to you; I called, "It is come. It is come. He is dead." You tried to silence me. The boatmen did not understand English. They told you they heard a cry, saw me jump in after my husband, then hurried to rescue me. The man had drowned. He was beneath the waves. He might in time be washed ashore.

The boat, drifting empty, was towed in, its sail loose.

The fishermen were witness to the story you chose to believe and which became the formal, legally recognized account of what had happened.

You informed the fishermen you were connected to my husband, instructed them to take me to the Italia, and told me that when you had dealt with the police and harbormaster you would come to me.

I waited in the hotel. I put on the turquoise necklace. You summoned doctors, telegraphed Sir Hugo and my uncle to come at once and bring Mama. I kept saying he was dead, that I was a murderess, that he called for the rope which I did not throw, that I let him drown. I implored you not to say I must tell the world what I had done, not to tell me I deserved disgrace. I could not bear for Mama to know.

I was like two creatures: one overcome by joy at release, the other burdened by guilt. Words spilled out: I had wanted to kill. I knew I must not act, but I was always waiting for the chance and it came; each day and night hatred worked in me; my consolation, my only way to free myself, was to contrive to kill him, at Ryelands, at Diplow, at Topping Abbey, at Grosvenor Square; I longed to use the sharp knife in the silver sheath locked in the drawer of my dressing case. I dared not unlock the case; in the yacht I dropped the key into the sea, I so longed to use that knife.

You drew a chair up close to where I sat and tried to reassure me. Grandcourt's death was an accident, I could not have prevented it, you said. He had fallen from the boat, he could not swim; I had leaped into the water with the impulse to save him.

But only thinking of what you would do made me pretend to try to save my jailer, my tormentor. And in my heart I knew it was a futile gesture and to my joy too late. Had you been overboard, I would have thrown the rope, maneuvered the boat, and swum with all force to save you.

I poured out my confession: how I used to think I could never be wicked, wicked people were distant from me, but within so little time I became wicked. Everything became a punishment to me, the very daylight seemed red hot . . . I ought not to have married. That was the beginning and end of it. I broke my promise to Lydia Glasher.

And then I was a coward. I ought to have left and wandered like a beggar, not stayed to feel like a fiend. I thought he would kill me if I resisted his will. At night in the cabin of the yacht, the sea, the stillness were punishment. You were my only hope. When I saw you in the Italia, I thought that if I told you everything—the locked drawer, the knife, the murderous thoughts, the temptation that frightened me—all would have less power over me. But he shut me off from speaking to you and took me out in the boat with no escape. And then the knowledge that at night his hated body would be on mine. Were he here again, I would wish him dead. But now his dead face will rise from the sea and be in the room, and I cannot bear more punishment.

You tried to quieten me, said I had resisted temptation to the last, that my fears were in my imagination, and that what was done could not be altered. But you could not lessen my aversion to my worst self, for though I had not murdered Grandcourt, you saw, or I think you saw, that a criminal desire impelled my hesitation in assisting him. I remember saying, "I make you very unhappy."

You told me to say no more, try to sleep, that you would see me again after I had rested. I saw my torment was not yours. I felt your desire to be gone from me. You promised to come when I asked for you the next day.

YOU CAME TO my rooms the next morning. You said you had not undressed or slept. I again implored you not to tell Mama or anyone else how I resisted throwing the rope as Grandcourt drowned. Again you said my thoughts and hesitation would have made no difference: he could not swim, he must have been seized with cramp. And then at last I told you of Mrs. Glasher, of their children, the will, the money, and how I wanted none of it.

I implored you to be patient with me. What I wanted, but could not ask, was for you to hold me. Instead you gave me lofty advice. I might, you said, become worthier than I had been thus far. "No evil dooms us hopelessly except the evil we love and desire to continue in and make no effort to escape from." You took my hand and held it in yours.

I had never before had from a man a physical sign of tenderness that I needed and wanted. The feel of your hand seemed my link to life. I said that if you were close

to me, I could be different, but that if you turned from
me and forsook me, I did not know what I would do. I
should not have said this. I was aware of urging you to make
promises you would not know how to keep. Again I had
gone too far.

You became pragmatic, said you would not leave Genoa
before Mama, Uncle, and Sir Hugo arrived, that my mother's presence would be a comfort, that I must save her from
unnecessary pain. I asked if it was your plan to live with
Sir Hugo at the Abbey or at Diplow. You reddened and
said you were uncertain where you would live.

Worn down, you said you must go to your rooms and
change your clothes, and that I must get well and calm
before the others arrived. As you went through the door I
felt like a banished soul, more alone than was bearable, with
the distance between us too great for me to bridge. I sank
to my knees and gave way to crying, and the attendant who
found me thought my display was of grief and despair
because my husband of a year had drowned in my presence.

When you held my hand in consolation, your touch was
a revelation. For you it was an unmemorable exchange, a
reassurance you would have offered any troubled soul. I
could not tell you I would have liked you to kiss my neck
below my ear. Forgive me, I could never have told you that.
Nor could I tell you, because I could not utter the words,
about the violation I endured from Grandcourt. At times
he did not wait for night. He dismissed the servants, turned
the key in the door of my room, mocked me with his pale

eyes, then stripped me of my clothes. I struggled and cried, but he insisted I be silent, unresistant, which was how I became.

NEWS OF THE drowning was in the *Times*. Mama and Uncle left for Genoa. They found me in a strange state of elation. I greeted them as liberators.

Sir Hugo arrived some days later. His delay was because, as Grandcourt's executor, he had gone to London to consult with Lush about the will. In Genoa he wondered about "the entanglement of our horoscopes," as he put it, yours and mine, that led us to be in the same hotel when this drama broke, but he was a man who could go one better with most stories: once by chance he had stayed in a Paris hotel on the night a former lover of his was abandoned there, without money, by her husband, an Austrian baron.

Sir Hugo had learned from Lush of the bad feeling between Grandcourt and me and about Mrs. Glasher and their children. The will stipulated, as I knew, that Grandcourt's estate go to Mrs. Glasher's boy. He left me two thousand pounds a year and the house at Gadsmere.

It was not that Grandcourt cared overly for his son, but he would not tolerate the notion that I might meet with you when financed by him. He knew you belonged to Topping Abbey, and how it pained me that you should be denied your home on his account. Sir Hugo was disgusted. Grandcourt, he said, intended his death to put an extinguisher on me. He had married me; he should have made provision for me to continue living in a style fitting to the rank to which he raised me. Sir Hugo thought I ought to have had four or five thousand pounds a year and the London house for life. He said he was not obliged to think better of Grandcourt because he had drowned, and in his view nothing in his life became him like the leaving of it. Nor did he hide his satisfaction that Grandcourt was not to be master of the Abbey. Your view was that Grandcourt's wrongdoing was in marrying me, not in leaving his estate to his son.

Uncle, deeply offended by the will, blamed himself for omitting at the time of the marriage to bind Grandcourt to provision for me. Only now did he choose to remember rumors of Grandcourt's entanglements and dissipation, which previously he found convenient to overlook. He resisted telling Mama about Mrs. Glasher and her children, but Mama, though too diffident to question me, had intuited something was wrong. I told her I was unsure what I would accept from the will and that she must not try to persuade or dissuade me on such matters. I implored her not to cry, promised to ensure she would have eight hundred pounds a year, and said I intended to be so wise, good, and sweet to her she would not know me.

You told Sir Hugo about my unhappiness with Grandcourt and how you thought I would not mind about the disposal of the property. He said this made me unlike other women, but you were right: I wanted nothing from Grandcourt and no reminder of him.

That same day, you left for Mainz. I resolved to ask you, on your return, whether I ought to refuse to accept any of Grandcourt's money. Within two days we all left Genoa. I never wanted to see the Mediterranean again. In a trance I did what was expected of me. I was compliant but not present. I feared causing anxiety to Mama. I could not talk to her about my marriage or the true manner of Grandcourt's death.

I did not want to reenter any of the houses I had lived in with Grandcourt. Kind Sir Hugo asked me to look on him as my protector and friend, called me "my dear," said my being badly treated made him feel nearer to me, opened his London house on Park Lane to Mama and me while mourning and other matters were attended to and for as long as we liked after that, and arranged for my possessions to be collected from Grosvenor Square and taken there. At Park Lane a bed was made up for me in the same room as Mama's. At night she lay wakeful, hoping to help me. I cried out for her, but when she suggested giving me a sleeping draft I chastised her.

Sir Hugo absolved me from any dealings with Lush or my uncle on practical matters to do with the will. He informed me I would have enough money to provide for Mama and my sisters and, as Offendene was again free, advised us to return there and try to re-create life as it had been only a year ago.

———

GRANDCOURT'S BODY WAS not washed ashore. A memorial service was held, which Mrs. Glasher and her children attended. With my face concealed behind a black veil, I held out my hand to her, but she turned away.

Sir Hugo spent some days at the Abbey, then returned to help us. I said in front of Mama, "Sir Hugo, I wish to see Mr. Deronda again as soon as possible. I don't know his address. Will you tell it me or let him know I want to see him?"

He said, "I am sure he will want to obey your wish," and that when you returned from Mainz, if you went to the Abbey he would give you the message or send a note to your chambers. Sir Hugo was convinced of my passionate attachment to you and supposed you to be in love with me. Though plans and expectations were inappropriate, mere days after Grandcourt's death, he viewed it as natural and right for us to be together now that the apparent obstacle to our being so had been removed.

You agreed to come to Park Lane. I waited alone for you in the white and crimson drawing room, with the lions on the pilasters of the chimney piece and Lady Mallinger's smiling portrait looking down. I thought of how, when we sat together on the small settee at her musical party, despite Grandcourt's surveillance, I told you my life depended on your not forsaking me, but it was Miss Lapidoth who sang "Per pietà, non dirmi addio."

I was joyous I could now see you without fear of reprisal. I wore black and no jewelry except the turquoise chain.

You looked apprehensive. It was good of you to come, I said, I wanted your advice: you knew the terms of my husband's will; ought I, in the light of my wrongdoing, take anything that had once been his? I admitted I married him because I was afraid of being poor and the dreary confinement of life as a governess, but in the marriage I had borne far worse things and could be poor now if you thought that right, though it would be hard for me to see Mama in poverty again. I was selfish, but I loved her, and even at my most miserable and desperate, knowing she was better off had in a small way comforted me. I was very precious to her, and Grandcourt had taken me from her and tried to keep us apart. If, I asked you, I took enough to provide for her but nothing for myself, would that still be wrong?

My tears came, though I tried to be calm. You did not hesitate with your advice: I should abide by the provisions of the will. The case was straightforward, and I should not punish myself further. Grandcourt chose to enter my life and affect its course in the most momentous way. He had an obligation to provide for me and Mama. If I took just eight hundred pounds for her and abjured the rest, it would create an uncomfortable predicament for her. She would not want income from me from which I was cut out. "You are conscious of something which you feel to be a crime toward one who is dead," you said. "You think you have forfeited all claim as a wife. You shrink from taking what was his." You then advised me not to speak about my guilt to Mama or anyone else, and to let my remorse show in the use I made of my monetary independence.

You took up your hat. You wanted to leave. It was as if, having had a duty to perform, you had done it and now wanted to turn to other matters. As ever, my heart lurched at the prospect of your going. I stood up. I said I would do as you advised, but what else must I do? I tried to check my tears as again on your face I saw that mix of compassion and desire to be gone. You asked if I was going with Mama to the country. In a week or ten days, I said. That was the best I could do at this time, you thought—to be with her and my sisters. Other plans would follow. "Think that a severe angel seeing you along the road of error grasped you by the wrist and showed you the horror of the life you must avoid. It has come to you in your springtime. Think of it as a preparation. You can, you will, be among the best of women, such as make others glad that they were born."

I felt unreal. You spoke of the promise of salvation and the prospect of a new life, but I had no idea what that life might be. I felt inseparable from you. With all the longing of my heart I wanted you in my life. Again you held my hand. You said you must not weary me, that I looked ill and unlike myself. I tried to be calm. I said I could not sleep, that memories tormented me, of Grandcourt's face as he rose from the sea, of the woman at the Whispering Stones. In time such memories would lessen, you said, but I did not know how, or with what they might be replaced.

I would have said anything, done anything, to make you

stay, but pleading was importunate. Again I asked if you intended to stay at Diplow or at the Abbey with Sir Hugo?

You were noncommittal, you gave a vague assurance you would visit Diplow, then moved to the door. I asked you to come to Park Lane once more before I left town. If you could be of use, you said, if I wished it, but there was reluctance in your face and hesitation in your words. I cried the more, implored you, said I had no strength without you. Yes, you would come, you said, but you looked miserable. I tried to control myself, to appear brave. I said I would remember your words, remember your belief in me. I asked you not to be unhappy about me.

YOU WERE MY world. I trusted and admired you and yearned for you to be with me, to redeem me, for you to know my better nature, not just my troubled heart. I had not consciously thought of marriage to you, but I could not bear separation from you.

I endured a difficult week, then dared ask you to visit again. I was in limbo, overwhelmed by the horror of what I had done. My summons disturbed you. You had seen too much of my despair. I was making demands on you that you were unable to fulfill. A year previously you might have moved to save me from sorrow and to carry to a conclusion the rescue begun with your redemption of the necklace. But unbeknown to me, momentous things had happened to you. I was too absorbed in my own world to observe anything of yours other than that you pitied me but could not respond to my appeal.

Mama spoke to you of the plan, now that I had decided to accept my income, for us all to return as a family to Offendene, and of her hope that I would piece back my life to what it was when we first went there and I was happy. You talked of the tranquillity of the countryside and the consolation and healing power of family life. I took your approval of the plan as rejection and a desire for others to bear the burden of caring for me. You revealed nothing of your life or intentions, and I asked you no questions. Not even why you had been in Genoa.

Some weeks later, on your next visit to Sir Hugo at Diplow, but before Mama, my sisters, and I had returned to Offendene, you called uninvited to see me at the White House. We sat alone together in the drawing room. I was composed. Jocasta brought us tea. I apologized for having caused you pain and being so full of grief and despair on your previous visit, and thanked you for all you had done for me in Genoa and after. You looked at me with concern. Hesitantly, you said you were troubled: you had things to tell me affecting your own life and future, which you should have told me before, had my own affairs not been so pressing. I thought you must be referring to matters concerning Sir Hugo and his property. I apologized for having been so bothersome and for giving you no choice but to think only of how to help me.

Then you gave your news: In Genoa you found out who

your parents were. You went there at the summons of your unknown mother, who, when you were a baby and after your father's death, had given you away to Sir Hugo Mallinger. You showed me a jeweled locket with her portrait in it. I supposed the locket had significance, like Grandcourt's diamonds. Her gaze was familiar; it was as if the portrait was of me. Although our coloring was different, she dark and I fair, I thought I saw reflected my own pride and loneliness.

She had sworn Sir Hugo to secrecy. Now, mortally ill, she wanted before she died to explain to you her motives for abandoning you to him. "Her chief reason had been that she did not wish me to know I was a Jew," you said.

"A *Jew*!" I am embarrassed to remember how I blurted the word and the look you then gave me of sharp reproach. To retract my blunder, I said, "What difference need that have made? I hope there is nothing to make you mind. You are just the same as if you were not a Jew."

You told me you were more than glad of it. You were overjoyed. A chasm widened between us. Why should you or anyone be overjoyed to be a Jew? Then you said how, in the past few months, you had become intimate with a remarkable Jew whose ideas so attracted you, you were going to devote the best part of your life to living out those ideas. To do this, you must leave England for some years and travel to the East.

I did not know what you were talking about. I had no clue what those ideas could be or what living them out might mean, beyond my exclusion. What I did understand was that you were going away. Afflicted with anxiety at the prospect, I felt my mouth tremble and I began to cry. I pleaded, "But you will come back?"

You huddled in your coat and moved to the mantelpiece. If you lived, you would return at some time, you said.

"What are you going to *do*?" I asked. "Can I understand the ideas, or am I too ignorant?"

You said, or I think you said, you were journeying to the East to restore a political existence to "your people," the "chosen people," who, though in a covenant with God, were scattered in different countries. You wanted to help restore them to Palestine to form a nation again. You saw this as your duty according to the Jewish scriptures. You were resolved to devote your whole life to this and to awakening this cause in others' minds in the way it had been awakened in yours.

What was I to think? Who were these scattered people, and how were you to find them and herd them in? I felt confused, crushed. I, it seemed, was not one of "your people," not one of the chosen. You intended a holy crusade from which I was excluded by birth. Your cause had nothing to do with me. I was the unchosen, without abiding connection to a people or place. No safeguard of birthright. I was to be consigned to Pennicote, in a rented house, my future without direction. "Marriage is the only true and satisfactory sphere of a woman," Uncle had told me. For me it had proved false and unsatisfactory.

My life seemed small and unlivable. Before my miserable marriage I felt all that happened was in some predestined and intimate relationship to me, even the stars in the sky, and the sea in which Grandcourt drowned. I had no curiosity about what lay on the other side of intimacy. It was as if I now stood alone with a void spinning round me into which you were disappearing. I felt like a speck of existence, an irrelevance, a nowhere person, unloved and unprotected.

After a time I said, "Is that all you can tell me?" I still almost hoped to hear you call this journey irrelevant in view of your love for me. You started to explain that the remarkable Jew who so influenced your thinking was Mordecai, the learned, emaciated brother of Miss Lapidoth. I remembered the afternoon when I called to see her. I heard you in the next room, she told me you and Mordecai were reading Hebrew, but I paid no more attention than if she had said you were playing whist.

"Did she tell you that I called to see her?" I asked. You said no, looked perplexed, and said you did not understand. And suddenly the truth came to me, and I felt my heart race and my breath halt. I asked if you could marry Miss Lapidoth. Yes, you said, you were going to marry her. She, her brother, and you would then journey together to the Promised Land.

It was not a dawning of error, as with my marriage to Grandcourt, but a sudden clarity of mortal wound, the piercing of a knife. I cried out that I was forsaken. For the eternity of a year all my hope and grief was directed at you. I had no life without you. I suppose I looked ill, you knelt beside me, held both my hands in one of yours, dried my eyes, said you were cruel, looked at me imploringly. Tears welled in your eyes too. You said you would write when you could and asked if I would answer. It was always your way to speak words of hope even when a situation was hopeless.

But all I really heard was that you loved someone else, were going, and I would not see you again. I tried to match your words of optimism. I said it would be better with me for having known you. You said had we been much together, we should have felt our distances more, but now, despite separation, you would be more with me than you used to be.

NOW I SEE such thinking as specious nonsense. I had been candid with you, but you had not been candid with me. Perhaps I gave you no opportunity. I had no inkling of how excluded I was from your life plan. You had made no mention of what that plan was. No reference to it. What could I have known of your being a Jew? I had seen you at Topping Abbey. You were its heart. An English gentleman. You knew every stone.

It had been a revelation to me to realize I loved you. I was punished for this love, first by Grandcourt, and now by you.

You had said what you needed to say, and you so wanted to be gone from my distress. I struggled to find courage. I told you: you had been very good to me, I deserved nothing, I would try to live, I would think of you, and I hoped I had not harmed you. We clasped hands, you kissed my cheek, you left.

Mama found me, said I looked very ill, and persuaded me to go to bed. She sat with me, and I cried in her arms for most of the night. In the morning when I saw her concern, I determined to console her. I commanded her not to be unhappy and assured her I would live to enjoy Offendene, annoy my sisters, and make the best of what there was. I did not say I felt I too had died.

III · Gwendolen

You had your Jewish wedding with your newfound Jewish friends. I was to hear about it from Hans Meyrick and Sir Hugo. Mordecai Lapidoth witnessed the betrothal of his sister and you, the two people whom he loved best in the world. Sir Hugo gave you as a wedding present all the equipment necessary for Eastern travel and for your wife a locket inscribed TO THE BRIDE OF OUR DEAR DANIEL DERONDA, ALL BLESSINGS, H&LM. It occurred to me Mirah Lapidoth was blessed with lockets, Sir Hugo's and your mother's, while I had been cursed with diamonds. The Klesmers gave you a watch. I sent you the following letter.

Do not think of me sorrowfully on your wedding day. I have remembered your words—that I may live to be one of the best

of women, who make others glad that they were born. I do not
yet see how that can be, but you know better than I. If it ever
comes true, it will be because you helped me. I only thought of
myself, and I made you grieve. It hurts me now to think of
your grief. You must not grieve any more for me. It is better—it
shall be better with me for having known you.

I had drafted the letter a dozen times. I wanted to bleach
it of self-pity or accusation. I was mindful of the letter I
received on my wedding day. I could better endure my loss
and pain at losing you than live with the apprehension that
once again I had been spoiling.

HOW BLEAK I felt after your departure. My life became inex-
pressible. Without your support I did not know how to continue. I could not speak of all I had endured in degradation
from Grandcourt, or say that through the deep winter of
that marriage you were my only hope. I could not talk of
my shame at withholding help from a drowning man
because I hated him. All I could not say raged like a contagion within me.

It was an effort to get from my bed to a chair. Nothing
interested me, everything disturbed me. My sense of guilt
was acute and of worthlessness entire. I could not concen-
trate on a book, receive guests, or easily look at my reflection
in the glass. Worse, I felt my return home was an anxiety to
Mama and depressing for my sisters. At night I cried out

because of my dreams. I dreamed I opened a door and found you there, but when I woke, you were not. I dreamed you called my name. Again and again I dreamed of Grandcourt's face rising from the sea. One night it was you who were drowning, and I could not get the rope to you.

Dr. Millington said my nervous system was exhausted, applied leeches to purge my despair, prescribed quinine and iron and Dover's Powder to coax me to sleep. A Nurse Pollock was hired but failed to tempt me with fish pie and chicken soup. Uncle said fresh air, sunshine, and exercise would restore me, but I felt incapable of venturing out. I think my aunt suspected I hastened Grandcourt's death, then acted the part of the bereaved widow.

Days and weeks passed in a haze. Sir Hugo feared for my mental and physical state and recommended that while Uncle organized the move from Jodson's back to Offendene, Mama take me to the spa at Bath for two weeks. He booked rooms for us in the Royal York Hotel. The queen had stayed there, he told us.

Bath was filled with white-haired people drenched of purpose but steeped in ailments: retired judges, generals, and their widows. I was put under the care of Dr. Myrtle, an unctuous man who exuded professional concern. I told him my suffering was to feel nothing. He diagnosed nervous exhaustion and a jaded brain and said my nerves were unstable, that I was worn out by menstrual bleeding, and that my depression was because despite being married I had borne no children.

Under his guidance I followed a regime. I began my day with a bath in hot spring waters, followed by a water-drinking session under palms to the sound of music. At considered intervals I had vapor baths, tepid baths, hot baths. I was wrapped in hot towels and massaged, soothed by soft music and hands gently pressing against my skull, prescribed a diet of fish and well-cooked greens, and advised to chew each mouthful slowly. I gulped the air and sipped the curious water, which was greenish and tasted fetid, apparently contained lime and iron, and was said to cure the most diverse ailments: sciatica, depression, eczema, paralysis, rheumatism, convulsions.

As I was wheeled in a black Bath chair to the pool in the mornings, dressed in my bathing clothes, in the company of the moribund and arthritic, I thought how the events of one year had turned me from the brilliant, self-confident Gwendolen Harleth, star of the Pennicote Archery Meeting, into a patient in the company of the old and ill.

Sometimes Mama and I went to Bath Abbey or for a drive and shopping, or we walked in the Spring Garden along the paths and parterres of flowers. We went twice to the play, drank tea in the public rooms, attended lectures on the arts and sciences (I do not remember what they were about). There was a bookseller where one might read the papers and a coffee room for ladies by the Pump Room.

I took little notice of any of it. I imagined, in my twilit

world, you might return to rescue me and that then my sense of unreality would end. You would divert me with explanations of the history of the city: what was Roman or Norman, the influence of Beau Nash and William of Orange and Thomas Baldwin (who had rebuilt the medieval baths), the story behind the large arched windows of the Pump Room. I had scant curiosity about such matters, though I accompanied Mama on two guided tours.

I wore the turquoise necklace. My talisman. I could not discard the hope I had invested in it. In the street I would see ahead of me a man with a certain walk and think it was you. At the Abbey I sat next to a man who used the same cologne as you. I scanned passing strangers. It was as if I was expecting you at every moment.

But behind my despair and bereavement I think I saw the possibility of freedom: Grandcourt was gone. Never again could he control me like his dogs, or abuse me. I was released from captivity. Vaguely, but without energy to act, I was aware my life was mine to shape if I knew how. But I was adrift. I did not have like you a destination, a mission. I did not feel I could save some part of the world, find roots, champion a cause. Klesmer had trodden hard on my fragile ambition. I had thought destiny would protect me and guide me to the happiness that awaited me. But in truth I had no idea what to do with my life. Without you I did not know who or what might in some way light the path ahead.

———

ONE BRIGHT SUNLIT day Uncle and Mama took me home to Offendene. The old house welcomed us, its creaking boards and lack of graces. Mama as ever was so patient, brought me broth and hot chocolate, called me her darling Gwen, told me I was special, and was oh so pleased to have me home.

Dr. Millington commended her as an excellent nurse, said rest and kindness were better medicines than he could prescribe, and advised me to look forward and not dwell on past pain. But I remained plagued by the image of Grandcourt's face as he floundered and called for the rope, which I did not throw, and of your awkwardness as you sat beside me and told me you were to marry Mirah Lapidoth and go together hand in hand to your promised land.

My sisters came to my room with flowers, spoke in soft voices, and tried not to giggle or annoy me. They brought news of Criterion and their outings and shopping expeditions. Alice said she was grateful to me for providing for Mama and her, Bertha, Fanny, and Isabel. Clintock was courting Isabel. She found him handsome and gallant. I asked if he had written poems for her, and she said he had, though she seemed unclear what they were about. Croquet? I suggested. Perhaps, she replied.

I gave her my emeralds and told her to sell them if she wished. She wondered at their color in the candlelight. I felt scorn for such possessions as I had and wanted no reminder of the price they had made me pay. I let my sisters each choose one of my dresses, a hat, and a piece of jewelry.

Sir Hugo was adept at managing and investing my inheritance, such as it was. He explained to Uncle, Mama, and me what must be done to derive the best income from it. He journeyed to inspect the Gadsmere property. Mrs. Glasher had moved with indecent haste into Grosvenor Square. Sir Hugo described a landscape black with coal dust, a gloomy mining village, and an isolated house of gray stone. That was where, by the terms of his will, Grandcourt wished to confine me. Only a monster, Sir Hugo said, would consign the woman he purported to love to a solitary existence in such an outpost.

He arranged the letting of it, to a man who worked in the coal business, at a far higher rent than Lord Brackenshaw required for Offendene. I had no wish to set eyes on the loathsome house, but it made me proud to provide Mama with a thousand pounds a year to pay for Miss Merry, Jocasta, the gardener, fuel for the fires, and even luxuries. And it gratified me to give my sisters a small allowance for clothes and see their delight.

I looked out at the garden, the downs, and fields of grazing cattle; I ventured into the lanes. The old house was a constant, and though it could not be to me the kind of heritage you found first at Topping Abbey and then from your Jewish forebears, the sense of unknown others having been in some way at home here, and now the door opening and

Mama or one of my sisters coming to greet me, was consolation of a sort.

I tried to find pleasure in small things: ferns and
foxgloves in the hedgerows, celandine in the ditches, the
songbirds, the stick nests of hawks in the cedar trees. One
afternoon I walked along the lanes with Mallow, the stable collie. One morning I rode Criterion with the same
abandon and recklessness as when Grandcourt was away.

My sorrow dulled. No one put pressure on me to be
what I was not, but I had changed. I wanted a room of my
own. My fear of sleeping alone had gone; so had my terror
of the face in the wainscot. I saw only a ridiculous image, a
practical joke poorly executed. I could not explain why it
had ever made me afraid.

But though those fears had dissipated, so too had my
joy. When life with Grandcourt became cruel, I thought I
would be content to return to the calm, uneventful life
that so frustrated me before I married, before I loved you.
But I could not settle into the small bed alongside Mama's,
the domestic routine. I could not again brave musical
soirées at the Arrowpoints, face the Klesmers in their
confidence, dine with Mr. Quallon at the Firs, take part in
archery shoots or the hunt. I had enjoyed the hunt before
I became a victim, before I was the hunter's prey. Or perhaps
it was more that I had enjoyed the speed of the ride, the
light on the corn and haystacks, the admiration accorded
me for my beauty and verve. Now I wished never to hunt
again, see fear in the vixen's eyes, spittle round her parched

mouth, watch her killed by hounds that bayed and slath-
ered, or ride home with her severed tail and head as tro-
phies.

Perhaps, though I felt at sea, I became a kinder person
because of all that had happened to me. You were my lien
to life, and I did not know where you were. I struggled with
my own unworthiness: I had burdened you, failed in marriage, and been complicit in a death. When I looked in the
mirror, I saw crow's-feet around my eyes and disappointment in the downward turn of my mouth. The sparkle had
gone from my appearance and my hopes. Or that was how
I seemed to myself. I was twenty-two.

SIR HUGO BECAME like a loving father. It was as if he
adopted me, the way I learned he had adopted you. Hitherto, his flippancy and facetiousness irritated me; now I saw
only a man of sensibility and compassion who was kind and
observant. He regularly sent a carriage to take Mama and
me to Diplow, or visited us at Offendene. I think he did
not want us to be dependent on Uncle again. He was cir-
cumspect in what he said, and never overtly critical, but I
believe he doubted Uncle's motivation and business acu-
men, and thought Uncle ought to have asked questions of
Grandcourt and not spurred me into a hasty marriage to
relieve his own parlous financial state.

He was outraged at what he knew of how Grandcourt
used and ill-treated me. And I think disappointed in you

for, as he saw it, encouraging me, but not catching me when I fell. He told me he had angered you by saying you and I made the perfect couple and that pity was a poor reason for selecting a wife. But he could not, in any deep or lasting way, be critical of you or your mother. She and you were the light of his soul, his unquenchable fire of love. Perhaps I became his crucial link to you because I grieved your absence as much as did he.

He invited me and Mama to Topping Abbey, suggesting I might further restore in that sequestered place. His daughters would be company, he said, and Hans Meyrick, your friend, would stay while painting a portrait of Lady Mallinger with her dogs. He suggested that to build my strength, I exercise the horses stabled at the Abbey. Again he said that now he neither rode nor hunted, that his horses could not compare with Grandcourt's; but he was concerned for them to be well tended and content.

Mama felt unable to leave my sisters but encouraged me to go. It was a sacrifice on her part, for she was happiest when I was near, but she so wanted me to be well. In my mind I saw the meadow surrounded by elms, the acres of forest, the river, the old bell tower, the choir of the Abbey church, the stained-glass windows, the little spaniel curled in the hackney carriage. At the Abbey I thought I might be close to you and again hear your voice explaining the history behind the stones.

I went for what remained of the summer, and in that enchanting setting, historical, romantic, and homelike, of gothic cloisters, fresh-baked food, woodlands, meadows, and summer breezes, my strength and courage returned.

A ROUTINE OF the visit was for Sir Hugo and me to talk in the library at around three in the afternoon. Lady Mallinger, calm and gentle, was pleased for him to have my company. She checked the tea and candles, then left us. I believe she felt I eased his pain at your departure. Theirs was a gentle love, imbued with grace and trust.

With views from the windows of oak trees and parkland, Sir Hugo talked of you. We missed you grievously, and I needed to hear your story. Sir Hugo described it as your "whim of Israel." "I thought Dan had gone mad when he wrote to tell me he was going to marry a Jewess about whom I knew nothing and go East to build a homeland for the Jews," he said.

I confided my bewilderment when you called at the White House and told me you were a Jew and were going away to Palestine. "I know nothing of the Jews," I said, "though clearly some of them are very clever. Herr Klesmer, of course. But I thought Mr. Deronda belonged here."

"Dan is the spirit of the Abbey," Sir Hugo said, and gestured toward the walls, books, portraits, and the grounds beyond the window. "You've seen his unfailing sensibility to every stone and cornice. His going gouges the heart from the place and severs a limb from me."

"And I have lost my anchor," I ventured to say. "Through the ordeal of my terrible marriage, Mr. Deronda was my hope."

I did not, I could not, tell Sir Hugo I loved you, but he knew, and put his arm around me.

"Madness," he said. "Madness, to leave all that with your heart and mind you love, to pursue a theoretical idea."

He asked, "Did Dan tell you why he was in Genoa on the day when Grandcourt drowned?"

I felt apprehension at the revelation that was to follow. You had told me of your reason for being in the city but in my heart I had supposed, I think I had supposed, you were in Genoa because you belonged with me. I saw your being there as fate and was unsurprised after Grandcourt was compelled to pull the yacht in for repairs, to see you at the Italia. A week later it seemed meant to be that you were at the harborside after I was dragged from the sea. I was so absorbed in my own drama, I had not wondered why else you might be there, other than to be with me. "I think Mr. Deronda mentioned his mother," I falteringly said.

Sir Hugo handed me a paper from his desk. "Here's a copy of the letter I gave Dan the previous week," he said. I skimmed the words. I had learned to fear letters.

TO MY SON, DANIEL DERONDA . . . I wish to see you . . . my health is shaken . . . no time lost before I deliver to you what I have long withheld. Let nothing hinder you from being at

the Albergo dell' Italia in Genoa by the fourteenth of this
month. Wait for me there.

    Princess Leonora Halm-Eberstein. Your unknown mother.

I did not know what to think. *Unknown mother.* The
words looked strange. "She was dying," Sir Hugo said, "and
wanted to see her son to explain why, when he was a baby,
she abandoned him and gave him to me. The approach of
death made her reflect on her past: her Jewish upbringing,
her father's control of her, her child's birth. She needed to
break a lifetime's silence."

Sir Hugo told me how apprehensive you were about the
meeting, how you wandered the city, went to the opera,
explored the Jewish quarter, then were summoned to her
rooms. You told him she seemed an unreal figure, theatrical, dressed in black lace, not like a mother.

"She gave Dan her father's ring," Sir Hugo said, "the
symbol of his Jewish allegiance. Her father had wanted her,
as a Jewish mother, to rear her eldest son as if he might be
the Deliverer, the new Messiah. His dying wish had been
for him to inherit the Charisi papers: the record of the family's origins, migrations, and lives. Written in Spanish, Italian, Hebrew, and Arabic, these papers were in a chest lodged
in Mainz with an old and trusted friend."

I remembered how you left Genoa to go to Mainz. I
felt ashamed it had not occurred to me to ask why.

"Then Dan astonished her," Sir Hugo said. He told her
it was momentous to find he had been born a Jew, that he

already instinctively identified with the Jews and wanted to travel East to help build a homeland for them. He told her about Mirah Lapidoth and her brother, Mordecai.

That, I learned, was to be your only encounter with this unknown mother. She did not want to see you again. Sir Hugo, in letters to her about you, extolled your wonderful mind, sympathy, and wisdom, but she asked no questions and showed no interest in you or desire to meet you. You collected the trunk from Mainz and took it to Mordecai in London. He helped you translate and study the archived papers and understand your true heritage and identity.

I listened to Sir Hugo with alarm. Your story did not belong to the portrait of you painted in my mind. I had thought you were in love with me, that you were in Genoa for me. But you had not been thinking of me. It was coincidence, not benevolent destiny, that had caused us to be in the same city at the same time. As Sir Hugo in his innocence spoke of your past and we walked the Abbey grounds, I felt an onset of the old terror that only my mother's arms could salve. It was as if the landscape, path, stone walls, and garden rose to consume me. I stumbled. A scream lodged in my throat as if in a dream. Here were the facts of it. I was alone and unloved. Some perverse equation of my mind had made me resist a man who loved me, succumb to a man who ravished me, lose my heart to a man as unavailable as you.

So much for me and men, I thought, and I remembered Captain Davilow. Sir Hugo's concerned face came into my view. He put his arm around me, said I looked ill, and insisted I sit for a while. I pleaded it was nothing more than that the day was hot and I needed water, and although I wanted the conversation to continue, perhaps that was enough for now.

WHEN NEXT WE talked Sir Hugo explained how he came to adopt you. He spoke of your mother's wonderful voice, her fame as Alcharisi, the opera singer, and how he pursued and courted her.

"I was madly in love with her," he said. "She was my once-in-a-lifetime love. We first met in Naples thirty years ago."

It was hard for me to imagine Sir Hugo madly in love, he seemed so elderly and uxorious, but as he relived in his mind what once he had felt, he became animated and youthful, like an actor who inhabits a different persona.

"She was newly widowed but wouldn't marry me. She said she couldn't love me or any man. Her father also had just died. Dan was two." Sir Hugo told me how your grandfather tyrannized her. "She counted as nothing to him. All he wanted was a grandson who would prove to be the Deliverer of the Jews, the new Messiah." She felt forced into marriage by him, when what she wanted was to be free and true to herself and her talent. "She could not love or care for Dan, she saw him as an obstacle," Sir Hugo said.

Sir Hugo told your mother he loved her so much he

would do anything for her. "One day Dan was sitting on my knees. I playfully said I would pay money to have such a boy. 'Take him,' she said, 'and bring him up as an English gentleman, and never let him know anything about his parents, and never let him know he was born a Jew.' She suggested you take the name Deronda after a branch of her family. Her father, she said, would have cursed her, but she was bitter about his rule: 'This you must be, that you must not be. A woman's heart must be of such a size and no larger; else it must be pressed small like Chinese feet; her happiness is to be made as cakes are by a fixed receipt.' Now, she said, it was her turn to say who or what her son should be and what she herself should feel. She wanted to relieve Dan from the bondage of being born a Jew and save him from the contempt in which Jews were held."

What a bleak beginning to your life, I thought. Mama's love was everything to me, and I could not countenance my fate without her. Nor could I understand her need to abandon you. "Why," I asked, "if Alcharisi's husband and father were dead, did she need to consider her son's Jewishness?"

Sir Hugo was unclear. He said she was contemptuous of the constraints and strictures of Judaism. "I was to feel everything I did not feel and believe everything I did not believe," she told him: "awe for the bit of parchment in the mezuzah over the door; to find it beautiful that men should bind the tefillin on them and women not, to dread lest a bit of butter should touch a bit of meat, to love the long prayers in the ugly synagogue and the howling and gab-

bling and the fasts and feasts and my father's endless dis-
coursing about Our People. I was to ever care about what
Palestine had been. And I did not care at all. I cared for
the wide world and all that I could represent in it."

Sir Hugo needed to talk about you, and I needed to hear
your story. We spoke of our loss and bewildered sense of
shame. He guided me toward understanding your life and
my own. I think this lessened the pain and insult I felt from
your actions. I stopped feeling so unworthy.

Sir Hugo told me how he kept assiduously to your mother's wishes, loved you as if you were his son, and brought
you up as a Mallinger, the perfect English gentleman. "But,"
he said, "I responded to Dan's questions with such awk
ward evasions he became embarrassed to ask what he needed
to know." He said his evasions were lies of omission that
turned you into an outsider, uncertain as to who you were,
and that he now felt abject about the confusion and loneliness his silence must have caused you as a boy.

We each admitted to selfishness in keeping our promise of secrecy. Sir Hugo wanted you for himself, as if you
were his son, and suspected the truth might take you from
him. And had I, before marriage, broken my vow to Mrs.
Glasher and told Mama or Uncle the truth about Grandcourt, I would have had to relinquish the tainted financial
privilege I obtained from marriage to him.

As Sir Hugo and I walked and talked on the Abbey
grounds, the river winding through the valley below, the
view of the hills beyond, I revisited the drama that took

place in the Italia that week: your past opening like Pandora's Box spilling out confusion, and I, by bizarre coincidence, in the same hotel.

I admired him for being "madly in love" with a woman as challenging as your mother: a young widow like me, a woman scornful of marriage and family. Her rebellion inspired me. If she dared defy the strictures imposed by men, then perhaps so might I.

I thought of her portrait in the locket she gave you, her proud face and aloof demeanor, and of the sense I had of seeing my own reflection. *I, like her, want the wider world,* I thought. I too shunned the customs and rituals of control, this to be done on that day, that on the other, because a certain man or men did it so five thousand years past.

I did not believe in God the Father, a Son born from a Virgin and a Holy Ghost, the importance of Moses, the divine authority of the Bible, the landscapes of heaven. Before marrying Grandcourt, I believed, tentatively, in myself. As Sir Hugo talked of your princess mother, I resolved to find my own courage again.

I had not met a woman like her. In Pennicote, Catherine Arrowpoint was gifted and clever, but she said *amen* to Klesmer. In London, Mirah Lapidoth would have drowned were it not for you. You were her deliverer. She said *amen* to you. Your mother broke free, greatly dared, and was the more loved and admired by men because of it. I wished I had met her. I felt I understood her, though of course I did not have her talent.

In Genoa you did not mention your mother or the coincidence that within days I was a widow in the same hotel. I wondered what might have transpired had she and I met. She might have wanted me to be your bride, commiserated with the oppression I had endured, admired my courage, liked my Englishness and impetuosity, and seen in me a kindred spirit, a woman who aspired to live an independent life.

My demeanor and beauty, my yearning for independence, and the spark in my eyes, Sir Hugo told me, reminded him of her when she was young. Like her, I was denied my own life because of domination by a controlling man. I endured Grandcourt and his grip on all I was: this you must do, that you must not. The jewelry and clothes I must wear because I was his wife, where I might visit, travel, to whom I might talk, what I must say or sing. But Grandcourt did not justify his control in deference to a higher power, a divine intention, or a force for good. He alone was the determining force.

Your grandfather's patriarchal ambitions were loftier. He looked to you to deliver exiled Jews to their homeland. He had not considered his daughter, her talent, wishes, or thinking. He overruled her, but she in time defied him and fulfilled her own ambition.

To Sir Hugo, I confided how Grandcourt controlled me and crushed my spirit. He said that when he heard Grandcourt was dead and you were in Genoa, he took it as a foregone conclusion you would marry me. Lady Mallinger too supposed it to be more than coincidence for you to be there when the drama of Grandcourt's death occurred. He took my arm and lightly said life seldom takes the path of true love and easy consolation, and we are obliged to learn the art of making the best of what happens to us.

We spoke of the irony of your wanting the life your mother tried to safeguard you against. She, Sir Hugo, and I would have liked you and me to be together in a scene of English happiness: the tall, dark, handsome Eton- and Cambridge-educated squire of a stately home, with his beautiful rose of a wife.

But I was not a true English gentlewoman: I had a wastrel father, subdued mother, lived in a rented house, with no money in the bank, no links to landed estates. I could no more be what by circumstance I was not than match your pioneering zeal, go to Palestine, and view it as my Promised Land.

I asked Sir Hugo if he thought you hated your mother for abandoning you, and if reversion to all she despised was your revenge. He did not countenance the idea. You were not a man ever to be driven by revenge or anger, he said, but nor would you be pushed in a direction in which you did not choose to go.

Sir Hugo had an uncensorious heart. Our friendship was a salve. He said without the truth we could not be free and urged me to accept that Grandcourt's death was all to the good. "See that drowning as a godsend," he said. "It could not have come too soon. The ocean befriended you that day. Now your life can begin."

IN THAT STRANGE summer between my old life and the new, I tried to go beyond my broken dream to the source and complexity of your feelings and actions and of Sir Hugo's and my own. You had said my life would be worth more if I had an interest beyond the drama of my small personal desires. I began to see the wider drama, its creation and implications, its sadness and muddle, and my part in it. Sir Hugo encouraged me to look forward and seek new opportunities, though he did not say how.

You did not write, just as your mother had not written to you. I knew you would not, not because you had forgotten me, but I supposed your wife would be jealous and you would not pain her. She had heard from Hans Meyrick how you and I made the perfect couple. She told him I was as beautiful as Princess Eboli in Verdi's *Don Carlo* and that she feared my hold on you.

Sir Hugo read me letters you wrote to him. It pained me to hear how you and Mrs. Deronda sailed from Brindisi to Alexandria, then by steamer down the River Nile. I learned about your life, saw the hopelessness of my love for you, yet hoped I remained with you as your mother's free spirit, though your wife was with you as your grandfather's dream.

HANS STAYED AT the Abbey. With his long blond hair he looked the part of the artist. He told me he was named after Holbein and that he took every commission he could so as to provide for his widowed mother and three sisters. Sir Hugo paid him a generous sum to paint portraits of his wife and daughters to hang in the gallery among the Mallinger forebears.

Hans painted my portrait too, not as the bejeweled van Dyck duchess, but dressed in black, my only adornment the talisman turquoise necklace, and seated in the gallery amid the brocades, plush upholstery, and formal elders frozen in their frames. Sir Hugo bought the painting and said he wished it might hang with those of his own ancestors.

As with Sir Hugo, I had, at first, found Hans irritating— voluble and keen to joke; but he too had a generous heart. He was enamored of me, and that tinged our friendship and made him keen to please, but he did not exasperate me with lovemaking.

It was a glorious summer, and in caring company and the calm of the Abbey I could not only be sad. In the mornings I exercised Ruben (a bay), Constance (a mare roan), and Pleasant (a gray). They were not as fast or spirited as Criterion, but I rode far and regained strength. For hours, as I traversed the fields and lanes, with all the joys and wonders of the English countryside, I felt I had discarded Grandcourt and my past. When Sir Hugo was in town, or occupied, in the afternoons I picnicked with Hans, alone or with the Mallinger girls. We swam and played croquet. Sometimes I allowed him to win. He sketched me picking cherries in the orchard and reading beneath a willow tree.

Hans was bereaved to be separated from you, his closest friend, Mirah, whom he hoped might love him, and Mordecai. He loved fun and laughter, took nothing too seriously except his painting, and was surprised to find I was neither haughty nor self-assured.

Used to the company of sisters, he was unafraid to tease, flatter, and befriend. I was taller and stronger than he, and we joked that I was more of a man: horsehair made him sneeze and his eyes stream, so he could not ride, boating on the lake exhausted him, and he splashed and paddled rather than swam.

He confided how, as students at Cambridge, he and you shared rooms and you helped him because he had no money. When he was afflicted with an infection in his eyes, you were so attentive you neglected your own study of mathematics and had to quit the university. He succeeded at your cost and wrote to Sir Hugo of your sacrifice. Sir Hugo called it your "passion for the pelted." Part of your allure was in the way you sought to protect the vulnerable. I think you would have liked to save me, but my needs alarmed you. Hans's sisters thought you as magical as Prince Camaralzaman from the *Arabian Nights*.

Hans showed me sketches of you rescuing Mirah Lapidoth from drowning in the Thames. He said he planned a

large canvas of the scene, a work of abstraction and ambi-
guity in which it would be unclear where the sky ended
and the water began, and whether you were pulling her
from the water or she drawing you into it. He never painted
this, but as I looked at his sketches, he revealed the story
behind them: How on a July evening you went boating on
the Thames near Putney and saw a girl of about eighteen
take her cloak, soak it in the river, wrap it around her as a
drowning shroud, and slip into the water. How you swam
across and saved her.

That was how the Jewess Mirah Lapidoth came into
your life. She had come to England to look for her mother
and brother but despaired of finding them. She had run
from her wicked father, who had tried to sell her into prostitution, and she had nowhere to go, no money, no friends.
You took her to Hans's mother and sisters, who welcomed
her into their small house. Hans showed me a dozen sketches
he had made of her. He thought her beautiful, was a little
in love with her himself, and jealous of her preference for
you.

The Meyricks exuded love and charity and did not show
caution at the allocation to them of a depressed and penniless stranger. Her despair and attempted suicide were soon
forgotten, and you, Prince Camaralzaman from the *Arabian Nights*, were her irresistible savior.

Six weeks after saving Mirah Lapidoth, you saw me in
the Kursaal in Homburg. Your gaze as if from an opposite shore, your return of my father's necklace, they were

my hopes of rescue. No one made drawings of those events. Your own family were lost to you. Instead, while I yearned for you, you scoured the streets of London's East End, searching for Mirah's mother and brother. Her mother had died but you found Mordecai.

Sitting with Hans on the grounds of Topping Abbey, I listened to this story with astonishment. I wondered at you reaching out to such a disturbed family. I thought the civility and privilege of your upbringing would have made you exclude connection with them.

But what again most affected me was that all the time I was yearning for you, you were searching for this Jewish identity, planning marriage to Mirah Lapidoth and emigration to a land I did not know existed. While you were winging six thousand miles from me in your thoughts, I saw you in everything, referred to you constantly, repeated your words of encouragement and supposed them to be of love. And at night when I heard with dread Grandcourt at my door, then endured his repeated assailing of me, my deliverance was to imagine I was with you, and that one day my dream would become reality because that was so much what I wanted. I only vaguely wondered where you actually were, and what business you were about, but never could I imagine you to be absorbed in the historical destiny of the Jews. I could as easily imagine you rising from the air on a brazen horse and vanishing into the dark as a twinkling star.

I appealed to Hans to explain to me what it meant to

be Jewish. I hoped to understand my own exclusion. He advised me to read *The History of the Jews from the Earliest Period down to Modern Times* by Henry Milman; I took it from the Abbey library but found it dull. Hans then tried to help me fathom the Jewish calendar: how their new year, called Rosh Hashanah, came in September and that at present they were in the year 5636. It was too confusing, and we agreed Christian strictures and rituals were impenetrable enough. He suggested we visit a synagogue when we went to London for there were none near Topping Abbey. He said you loved the Jews for the duration of their sorrows and the patience with which they bore those sorrows, and that your rescue of Mirah Lapidoth from drowning seemed portentous to you. But I was drowning too, and was there not a multitude of women like me, drowning unseen?

Hans was as surprised as I about your Messianic plans. Though you shared rooms with him, you scarcely confided. He thought your being an only child of uncertain parentage made you withdrawn and disinclined to speak of affairs of the heart. He had no idea of your romantic interest in Mirah Lapidoth. He thought your passion was for me but that you were too moral a man to pursue a married woman. He was embarrassed to have boasted to you of his own interest in Mirah. When he read in the *Times* of Grandcourt's drowning, he supposed you then hurried to Genoa to declare your love for me. He, like it seemed the rest of the world, had observed I was in love with you.

———

AS HANS SPOKE of the Genoa drowning, I again saw Grandcourt's face rising from the water and heard him call: "The rope!" I asked Hans if he had a mind to paint me jumping into the sea as I failed to save from drowning the husband I hated. I did not tell him of my guilt, though I yearned to do so and to speak out about how I was not married but held captive by a monster.

With difficulty I told him something of Grandcourt's brutality toward me: how he watched me like a praying mantis, visited his mistress as and when he wished, kept me from Mama, and controlled what I wore, where I went, and whom I spoke to. I wanted to admit to him the torment of the nights, but I could not shape the words. I recounted how Grandcourt put the diamonds around my neck and in my hair and ears and how he tore my clothes, but that was as much as I could say.

Hans put his gentle, spindly arms around me and said Grandcourt had not touched the heart of me, that I must rid my soul of him and not dwell on his contempt. He said I resisted him with courage, and thank God neither I nor anyone else need ever see him again. He impersonated him by stroking an imaginary mustache, sucking at a pretend cigar, and tormenting a nonexistent dog. Drowning, he said, was too good for him, and he wished he were still alive so he could kill him.

Hans's mischief was a help. Look to the future, he said. The past is a closed book.

MANY OF HIS sketches were illustrations to the story of your life: the Abbey, the cloisters and library, Sir Hugo and Lady Mallinger, the dogs and the river, the Meyrick family, Mirah Lapidoth, Mordecai. Looking at them, I gained some hold on the fleeting days, though it pained me to see how, in drawings of you, he captured your look of thoughtful appraisal.

Hans was also a friend of Rex, whom, like you, he met at Cambridge. When he showed me sketches of him, remarked on his fine face, the strength of his upper lip, and said what "an uncommonly good fellow" he was, I felt another loss and such a desire for Rex's honest company. Rex confided to Hans that he had been so in love with me he could no longer bear to go to Offendene if I was there, or see me since I became a widow. He was resolved to remain a bachelor and devote himself to the law. Hans thought that unlikely. He told me of your annoyance when he joked to you that if Grandcourt had not got himself drowned for your sake, it might have been for Rex's. "Is it absolutely necessary that Mrs. Grandcourt should marry again?" you had said sharply, and Hans sensed ambivalence in you and jealousy, or some cousin to it.

I and Mirah in love with you, Hans in love with Mirah, Rex in love with me, you in love with Mirah and me. Hans said God must be choking himself with glee. He and I talked and talked and after a while laughed at such muddles of the heart. He said knowing me assuaged his bereavement at losing you, Mirah, and Mordecai; that knowing me made him happy and glad he was born.

I STAYED AT the Abbey for seven weeks. The beauty of the surroundings, the wisdom of Sir Hugo, the kindliness of Lady Mallinger, the friendship of Hans—all worked magic on me to bring me to a wiser version of my former self.

I admitted to Hans I was unclear what to do next. I cried when I told him I felt too punished by life and too at odds with myself to continue. He said I must see a wider world than Pennicote. I should go with him to London, shake off the dubious status of the widow denied her duplicitous husband's inheritance, and reemerge as Gwendolen Harleth. A new life would beckon. But for now, Hans said, it was enough for me to be alive and, if not happy, free from entrapment and anguish. He told me I was lovely, humorous, energetic, witty, and intelligent, that I enlivened and would always enliven whatever company I was in, that his mother and sisters would welcome me, and that he was sure when a little time had passed Rex would gladly be friends with me again. Hans made me feel less alone, less sullied. He said I knew what love was because I had felt it for Mama and you, and that I did not have to go and find the Promised Land, save the Jews, sing like Alcharisi, compose like

Klesmer, marry for wealth, or populate the planet. "You have suffered," he said, "and now you owe it to yourself to live happily, free from pain and guilt." Then he took my hand and we went swimming in the lake, I much faster and stronger than he.

ONE AFTERNOON IN the library I asked Sir Hugo how long it took him to recover from his grand passion for your mother, the beautiful, gifted Princess Leonora Halm-Eberstein. He laughed and said a lifetime and that we should not expect or desire to recover from what affects us most. What has happened lives on in us, he said, and the art was not to stay fixed in the past but to move on in a state of acceptance: not to be bitter or pine for what we have lost or clearly cannot have, not to want blue eyes if we have brown, or seek to be young if we are old, not to let regret and disappointment define us.

"I had Dan to remind me of her," Sir Hugo said. "He was my beautiful, special son, gifted and wise, solemn and apart, abiding proof of my love for his mother."

He told me how, as you grew up, you modeled your manners and appearance on his and dressed, ate, and worshipped like a Mallinger, as English as the crest embroidered on your handkerchiefs (but torn from the handkerchief in which you wrapped my father's chain).

"But then when Dan went away to Eton, I was lonely," Sir Hugo told me. "I was forty-five and troubled at having no legitimate son and heir. I wrote to tell him I had married Miss Raymond, of whom he had never heard. I am ashamed of how he must have felt as he read my letter."

I recalled how devastated and cast out I felt when Mama told me of her marriage to Captain Davilow.

Sir Hugo said I should not imagine he was disappointed in Lady Mallinger, who was the sweetest soul, and they delighted in their daughters. He called the absence of unhappiness a freedom and a privilege. He enjoyed family life, his political work, the Abbey, friends, the social exchange, his London clubs, the ordinary things of every day. "But, dear Gwendolen," he said to me, "our lives seldom go according to plan. We must accept what we cannot change.

"I thought Dan would choose a profession: barrister, politician, writer. When he said he wanted to travel abroad to understand other points of view and rid himself of merely English attitudes, I was supportive, though I asked him to keep an English cut of clothes, smoke English tobacco, and not carry difference too far. 'Know where to find yourself,' I told him."

Sir Hugo felt he had failed you and your mother. "He will return," he said to me, with hesitancy in his voice and loss in his eyes, and I cried for him as well as myself. All you turned your back on!—the pastures of England, the seasons of the year, your beautiful Abbey, and the secrets coded in its flagstones. And I knew nothing of the world in which you were transplanted, though I had seen engravings in books of such a place of desert and scalding sunlight.

———

AS EXECUTOR TO Grandcourt's will, Sir Hugo was compelled to meet with Lydia Glasher and Lush. I told him of
the poisonous letter to me on my wedding night and how
it lay like a nemesis on Grandcourt's fetid parure of diamonds, the diamonds I loathed and wanted sent back to
her. Sir Hugo suggested I pawn them, then gamble away
every penny they fetched, for that might at least give me
a diversion. More seriously, he said to return them would
be open to misinterpretation, as if I was intent on moral
victory. My inheritance was not large. He would arrange
for their sale in Hatton Garden.

He viewed Mrs. Glasher as trapped, and warped by
Grandcourt's years of ill treatment of her. He described her
as avaricious, said she spewed jealousy and resentment of
me despite the triumph of her inheritance, and as for Lush,
it was a pity he had not gone overboard with his master,
for they belonged together on the ocean floor.

Lydia Glasher's life, Sir Hugo said, was shaped by
impulse, punishment, and desperation. Ten years back, aged
twenty-eight, after five years of violent marriage to Colonel Glasher, she left him and their three-year-old son for
Grandcourt, who was five years her junior. The colonel challenged Grandcourt to a duel. "The bullets merely grazed
the air," Sir Hugo said. At first Grandcourt wanted to marry,
but Colonel Glasher would neither divorce nor allow her

to see their son. The boy died within two years, uncom-
forted by his mother.

She and Grandcourt moved from place to place abroad
and had their four children. When her beauty faded, he
tired of her. Her social isolation grew, she felt tainted by
the irregular relationship, and it became her dominant wish
for him to marry her. Her husband's death removed all
impediment in law, but Grandcourt no longer wanted the
family he had created. Three years back he broke free and
banished them all to Gadsmere, out of view of Society.

In that bleak outpost she aroused no comment. In
church she was viewed as a widow, tenant of a house owned
by a Mr. Grandcourt, a name not known in the district.
Grandcourt visited her, stayed, and left as he chose, while
appearing in Society as the most eligible of bachelors. She
and their children were entirely dependent on him. He
provided two ponies, dogs, toys, a wagonette, good clothes,
but would make no commitment except through a will.
She had no contract, no binding agreement, no sense of
belonging anywhere.

Listening to Sir Hugo, I felt dread lest my future too
be infected by such isolation. I was alarmed to hear that
Colonel Glasher, like Grandcourt, was violent and punishing. I wondered if both Lydia Glasher and I at root were
victims who sought out pain and punishment, or doomed
alike for seeking to build happiness on another's pain. Perhaps I, like her, would find no place I might safely call

home, no true address. You traveled to find your roots, Sir
Hugo was assured of his, but she and I could not plant on
shifting sand. I recalled her words at Cardell Chase and the
venom of her second letter.

> *When Mr. Grandcourt first knew me, I too was young. Since*
> *then my life has been broken up and embittered. It is not fair*
> *that he should be happy and I miserable and my boy thrust*
> *out of sight for another . . . The man you have married has a*
> *withered heart. His best young love was mine; you could not*
> *take that from me when you took the rest.*

Perhaps with Grandcourt's death and money her life would
be less broken up and embittered. She could speak of "best
young love." "The rest" for me meant loathing and ice-cold
diamonds. She must have had more strength than I to with-
stand his treatment of her. That afternoon when she stood
with their children on Rotten Row and he rode past without acknowledging her or them . . . Why did she subject
herself to such humiliation? Why did she want to marry
such a man? Compelled to more time with him, I would
have murdered with that steel blade, lost my reason, drowned
myself in the Thames without your rescue. I could not tell
Sir Hugo of my self-loathing or confide my disturbed dreams
and memories, but I confessed to my relief at having borne
no children to remind me of Grandcourt, and to my wish
to forgive myself for my impulsiveness and Lydia Glasher
for her bitter desire for revenge.

Sir Hugo learned that Lydia Glasher intended to keep the repellent Lush as her factotum; employment that absolved him from the effort of providing for himself, allowed him limpetlike to adhere to her in the same way as he clung to Grandcourt for fifteen years, have his own rooms in all and any of her houses, feel superior to any servant, be impervious to insult, intervene over scheming arrangements of her heart, and carry out all poisonous errands.

I was shielded by Sir Hugo from further dealings with him. Did he think, I asked, Lush more resembled a toad crouched in a damp dark corner, or a parasitic wasp that feeds on its host? A cross between the two, Sir Hugo said.

Lush tried to turn him against me. He told him I married Grandcourt in haste to avoid the humiliation of work as a governess and penury for my family. He said he warned Grandcourt that if he married me he would have to provide for Mama and my sisters and would repent of it within a year. He admitted he would have found Catherine Arrowpoint acceptable as a wife for his master because of her inheritance.

"Put Lush, Grandcourt, and Mrs. Glasher from your mind," Sir Hugo told me. "You need never see any of them again." His advice was welcome, though not easy to follow.

MY STAY AT the Abbey was a time of enlightenment and transition. I recalled the New Year's Eve there, so soon after my marriage, when you and I looked out at the moon and I asked what I could do, should do, to bear the guilt I felt and the punishment to which I could see no end, and you said, "Look on other lives besides your own. See what their troubles are and how they are borne."

With the kindness and counsel of Sir Hugo and Hans, I more clearly saw your troubles and the tribulations and struggle of those who shaped my destiny. I dared hope my actions were no worse than those of the other players and less heinous than Grandcourt's and his henchman, Lush. Better too than those of my uncle, who was so forceful in thinking himself right.

That New Year's Eve you also exhorted me to "try to care for something in this vast world besides the gratification of small selfish desires. Try to care for what is best in thought and action." I like to think that with the encouragement of Sir Hugo and Hans, I was freed from the worst thoughts that had warped me. But I had learned too much of what I could not do and did not care for. I do not know if my desires had ever been small and selfish. I had not found much gratification. I had hoped for love and ambition to guide me.

IN MID-AUTUMN HANS accompanied me home to Offendene. As our carriage neared the lane that led to the house, I felt excitement and delight. Mama, Alice, and Fanny gathered on the porch to greet us. Mama was so happy to see me well, at ease with myself, and in the company of a young and cheerful friend. The house looked small and shabby after the grandeur of Topping Abbey, but entering it I felt reunited with a loving friend. I again was proud to have restored the house to Mama and my sisters so that they need not sew for sixpences or go cap in hand to anyone.

Bertha, to Mama's pride and concern, was now living away from home. Hans took her room, and I went back to the little bed beside Mama's. Bertha was emphatic that for herself she would consider neither marriage nor a governess's post. She said that having observed Mama's marriage then mine, she would sooner be a strumpet. She was working at Upton Manor, twenty miles away, as a gardener. Mama praised her talent for botanical drawing. I was surprised. I had always thought Bertha slow and unimaginative, and I had derided her artistic efforts, but she had so impressed the owners of the Manor, Sir Roland Myre and his wife, Anne, with her horticultural knowledge, they hired her to help maintain their arboretum and commissioned her to illustrate a calendar with a different tree for each month of the year.

Mama adored Hans but I think was relieved not to have to view him as my suitor. If a button was loose on his shirt she sewed it, if his boots were scuffed she saw they were polished, if he sneezed—as he did much of the time because of the flowers, the grass, the horse, the dog—she tended him with balsam and menthol. He made her laugh, and that was a joy to hear. She plied him with cake, hot chocolate, and sweets. He called her Mrs. D and said she was his country mother. It amused me to see how Mama would have loved a son like Hans, boyish and mischievous, a bit wayward but vulnerable and good-natured too. Most of all I think she adored him because he watched out for me in his concerned yet carefree way.

At ease with my sisters, Hans teased and flirted just a little, amused them, gave them sketches he did of them. A spirit of joy and ease imbued the house. Together we walked the lanes and picked crab apples in the woods. I was glad to be reunited with Criterion and to ride fast each day. Alice had cared for him all summer and was rueful to be consigned to Twilight, the slower horse.

One fine warm day Rex and Anna joined us—my sisters, Hans, and me—for a long walk and then a picnic near Cardell Chase. I was apprehensive about Rex's state of mind, and Anna, I suspected, would be subdued and watchful. But the countryside was pure and lovely, Mama had seen to it we had a pie, cheese, sourdough bread, and apples, we spread ourselves under a beech tree, and our joy was light and without care or undercurrent.

Rex made no mention of my troubles. I was glad again to see his honest, intelligent face and hear his respectful voice. I had heard Lord Brackenshaw's eldest daughter, Beatrix, was smitten by him, but I did not know if he was flattered at her interest. He asked what my plans were if I went to London, and I said I did not know, that I hoped to find a creative path but was unsure what that might be.

He said whatever I put my mind to he was sure I would excel at and that I enhanced any gathering. Hans reiterated the important thing was for me to enjoy myself. Neither of them made any mention of you.

Anna was enamored of Hans. She transferred her devotion from Rex to him and fussed that his fair skin might burn in the sun or that he might have chosen the lesser piece of pie. At ease with her attention, he teased and complimented her. It occurred to me that she would love the man she married with the same wholeheartedness and ease as Mirah Lapidoth loved you, whereas I could never be unequivocal or entirely straightforward.

THE DAYS AND weeks passed. I thought often of Sir Hugo's words *The absence of unhappiness is a freedom and a privilege.* I was no longer unhappy, incessantly watched, or answerable to the command of a savage keeper. Safe again at Offendene, with Mama and my sisters provided for, not lavishly but adequately, with Sir Hugo as my protector and Hans as my friend, I rejoiced in my freedom. And though a weight of guilt and wrongdoing burdened me, and I could not quite see how I might meaningfully occupy the days, I dared to admit that the greater conflict would have been had Grandcourt lived. He was mourned by no one.

But I could not go back to who I was before my marriage or to the life I had lived. I did not want to appear in Wancester Society as the ill-treated widow; nor could I again be Mama's spoiled darling, sharing her bed, her coiling my hair. When suffering so with Grandcourt, I thought the old routines were all I wanted: Mama and the house, reading by the fire, dinner parties, charades, and picnics, the archery contest, the hunt, galloping over the downs. But I could not settle into such a life again, and I refused the social invitations with which Mama tried to tempt me.

My fears had gone, of the dark, of the vast night sky, the face in the wainscot, the serpent in the diamonds. I could think of death without particular dread. But Offendene, though loved by me, was not a place where I now could stay. The ghosts of the past confined me. If I was to become an adult, if I was to become Gwendolen Harleth, I must move away from Mama and Pennicote.

SOON AFTER HANS returned to London, I followed him there. Mama agreed to my going. I believe she would have agreed to any move I wanted and thought might bring me a chance of happiness. Hans promised to chaperone me and that his family would care for me. Sir Hugo assured her of my safety and well-being in his Park Lane house, with his servants to look after me, and he, Lady Mallinger, and their daughters frequently in town, and I assured Mama of my frequent visits home. I said she would see so much of me she would grow bored, that I needed her company more than she needed mine, and that she and my sisters must stay with me at Park Lane when in town.

In Sir Hugo's town house I was accorded a bedroom in
pale green and cream, and an elegant sitting room with
writing desk, chaise, and view over Hyde Park. As the maid
closed the door I felt calm and safe, but I yearned for you
to call, see me in these surroundings—free and determined
to be myself—be pleased for me, and give me encouragement. The wish passed, and I realized, with strange sorrow,
that I thought about you with less pain, and only with effort
could I conjure you in my mind, your still and thoughtful
presence, your eyes that seemed to take me in, and although
I still revered you, the day might come when you ceased
to be the person to whom in my heart and soul I addressed
my every wish.

I was sad that despite you saying you would write to
me and remain close, you did not because you could not:
not as a married man. Sir Hugo and Hans always read to
me their letters from you, but what could I care about this
place called Palestine and your other life and adventures
from which I was so excluded?

LONDON SEEMED FULL of secrets, promise, and destinations. From my windows I looked out at trees and lawns,
people strolling, talking, hurrying, smart carriages, buskers,
lamplighters. I thought of my sister Bertha and my surprise
that she should find a singular talent and the strength to
pursue it. I hoped there might be a similar fate for me.

Hans promised to escort me to the theater and circus

and on boat trips along the Thames; to introduce me to his clients, friends, and fellow artists. He encouraged me to wear simpler clothes and to coil my hair more freely. I wondered about getting it cut short like some of the suffragists. Hans said he would cut it for me with his mother's kitchen shears and that when he had finished I need never again fear the amorous intentions of any man.

One of the first visits I made with Hans, in late autumn, was to Mrs. Lewes and her husband. We were invited to one of her Sunday salon afternoons. "She wants to know more about you and your feelings for Dan," Hans said. "She misses her conversations with him."

I had first seen her at the Abbey at Sir Hugo's New Year's Eve party, when you and she were talking about the Jews, then a few times more at Park Lane, at the Mallinger gatherings. Hans told me it was you who inspired her to study Jewish history, and you who introduced her to Mirah Lapidoth, who then sang Hebrew songs at her musical soirées.

I had thought little more of her for she seemed ugly and erudite, but now, widowed and uncertain of my social status, I was trepidatious at the prospect of meeting. I feared that, like Klesmer, she would confront me with her genius and my middlingness, and I had had sufficient of that mix.

Hans said she had her own muddles, just like the rest of us. "She's not really Mrs. Lewes, even though she insists on being addressed that way. She always corrects anyone who speaks of her as Miss Evans, but that's who she is. She can't marry him because he already has a wife, Agnes, whom he can't divorce."

Mr. Lewes had been Agnes's tutor. He married her when she was nineteen. She was blond, beautiful and clever, translated books from French and Spanish, believed in free love, and had eight children. "Lewes was the father of the first four," Hans said, "and Thornton Leigh Hunt, editor of the *Daily Telegraph,* fathered the others." Leigh Hunt also had another ten children with his legitimate wife and on two occasions was the father of a child by her, then one by Agnes, born within weeks of each other. He had wanted to be an artist but paint made his skin fester and itch, so he turned to journalism. Hans sympathized, because he himself was allergic to many things, though fortunately not to paint.

Apparently, Lewes was at ease with this unconventional marital arrangement and cared more for the first of the babies fathered by Hunt, but born to Agnes, than for any of his own children, with whom he was rather distant. He put his name as father on the birth certificate, though the child was "very brown with unmistakable Hunt eyes."

Hans was unclear when Mary Anne Evans and George Lewes became lovers but thought it was early in the 1850s. Before she would agree to live with Lewes, she wrote to Agnes for assurance their marriage was over in all but name. Agnes replied she would be delighted for Mary Anne to marry her husband, but as he had condoned her own adultery they could not be divorced. So Miss Evans lived in a loving and committed relationship that she could not grace with legal status. Her eldest brother, Isaac, whom as a child she adored and revered, would not speak to her because of it and only communicated about unavoidable family matters through solicitors.

I thought of Grandcourt and Mrs. Glasher when they had become lovers, their "best young love," and Colonel Glasher had refused to divorce his wife. Mary Anne Evans avoided social ostracism by calling herself Mrs. Lewes. She was wiser than the law.

Apart from such tiresome practical obstacles, the Leweses and Leigh Hunts were civilized and supportive of each other. There was no vengeance or malice: no lying in wait at Cardell Chase, no wedding day letters about withered hearts, no menacing appearances on Rotten Row. Mrs. Lewes wrote her successful novels under the name George Eliot, so I, like many of her readers, had supposed the author to be a man. George was Mr. Lewes's Christian name, and Eliot, she said, was "a good mouth-filling easily pronounced word." Writing earned her wealth as well as fame and financed Mr. Lewes, his wife, and their offspring, whom she viewed as her stepchildren. The children called their mother "Mama" and the second Mrs. Lewes "Mother."

My eyes were being opened to London life, and I resolved to choose my time to explain such complexities to Mama. But hearing of such temerity gave me an inkling of how I might perhaps for myself, by some act of daring or rebellion, achieve liberation from the fixed receipt of a woman's happiness. I might yet, like Hester Stanhope, dress like a Bedouin and travel with a caravan of camels across the desert.

I doubted I could be a writer, like Mrs. Lewes or Mrs. Arrowpoint. I could not conjure unborn people in my mind or bring myself to care about the truth or otherwise of Tasso's madness, or whether his seventeenth-century Italian love life was one thing or another. I cared about my own love life, and yours, and Hans's and Rex's and Sir Hugo's and Mama's and Bertha's.

Mrs. Arrowpoint of course did not shine outside of Wancester, whereas George Eliot was admired worldwide. Queen Victoria had twice read *Adam Bede* and was so taken by it she commissioned the artist Edward Corbould to paint two watercolors from scenes in it: one of Dinah preaching, the other of Hetty making butter. Hans said these pictures hung in Buckingham Palace, though he had not seen them. He admired Corbould's technical skill but considered his subject matter stiff and traditional.

Hans and I went in Sir Hugo's carriage to the Priory, the Leweses' house by the Regent's Canal. I told him I would like to arrive a little late to give other guests time to gather. I did not want to be conspicuous. I wore pale green and white, a simple pearl necklace, and of course the turquoise chain.

The house, secluded and pretty, was set far back from the street. Late roses still bloomed in the front garden. The rooms, spacious with large windows that reached almost to the ceilings, had been arranged and furnished by the architect Owen Jonès, who designed the interior of the Crystal Palace for the Great Exhibition of 1851. All had bespoke wallpapers and carpets and were filled with paintings, engravings, sculptures, and exotic fabrics. The Leweses each had a book-lined study. They shared a music room.

I was discomfited when on arrival Mr. Lewes took me into his study, ostensibly to show me a portrait of "Polly," as he called Miss Evans—to add to the confusion about names—which hung over the fireplace. I recoiled at the way he took my arm and looked at me. He asked Hans for his view of the portrait, and I knew by Hans's circumlocutory reply he thought it of little merit. Mr. Lewes wanted to commission him to do another, of Polly reading in their garden with her dogs beside her.

The setting was warm and welcoming, but I felt apprehensive among the mix of such confident, self-important people. I made Hans promise not to leave my side. He said it would be easy to stay with me for I was the most amusing and beautiful woman in the room. There were perhaps a dozen men but only five or six women. Barbara Bodichon was there—I had heard of her—and two other "Ladies of Langham Place," feminists who wrote pamphlets about women's rights. Through their campaigning the Married Women's Property Bill was passed in 1850-something, which meant husbands could no longer be entitled, in marriage or divorce, to have all the assets that belonged to their wives. I remembered Grandcourt's derisory comment on this jurisdiction in support of women: "They'll be wanting to enter Parliament next," he had drawled.

I knew almost none of the guests, though I recognized the Hebrew scholar Immanuel Deutsch, with whom you had studied. He was at Lady Brackenshaw's musical evening when Mirah Lapidoth sang. He was Jewish too. He had dark hair and eyes, was small and sad-looking and wasted with cancer. Hans told me he had been to the Holy Land some years previously to visit the Wailing Place in Jerusalem. I supposed that to be your destination.

I was glad Herr Klesmer was not among the guests, though even without him I feared the talk was disconcertingly erudite. I was aware of Mrs. Lewes's repeated scrutiny of me in a way I could not interpret but that seemed unfavorable. I felt weighed in the balance and found wanting. She keenly observed my appearance, though her clothes were a veritable mishmash of ill-assorted things. I thought her so plain and evidently fiercely clever that not many men would want her as their wife. It was as well Mr. Lewes was devoted. I suspect she viewed herself as ugly, which she was, hers was such a heavy face—her big nose, severe jaw, and rather tired eyes. Perhaps she had been led to believe she was ugly as often as I had been praised as beautiful.

Mr. Lewes told Hans that Polly was much troubled by her teeth, and indeed she kept putting her hand to her cheek in a way that indicated pain or at least discomfort. Two of her canine teeth had recently been pulled after she was first made unconscious with nitrous oxide.

Mr. Lewes was if anything uglier than she, with wispy brown hair, a straggly mustache, pockmarks on his skin, wet lips, and a head too large for his tiny body. He was illegitimate and so was Barbara Bodichon, Hans said. I thought of Mrs. Glasher's brood and began to wonder if half the world had been born out of wedlock. Even when living with his young, beautiful wife and four sons, Mr. Lewes had had affairs with other women. I found it difficult to believe women could find him attractive in that way.

But all that was in the past, Hans told me, for now George Lewes and Polly were everything to each other and never apart. He adored her, encouraged her genius, helped and guided research for her books, and loved her so much he was not tempted to be unfaithful.

Seeing them together, I had the sense that the man's role and the woman's merged. He fussed in case she was in a draft or if the tea might be too hot for her teeth, whereas she paid all the bills. Both he and she were clever, witty, and self-assured, with languages to learn, countries to visit, and books to write—his were about philosophy and psychology, I think. I thought her brave, openly to live with a man who was married to someone else, but I wondered what her view would be of my marriage to Grandcourt and if she would consider Lydia Glasher's venomous behavior toward me justified.

As if reading my thoughts she beckoned me over. In anticipation of meeting her, I had rehearsed a small speech. I told her I had read several parts of her recent novel *Mid-*

dlemarch and found Mr. Casaubon perfectly awful, though
not as horrible as my husband had been, and that I feared
Will Ladislaw was not much better. She seemed immod-
erately hurt by my remarks and looked across to Mr.
Lewes, who again held my arm, took me to one side, and whispered that criticism plunged Polly into despair and we must
try to shield her from it.

I had not intended criticism. I felt like telling him that
apart from you I considered no man worthy to be anyone's
husband, but it seemed best to say nothing if everything
was open to misinterpretation. Mr. Lewes then said something to her, I think in Hebrew, which is how they communicated when they wanted no one else to understand.

She then told me she had recently received a letter from
you. Again I felt a stab of jealousy that you wrote to her as
well as to Sir Hugo and Hans but not, as you had said you
might, to me.

"What is his news?" I politely asked, though my voice
sounded strained.

She said you wrote of palm groves, pelicans, barren hills,
mud dwellings, and fields of sugarcane. You had climbed
Mount Sinai to see where God gave Moses the Ten Commandments. You were studying Sanskrit, Aramaic, and
other strange languages in order better to understand the
Talmud.

"What is the Talmud?" I asked, supposing it to be a
building like Topping Abbey.

She gave me an amused, condescending glance and said

it was the encyclopedia of Jewish law: "civil, penal, ecclesiastical, international, human, and divine."

"I see," I said, though in truth I did not quite see, and
the familiar bewildered feeling of unreachable worlds from
which I was excluded afflicted me.

Your knowledge of Jewish matters interested her greatly.
I asked her if she was Jewish. I thought she perhaps was,
given she had such a large nose and was rather plain.

"Unfortunately not," she said. "They are such a cultured,
creative people."

I did not know what to say. I knew little of the Jews,
knew only of my hopeless love for you. I longed for your
news, not of holy shrines, synagogues, temples in Egypt and
Palestine, and the fate of the Jewish nation, but of you and
your feelings for me.

There was a silence in which she scrutinized me with
her shrewd blue eyes. I found this unnerving, as if she was
weighing me up for I did not know what. Then she leaned
forward and in a whispered hiss asked, "Why did you marry
Grandcourt? You're not foolish. Surely after the most per-
functory acquaintance you could have seen his character?
And you knew of the other woman and his children. You
did not have her permission."

I was taken aback by such sudden intense intimacy, the
abrupt change of direction of the conversation, the impli-
cation that she knew much about me and indeed about
us all.

"It was a mistake," I said nervously. "We make mistakes.

It happened so quickly. I married in haste. We hardly talked. He did not reveal his character. I saw what I wanted to see. When I realized my mistake, it was too late. Marriage to him was a steel trap. It snapped shut. I could not escape. I paid so fiercely."

She looked at me as if she knew all that. She nodded. "Grandcourt was polite, charming, and attentive," she said. "That was his tactic of capture before punishment, an aspect of his control."

I wondered if she pitied or even despised me. I thought of her unorthodox domestic arrangement, her proxy mothering of Lewes's children. I dared to say, "You did not swear promises you could not keep. You could escape at any time."

"Mr. Lewes and I love and cherish each other," she said. "We are in the best sense married. We see the world through the same eyes. Without him I would achieve nothing. I provide"—she swept her hand to the furnishings, paintings, ornaments—"and for the children."

"Yet you feel the approbation of Society," I countered, for her air of moral superiority discombobulated me almost as much as her apparent clairvoyance. She did not reply. I felt accused. I said I did not see why all women had to marry. For myself, I did not like men, and marriage had brought me to my knees. I entered into it all too hastily for unworthy reasons, and I did not intend to attempt it again. I did not reveal that had you married me, I might have thought myself in paradise.

"If you reject men, you must perhaps make do with

women," she said. "You must meet Barbara. Though I doubt she will turn you into a feminist or suffragist. And you should meet my adoring 'daughters,' as I call them, Elma and Emilia." She showed me a table and mirror carved by Elma, a soldier's widow who lived in France, called Mrs. Lewes her "spiritual mother," and bombarded her with gifts: woodcarvings, shawls, paperweights, slippers, photographs of her dogs, Watch and Dora, and letters saying she longed to be her servant and to kiss the hem of her dress. I wondered if Mrs. Lewes encouraged such attention. I should not like it. Emilia, I gathered, had a very old husband, the rector of Lincoln College, Oxford, with whom she was unhappy.

Marriage, Mrs. Lewes told me, was a moral state. She said the shackling of women to men in bad relationships appalled her. Herr Klesmer and Catherine Arrowpoint were meant to marry; they were in love, they respected each other's talent. Catherine was right to defy her parents; she and Klesmer would not have their pure hopes sullied by the venality of greed or the prejudice of race. "Your uncle," Mrs. Lewes said, "his interests were venal too. He should not have put pressure on you to marry a man of low character."

How did she know of my uncle Gascoigne and his insistence that I should marry Grandcourt? I was unnerved. I had made no mention of him, I had not spoken of him to you, Rex would not have criticized his own father, and Hans cared for the good name of us all.

I feared she had power over me, a psychic ability to read

my mind and innermost thoughts, and would know were
I to lie or dissemble. I wondered if she disliked me because
I was beautiful and perhaps felt I used my beauty to under-
mine her. I did not know why she was questioning me or
what she really wanted to know. Yet I was intrigued by
her and hoped she would advise me what to do next with
my life.

She leaned forward again. "In the harbor at Genoa," she
whispered, "you withheld the rope."

I did not answer.

"You saw him sink?"

"Yes."

"And then what?"

I thought of the Catholic confessional, the shield between
confessor and priest, which offered an illusion of privacy,
whereas Mrs. Lewes's blue eyes absorbed my deep blush,
shortness of breath, struggle to confront the darkest deed
of which I ever could be guilty. Were I to lie, she would
know, of that I was sure.

"He came up farther off," I said, though my voice, like
Grandcourt's as he drowned, seemed not to belong to me.
"The boat had moved, I stooped for the rope, I had the
rope in my hands, and I was sure he could swim."

"But you hated him," Mrs. Lewes said. "You wanted
him to die."

"I dreaded him. He went down again. My heart said
die. He sank. And I felt it was done, and that I was wicked
and lost."

She gave a strange satisfied smile as if I had confirmed what she wanted to hear but already knew. But did she, I wondered, know my desperate hate, my murderous rage, was born from his ravishment of me? Was she going to ask about that, or was that taboo, so embarrassing and terrible it must not be mentioned? I waited, aware of my racing heart, hoping she would ask and help me talk of it, so that I might rid myself of the blight of shame and self-disgust. She said nothing, and silence hung there, like an undisturbed curtain.

"Did you not think it strange," she asked, "for Deronda to be at the harborside when you were taken ashore by the fishermen? Were I writing a fictional account, I'd hesitate to include such a coincidence, such synchrony. It would strain my reader's sense of credibility."

I said I had not wondered. I was disturbed when hauled ashore, and you were so continually on my mind I was unsurprised to see you.

"It was not all mere coincidence," Mrs. Lewes said. "Deronda deferred his departure from Genoa because he was sure you needed his help. When he first met you on the stairs at the Italia and saw your troubled state of mind, he resolved to talk with you, however counter that ran to Grandcourt's wishes. On the afternoon of the drowning he asked at the desk if you were both still in the hotel. He learned you were out boating. He went to the synagogue, then took his evening walk along the quay, hoping to catch you as you came in from the sea."

Our lives, it seemed, were in Mrs. Lewes's hands. She knew not just our stories—the facts and details of what happened when and where—but our motivation. I felt dazed, drawn back to that terrible day, afraid I might be forced to live it again. But I was thrilled to hear you had been waiting for me and wanted to talk to me. In the precious chamber of my heart I stepped on a summer's evening from a wrecked boat to a safe harbor and my ordained union with you.

I must have swooned into a trance for next I heard her say sharply, "That's enough," and I started, as if woken in an unfamiliar and for a moment unrecognized place.

She became more formal. "Do you know anything of Jewish history?" she asked.

I spoke of my effort to read Milman's *History of the Jews* and inability to get far with it. I said I preferred novels, romances, and mysteries, though I had a fondness for Shakespeare, particularly *A Winter's Tale*.

"'To unpathed waters. Undreamed shores,'" Mrs. Lewes said. I gave a slight smile and a nod, to pretend I recognized the quotation. "If you knew something of Jewish history, you would better understand Deronda and his departure." She guided me to her study and showed me shelves of books about Jews. Yours was a religion of sublime far-off memories, she told me. "You must talk with Mr. Deutsch. He has visited Palestine many times and written eloquently of the Jews and their thousand years of collective suffering."

Your connection to Genoa, Mrs. Lewes told me, was
time-honored and symbolic. While waiting for your mother,
you searched the city's archival records. She too had studied them. Your forebears, Sephardic Jews from Spain and
Portugal, fled to Genoa from persecution at the time of
the Inquisition. They arrived as refugees, were herded into
a ghetto by the harbor, and could not go through the city
gate unless granted a license and displaying a yellow badge.
When they wore these badges, they were insulted by the
indigenous Genoese. If they failed to wear them, they
were fined. Mrs. Lewes told me of a Jewish man who put
candle wax in his ears so as not to hear the insults hurled.

In Spain and Portugal the exiled Jews had been doctors,
musicians, clockmakers, shop owners. By Genoa harbor
they hawked fabrics, coffee, woolen stockings, shirts for sol-
diers. They were not allowed to wear swords, or walk about
at night.

Sometimes the doge took action against those who
threw stones and repeatedly insulted the Jews, but in 1686,
in the name of the pope, he decreed that all Jews living in
Genoa should be deported.

Such were the iniquities and a thousand others like them
against which, Mrs. Lewes told me, your soul rebelled. They
were a people who were *pelted*, to use Sir Hugo's word.
Among those who survived, in whatever country would
permit them entry, many kept alive their racial and cultural identity through language, diet, customs, and worship, in obedience to rules laid down by Moses on Mount

Sinai. You wanted to help deliver your people to the homeland from which they had first been exiled.

I LISTENED TO Mrs. Lewes with some interest, but I felt
discomfited. None of this was what I wanted to hear. Talk
of the Jews bewildered me and distanced me from you. That
was then, I wanted to say, but it is now that matters. I felt
the same frustration and uninterest as with Uncle Gascoigne's sermons at Pennicote. I preferred galloping across
the fields. I did not care about Moses or Jesus. I could not
match your Jewish suffering, your collective memory. Mine,
it seemed, were the less than sublime not-far-off memories of Pennicote and twenty other unremarkable places to
which I no more belonged than did the swallows and peonies of an English summer.

Mrs. Lewes then confounded me by saying that although
religions interested her, she believed death to be the end
of life and the utter annihilation of the individual. That
seemed a view too far.

As we went back to her drawing room to talk to her
clever guests, Mrs. Lewes told me she would like me to visit
again in a month's time at another of her salon gatherings
or, if I preferred, tea and a quiet tête-à-tête. In the mean-
time she and Mr. Lewes were packing up, taking their dogs,
and going to the countryside to write; they liked and needed
long spells without distraction, away from Society. But I,
she said, intrigued her, and there were a dozen questions

she wanted to ask me, questions that she hoped I would answer. I felt a mixture of flattery and perturbation. What was it about me she could want to know? Why should I be of interest to a famous writer, a bluestocking immersed in different cultures and history who translated books from French, German, Italian, Latin, Greek, and Hebrew and whose novels Queen Victoria admired and read aloud to the prince consort?

I was relieved when Hans signaled to me that he wanted to leave. In the carriage back to Park Lane I told him I had found the afternoon intriguing but I was unsettled by it. What was I to Mrs. Lewes or she to me that she should be so interested in me? Had he seen how she singled me out? Who had given her all this information about me? Moreover, such a gathering of clever purposeful people emphasized the now familiar feeling of my own inadequacy and limitations. I neither wrote books, fought for women's rights, nor studied ancient scriptures. My father had been an inconsequential man of whom I had scant memory; my mother was sweet, long-suffering, and uneducated. We had scarce money; I had made a disastrous marriage, and love eluded me.

Hans said it was invidious to view oneself in such a way, that I should not underestimate the vulnerabilities and self-doubts of others, and that my compelling presence was evident by the way all eyes turned on me when I entered a room. "You don't know your own power, Gwen," he said.

"Even Mrs. Lewes is intrigued by you above all her other guests."

I was flattered by his appreciation of me, though I doubted whether being an object of regard was sufficient justification for my existence. I was the statue that had yet to come to life. Uncertainty trapped me. My heart was in turmoil, my frustrations were acute, and all around me others succeeded while I stood still.

ONE DAY HANS said to me that as part of my education, I must meet Juliette, his latest friend. This was the time of Hans's "circus phase," when he was commissioned by the *Graphic* to illustrate circus life. I had not hitherto been to a spectacular circus. In our first autumn at Offendene a touring company pitched their tent in Pennicote; the display comprised two clowns, two dwarves, one juggler, two performing horses, a tightrope walker, a fire eater, and an acrobat. We marveled, but only slightly. The city circus was of a different order.

I went with Hans to performances in various towns and cities. He filled sketchbooks with drawings of elephants and lion tamers, equestrian acts with seventy horses in the ring at once, dwarves, giants, bearded ladies, and trapeze and high-wire acts. In Paris we saw Miss La La hoisted upward by a rope in her mouth until she reached the high wire. We gasped at the danger.

I was witness to no serious mishaps beyond a dropped baton and a slipped step, though Hans told me of Madame Blondin, who, in front of thousands at Aston Park, Birmingham, shackled and blindfolded and with a bag over her head, held the balancing pole, took three steps on the high wire—which broke—then fell to her death. She was eight months pregnant. The queen then complained to the mayor of Birmingham.

When the circus came to Olympia Hans and I, on several nights, sat in the third row. I enjoyed the antics of the clowns, the displays of acrobats and gymnasts, but it disturbed me to see the exploitation of damaged people: dwarves, giants, bearded ladies, and fat men, and of animals, lions, elephants, horses, forced to behave in ways alien to their nature. It was not their choice to parade in such a way, and my time with Grandcourt made me recoil from such shows of captivity and control.

But then came Juliette. The arena plunged into darkness, gaslights flared, and she appeared, adorned with paillettes, feathers, and lace, at the top of a thirty-foot column. Her bodice and headdress glittered with silver lamé, her huge gauze skirt fanned over the length of the column and spread wide on the floor, she began to twirl on the top of the column, and as she did so the skirt gathered momentum, lifted off the floor, and spun like a wheel. It was an aerial ballet. The audience roared.

Next she appeared as a circus girl, swathed in ostrich feathers and jewels. Then she shed her headdress and clothes and became in turn an elf, a fairy, an angelic creature, a statue that came to life and then performed. Wearing little but jewels, and flaunting her perfect figure, she walked backward and forward on a high tightwire, then a slack wire; she pirouetted on rings and the trapeze to music by Wagner and Rimsky-Korsakov; she pretended to fall and caught herself by a last-second hook of her foot. We were aghast, amazed; we gasped, groaned, and shouted. In another act she hung by her teeth and whirled.

Then at the end, to the disbelief of us all, she threw down the balancing pole, leaped down to the stage, gave a bow, and tore off her wig to reveal—how loud we gasped—a boy's head. Juliette became Julian, who to wild applause made a salute with a clenched hand. He returned many times, put on his wig, then doffed it to show his cropped hair and remind us we had marveled at a man playing at being a woman.

My own astonishment was intense. I could not put him from my mind. Hans took me backstage and introduced me as the van Dyck duchess. Julian laughed and said he imagined I was less laced up than any duchess.

I met him many times while he was in London; at Hans's studio, where he went to model for him, Hans sketched and painted him as Julian transmorphing into Juliette, and on several occasions I visited him at his lodgings. He rented a room from a grim landlady in King's Cross in a house that smelled of cabbage. The room was damp and cold with stained wallpaper and dirty windows, and I marveled that great beauty could emerge from such squalor. Some afternoons he called at Park Lane, usually when I was alone. He was the most exquisite creature, and I felt his beauty matched the elegance of the Mallinger house. I suspected the tea and cakes Avril the maid served were his main meal of the day.

I had confided to both Sir Hugo and Hans and drawn strength from their affection for me and their kindness, but with Julian there were few taboos in our conversations. He was outside of Society. We talked of face powder, blushers, unguents, and my menstrual pains. Despite his femininity, he exercised to a peak of physical fitness and was as strong as any stevedore. I saw how callused and scraped his hands and limbs were, yet his acts on the wire and trapeze seemed effortless. He said when he dressed in women's clothes he became a woman, but that was not his quintessential self, and that identity need not be fixed, neither his nor mine.

To Julian I managed freely to talk of all that had happened to me, to confide how I loathed men to touch me or make love to me, and yet I loved you and longed for you, though in reality you were quite out of reach to me.

Remember that life can change from minute to minute, he said. He advised me not to view all that happened as just one event; some things were good, some lucky, some bad, some terrible. Other possibilities would happen if I allowed them, if I was open and receptive: new friendships, distant countries, diverse experiences.

His life inspired me. He spoke with a soft American drawl for he came from Texas. His mother had been a milliner, but he had no recollection of his father. His name was Julian Hope, and when, as a boy, he saw his first circus, mesmerized by the high-wire acts, he determined to be a tightrope walker. He practiced on the clothesline in his mother's yard, worked in the cotton fields, and, using the money he earned, traveled to where circuses were being held.

When he was fourteen he answered a billboard advertisement for auditions with the Giuliano Sisters, "World Famous Aerial Queens." One of the three sisters had died, and a replacement was needed. He was hired, provided he would perform as a sister. So Julian became Juliette, though such friends as he had called him J.

He learned a great deal with the sisters but felt constrained to be part of a troupe and aspired to perform alone, not as an acrobat in a woman's clothes, but as a solo star of the theater, a vaudeville artist, or graceful daredevil. Shakespeare's heroines were his influence. They were played by men, he said. When he performed he aspired to become the depicted woman, statue, bird, or two lovers in one body.

At his solo debut in Harlem, audiences were ecstatic. He was hired to perform in revues, circuses, music halls, at the Casino de Paris, the Folies Bergère, and in Covent Garden in London.

———

I WONDERED IF you might have understood the allure I felt toward Julian, or if you would not have countenanced him. Uncle might have viewed him as an envoy of the devil and Grandcourt not have acknowledged his existence. I doubted Mrs. Lewes would have found a place for him in one of her books, and neither Julian nor Juliette would be invited into the living rooms of the Arrowpoints, Brackenshaws, Quallons, and Klesmers, but to me he was in every way aerial and free. He said we were similar, called us the narcissists whose beliefs came only from inside ourselves, and said neither of us had, or could have, roots or a place or person where we belonged.

I confided my fear of having no place or profession, how I found it difficult to separate from Mama, and that when playing the part of Hermione in *A Winter's Tale,* instead of coming to life at the appointed time, when I saw the image of the dead face in the wainscot I screamed. Fear, I said, stood between me and life. As I spoke I remembered your words *Take your fear as a safeguard. It is like quickness of hearing.* I had some glimmering of what you perhaps meant.

JULIAN SAID HIS body was all he had, and that he did not care if romance was between a man, woman, or idea; it was the theater of it he loved. One afternoon he told me of how he had been caught kissing a man and the theater manager forbade him to return and said he could not get work there again. My response to this was the same as when you told me you were a Jew. At first I blurted with shocked surprise, "A Man!?" But then when I saw disdain on his face I said, "What difference need that have made? If you wanted to kiss, it is just the same as if you kissed a woman." And he said, with kinder rebuke than you leveled toward me and with less defensiveness, that it was not the same, that he would never kiss a woman. It was men he desired and wanted to kiss. That was a fixed point of feeling of which he was sure.

And I felt bewilderment, yes, but beyond that a sense that perhaps my play was never *A Winter's Tale* but *The Tempest*, and that I might, like Miranda, say, "O brave new world, that has such people in it," one of whom, or maybe two or even a few, might if I were lucky guide me to a newfound home.

I thought how Mrs. Lewes was not Mrs. Lewes or a Mrs. at all. Nor was she a George. Juliette was Julian. You were really Daniel Charisi, Mrs. Glasher wanted to be Mrs. Grandcourt, and Hester Stanhope dressed in embroidered trousers and a purple velvet robe and wore a saber to greet the pasha. I thought how alarming for your mother to give you away as a baby to an unmarried man, then take no interest in your fate; how mystifying that I should be repelled by lovemaking, and how marriage to Grandcourt was the worst fate that could have happened to me, but perhaps had brought me to the place where I now was.

Don't look to the past, J said. Look forward, find happiness through whatever door it comes. He said he was glad to have met me, he found me beautiful and sympathetic, and how important it was to love someone or something, because only that way could we ever hope to love ourselves.

I asked if he thought, if I learned to walk the high wire, I might find employment similar to his, not on the same level but perhaps as a supporting act. I said I was adventurous and very good at most sports, I could jump any brook on horseback, was a fair dancer, and I liked to act. J said it was not impossible, my elegance and grace would captivate any audience, but I was coming to it late so it would be hard to make up for the childlike fearlessness and ease that came with an early start.

Unlike Klesmer, Julian discouraged me gently. The pay, he said, was derisory, work opportunities were uncertain, and risk of injury was high. He thought I might get to dread, as did he, finding myself alone on tour in dingy lodgings in provincial towns and cities. He said for himself he had always known the tightrope was where he needed to be, but without such compulsion it was not an existence to envy.

HANS INTRODUCED ME to strange people and brave excitements. In the world into which he took me I found freedom of thought and action beyond the social round and searching for a husband I did not want. I could not now care about winning at the archery contest, marking every dance on my card, coiling my hair just so, or riding with the hounds. I found courage and a determination that was mine alone. One day I told him I felt hopeful and were a chance of happiness, however passing, be open to me, I believed I might take it.

REX AND HANS were good friends and saw much of each other, so it was inevitable Rex and I should meet again. Uncle feared that Rex, now a pupil in chambers near the Royal Courts of Justice, might revive his infatuation for me, but I gathered from Hans he had given up hope of my loving him, the pain of rejection had diminished, and he felt no ill will. Rather, like Hans, Sir Hugo, and Mama, he wished for me to find some joy in life. Hans said it was absurd to allow one falling-out to break a lifetime of friendship, and I agreed. But I was disappointed that Rex at social occasions seemed to avoid me, for when we picnicked at Cardell Chase some months previously I had dared hope our childhood closeness might be restored.

Then one afternoon, at a gallery viewing of Hans's work, I saw Rex standing alone. I went up to him and asked if he would call and have tea with me the following day. He looked startled but delighted, and he agreed.

In the formal setting of the Park Lane house we were reserved. I was aware how much we both had changed.

I was less confident, he was more: a well-cut suit, his hair stylishly barbered, his manner authoritative though without conceit. Rex within two years had changed from a boy to a man, whereas I had changed from a girl who was witty, bright, and impulsive to a woman more troubled and unsure. Uncle's pride in him was not misplaced, and he was set for a distinguished career. He was ambitious for law reform and outraged at the denial of women's rights and the severe punishments given to children—he told me of a twelve-year-old boy called William sent to Wandsworth Prison for stealing two rabbits to feed his family.

I should have hated Rex to pity me. Pride made me stand by the mantelpiece, seemingly composed, assured, and poised but, with the ghost of past vanity, with the intention for him to admire my long neck, profile, and retroussé nose. I wanted to dispel the shadow of that awkward afternoon at Offendene when I met his marriage proposal with scornful impatience. "All the happiness of my life depends on your loving me—if only a little—better than anyone else," he had said.

He did not look unhappy now, so perhaps he had kept a little happiness back for himself. Unfair though it was, for I did not want Rex for myself, I was jealous to think he might entirely have recovered from his passion for me. I knew from Hans that Beatrix Brackenshaw was interested in him. I wondered if the interest was shared, or if he was deterred by her father's conservatism and belief that women should dine separately from men. Apparently, Beatrix was headstrong and clever, a rebel and a suffragist, and intended to study to be a doctor like Elizabeth Garrett Anderson.

"I am sorry you have endured misfortunes," Rex said, and his concern was sincere, though his words sounded stilted. "But you seem restored and are as beautiful as ever." He looked at me in his familiar, tender way, and I again thought had I been able to love him, be wife to him, mother to his children, how solicitous, kind, and generous he would always have been to me. I might have had the direction and safety I felt I wanted but could not find.

He spoke of his anxiety for me when he heard of the boating accident and Grandcourt's drowning and his relief that you had been there to help me. I did not know if he knew the circumstances of the drowning or quite how terrible the marriage had been, or of Grandcourt's dubious private life and the humiliation intended to me by the terms of his will.

Then Rex looked at me as if to determine whether I was strong enough to hear uncomfortable news, and with a prescience worthy of Mrs. Lewes I knew what he was about to say. I thought again of that afternoon at the White House, the last time I saw you, when you told me with embarrassed hesitancy of your intention to marry Mirah Lapidoth. And now Rex wanted me to know he was to marry Beatrix Brackenshaw. He believed they would create a happy life together, which did not mean, he said, that I did not have an enduring place in his affections.

For a moment I was silent, then I sat on the sofa, bent forward, and shed tears I could not check. I do not know why I wept so copiously, for I did not love him in a way that might fulfill his life: had he kissed my neck below the ear, I would have recoiled; had he told me, with an equally careful choice of words, that his feelings for me were unchanged, that all the happiness of his life depended on my loving him a little and becoming his wife, I should again have rejected him, though with more kindness, tact, and concern for his feelings than on the previous occasion.

He implored me not to cry, spoke my name again and again, reiterated that I would always have a place in his heart—I was his cousin, his childhood sweetheart—the love and affection he felt for me could never be excised. And then he said his news brought the chance of good fortune to Mama and my sisters, and that was what he most wanted to tell me about, and was so glad of my invitation because of this opportunity it gave him. He was now legal adviser to Lord Brackenshaw over his estates. He had talked with him and Beatrix, and all were agreed that Offendene should, in perpetuity, be a grace-and-favor home for Mama, my sisters, and me. Moreover, the estate management would be responsible for repairs, renovations, and upkeep. A carriage was to be provided, a groom, a gardener to attend the grounds; there were already plans to retile the roof, reframe the windows, and redesign the vegetable beds. All of course in consultation with Mama.

Such kindness and honor made me cry the more. I

believe Rex would like to have put his arms around me but feared such an expression might be unwelcome or misconstrued. He walked to the window and waited, with his back to me, until I had calmed. I saw, even though my heart was troubled, what a gift this was to Mama and the girls. Henceforth they would be more than secure, Mama free from any anxiety of financial pinching, my sisters free from pressure to marry or to suffer as governesses in unfamiliar households. If they had aptitudes, there would be no impediment to their following them.

I half wondered if Rex was entering into this marriage in order to help me in the only way he could, but I dismissed the thought, for he was too honorable a man to calculate in such a way or compromise Beatrix's feelings.

I thanked him and asked perhaps rashly if he loved Beatrix Brackenshaw. I said I had heard she was freethinking and high-spirited. "There are different ways of loving," Rex said. He was hopeful they would have a good life together of independent pursuits and shared interests; they saw life from the same point of view and got on well; she was more lighthearted than he, but ambitious in her own right. She was not content merely to be a wife and mother. They had much in common, and there were reforms in Society they both wished to strive to achieve.

He laughed when he said had she not sought him out, he doubted his courage to have shown an interest in her, for fear of being viewed as avaricious. At first Lord and Lady Brackenshaw were antipathetic to him; he came with no inheritance, was a poor horseman, and encouraged their daughter in her wish to be a suffragist, doctor, and social-ist, but now they accepted and even liked him, for it was clear he would excel in his chosen profession.

As Rex left, he said he hoped he and I might from now on meet easily, for I was too precious and important to him to disappear from his life. I tried to reassure him, but with the same effort as wishing you success in your marriage, for in my heart I cried for my own safety. Again I saw a door that might have opened, and through which I might have gone, close shut as others walked through it into what might be happiness. Again there was direction and pur-pose for others' lives but not my own.

HANS HATED TO see me sad. He said I was only outside of things if I chose to put myself there, and that he was deter-mined to lure me into the activity of the present and the promise of the future.

One morning in May, soon after breakfast, he visited unannounced and said we were to go shopping together. For what? I asked. For clothes, he replied, after which I must keep the next day free. We went to a store on Aldgate Street, where I was fitted out in a blue knickerbocker suit trimmed with gold, and a pair of high-legged boots. As I postured in this rakish costume, I felt a glorious sense of freedom and defiance, and Hans agreed I more resembled Hester Stanhope than the van Dyck duchess.

I could not guess what adventure was planned. I questioned Hans, but he gave me no clues. He told me to get a good night's sleep, have only a light breakfast, and be ready at eight the following morning. "Are we to go to Ashkelon?" I asked. "Shall I shave my head? Will there be camels to carry my baggage?" He looked enigmatic and would not be persuaded to enlighten me.

I woke several times in the night wondering what awaited me. Perhaps Julian had talked to Hans about my hope to perform in a trapeze act. This might be the start of my theater career.

IN THE MORNING I put on this daring garb, coiled back my hair, and thought I looked like an androgyne. I again fancied I would have my hair cut into a bob like the suffragists, and felt mischievous delight at what Uncle Henry and Mrs. Arrowpoint might say.

Hans laughed when he saw me. His clothes were not dissimilar to mine. "Where *are* we going?" I asked, but he would not tell me.

We took a carriage to the rebuilt Alexandra Palace in north London. I had not been to that part of town before. We alighted in a field near the palace, and I was introduced to Captain Lucas, a military man with a bushy mustache and a loud voice. "Ah, my parachutists," he boomed.

Parachutists. My excitement was intense. Was I to fly and outdo Julian on his trapeze and high wire? The captain stood by a huge basket, which ten men held anchored to the ground, and supervised the slow filling with gas of a vast golden balloon. "You are pioneers," he said to Hans and me. He told us there had been ascents in hot-air balloons for the past hundred years and jumps using parachutes with rigid frames but that he had revolutionized parachute design. His inspirations, he said, were the flying squirrel and the dispersal of winged seeds, and he was working to perfect the design of a trapeze bar and sling. Twenty volunteers had so far jumped from his balloon, and the only injuries were a broken ankle and a grazed forehead. His eldest volunteer had been a postman aged seventy-two. I was the first woman.

"Is she adequate to it?" Captain Lucas asked Hans, as if I were not there. Hans told him I was stronger than himself: an archeress, a horsewoman, a swimmer. "This will be more thrilling than any of that," the captain said. "This will be the most exciting event of your life."

As if explaining an everyday affair, he said we were to rise two thousand feet in this odd contraption, then jump from it with parachutes that would waft us down to earth. First he showed me how to fall. "Never land standing up," he said. "You'll break your ankles and damage your knees and back." The moment my feet brushed the ground I was to roll onto my back. I practiced. It was not difficult for I had learned to fall from a horse.

Captain Lucas showed me how to work the parachute, which hung from the balloon. Attached to it was a trapeze bar with cords and a sling of webbing about six inches wide. I was to step astride the sling, and as I jumped and held the bar above my head, the webbing would rise up between my legs and take my body weight. "You must keep a firm hold on the bar to balance yourself," he said.

A crowd gathered to watch the spectacle. The golden balloon, as it filled with gas, swayed in the breeze and pulled at the ropes that tethered it. The tops of the limp parachutes were tied to the balloon's netting with cocoa string, which, we were told, would snap under the weight of our falling bodies. The released parachutes would then stream and fill with air.

Hans and I were to be carried up with Captain Lucas and another instructor, a burly, much-tattooed man, in the huge basket suspended under the balloon. As the balloon went up, we were to sit on the basket's rim, our legs dangling over the side, the webbing of the parachute between them, one hand holding the trapeze bar, the other holding the supporting ropes. When we were high enough in the sky, and at Captain Lucas's command, we must jump forward from the basket. He said we would probably land a mile or so from where we took off, depending on the strength and direction of the wind. A pony and trap would pick us up and take us back to the palace. I was to jump first.

We perched on the edge of the basket. Captain Lucas gave the order for the men holding it to release their grip. Onlookers cheered and waved hats, hands, and parasols. There was no feeling of upward movement. It seemed as if we were still and unmoving while the earth and all those on it fell away. There was a strange silence. I saw the world as if I were a bird. It was as if my life was beginning. The landscape formed beneath me, a patchwork of fields and lanes; the crowd dispersed and became little figures who crawled away. I saw Lilliputian dolls' houses and specks that were animals. Captain Lucas pointed to my destination, a small green square, which I supposed was a field.

We floated on, above the clouds and upward into heaven. The air was light and pure. Here was my escape from the earth, my happiness. Captain Lucas said we were over two thousand feet high and told me to be ready to jump. "Now!" he said, then "Go!" I gripped the trapeze bar with both hands and flung myself down, exhilarated, fearless, not knowing if the parachute was going to open. I heard the canopy of the parachute break from the balloon. There was a rush of air. I plummeted so fast and far my breath was knocked out of me. The sling tightened between my legs, I held the trapeze bar tightly with both hands, and it pulled at my arms, and then I saw the silken dome of the canopy of the parachute stretch over me, billowing in a gentle breeze.

I was suspended in clear, warm air high above the land. Above the symmetry of roads and farms, the shadows of trees on wooded hills, I felt such freedom. I was flying high. I laughed and shouted and thought how you would deplore it, how Mama would be alarmed, how Uncle would preach a sermon, and Grandcourt not rescue me no matter if I nearly died. My heart for this eternal moment was not pressed small. My unbounded future was everywhere and everything. The fixed receipt for my happiness was not determined by a husband's permission or Society's approval. I need not care about the wheel of fortune nor strive to win the golden arrow or the silver star. It did not matter that I could not be the best of women or make "my people" glad that I was born. I did not have to act like Rachel, sing like Jenny Lind, compose like Klesmer, or write like Mrs. Lewes. Humiliation and disappointment evaporated. I was above time or place, achievement or failure. I was in my element. Life and death seemed to blow with the wind. I looked down and saw the curve of the world, the patch of green that was my irrelevant destination. I did not want to hurry to reach it. I wanted to stay poised in the air, to float forever, to circle the globe, never to land, not because of fear of broken bones or dislocated shoulders, like poor Rex tumbling from Primrose, but so that this wonderment would never end. I had told Rex I wanted to go to the North Pole, ride steeplechase, dress like a man, and be queen of the East like Hester Stanhope. I should have told him I wanted to parachute jump from a hot-air balloon. I was not Lady of the Bow but Queen of the Skies. I was Gwendolen.

HOW LONG IT was before the earth drifted back to greet me, and houses and trees took on familiar proportions, I do not know. The elected field approached slowly, then with a rush. The grass rose, and as it touched my feet I circled onto my back; no broken bones, no pain. I undid the belt, stepped out of the sling, breathed the scent of grass, and saw the parachute lying beside me. I looked up, and there was Hans gliding down, and high above him in the sky the seemingly tiny balloon sailing on its way.

Hans and I laughed and hugged. He said he found floating down to earth strange and beautiful and that it made him understand abstraction and the severance of the new world from the old and that he would not paint in the same way again. I said I dared do anything now. People ran from the lanes to greet us. We were birds that had descended from the sky, from the realm of the rainbow and the sun. Wasn't I scared? Did my mother know? Where was my husband? they asked. Hans and I were driven to the palace in the pony and trap, given hot tea and scones, and interviewed for the *Graphic*. "Are you beginning to see how wide and full of possibilities the world is?" Hans asked me, and I thanked him and agreed I was.

AND SO I moved on. I forgot I was a widow except in haunting dreams. I woke to relief that Grandcourt was forever gone. My unrequited love for you merged with new preoccupations. I wore the turquoise necklace as allegiance to a memory but not with a sense of hope.

The here and now were not much changed. What had changed was my acceptance of it. I still did not much care for the formal social round; my self-belief remained frag-

ile, and so did my ability to trust the love of anyone but
Mama. Hans partnered me at dances and dinner parties. I
am not sure I would have been invited unaccompanied.

The Mallingers gave musical soirées and held dances
at the Abbey; they now wanted suitors for their girls. Klesmer, when he saw me, invariably told me I was lovely. I
felt by thus describing me he was telling me I was quite
without interest, except as a valued painting to adorn a wall.
Catherine was expecting their child: a little genius no doubt.
Lord Brackenshaw was disappointed I now declined to hunt;
he said he feared the modern generation was losing its vim
and verve. Anna and my aunt and uncle stayed at Park Lane
when in town to visit Rex. Anna was evidently in love with
Hans, and I met this observation with unequivocal hope
for them both. My aunt did not revise her opinion of me:
I was a threat to the male of the species, a spoiled child,
and probably a heretic. Uncle made no further mention of
my marriage or his encouragement of it, and dropped his
paternal manner toward me. Rex's move into the Brackenshaw dynasty meant meat for breakfast for him and a
pedigree companion for Primrose.

Often Hans accompanied me when I went home to see
Mama. He was a loved guest. I have on the wall before me
his sketch of the family grouped on the porch at Offendene
as I arrive and Mama and my sisters greet me. It was how,
on so many occasions, I remembered the scene. It was my
delight to arrive like a meteor bearing gifts of hats,
scarves, perfumes, and a hamper from Fortnum & Mason.

On that visit, Mama told me I looked radiant, and in truth so did she: her face less lined, her eyes bright, her clothes fashionable. She proudly showed me her wardrobe of new gowns. She told me Mr. Quallon, the banker, was her new adviser on financial matters. Offendene was smart, its management supervised by Rex: the hedges clipped, the stables extended. There was a full-time groom, a carriage for Mama to go visiting. Refitted windows made the house warmer; Jocasta and Miss Merry acquainted me with the new and gleaming kitchen. Rex's generosity was an act of loving kindness; he wished for nothing in return but our well-being.

I doubt Mama could see me with a man without wondering if he might become another husband, but fortunately she was too reticent to ask questions about Hans. We all gathered around the dining-room table, and my sisters quizzed me about the life of balls and lovelorn swains they supposed I lived in London. I gave some account of Mrs. Lewes and her salons, the circus, opera, and latest hats and plumes in the shops, but I did not talk of Julian's wondrous shift to Juliette, my ascent in a hot-air balloon and descent to earth in a parachute; these seemed like flights too far for Pennicote.

Mama's delight was to see me happier. She confided her fear of my being lost, in grief and disappointment, to myself and her. With simulated nonchalance she asked whether you had written to me. I said you had not, but that from others I heard of your sunlit journey to the Wailing Place.

Clintock called at every opportunity and was so ardent in wooing Isabel he seemed scarcely now to notice me. His habit was to hold forth on tedious matters as if they were of supreme importance; how not to clean a hen coop was one. It was a mystery to me that Isabel tolerated an hour of his company, let alone the prospect of a lifetime of it, but I had learned that many life choices defy understanding.

Bertha came home for a visit, knowing I was there. I told her about Julian for, in knickerbockers and with short cropped hair, she now looked more of a man than did he. It was her view that all people should be free to follow their hearts. She enjoyed her work as a landscape gardener and spoke with unconscious frequency about Marjorie Millet, a stable girl at the Myre estate, with whom she rode, picnicked, and roamed the countryside.

When I left with Hans for London, Mama did not say good-bye with the same puzzled and disappointed countenance as when I was married to Grandcourt. As our carriage drove away, she and my sisters waved and waved from the porch, and I waved and my heart was wrenched, but more from a sense of the fragility of their lives and hopes, and the awareness of all things passing, than from remorse at leaving Offendene for the still unknown.

"YOU MUST MEET Barbara," Mrs. Lewes said at my next attendance at her salon gathering. She gave her now familiar scrutiny of me, as if reading every detail of my appearance and thoughts.

Mrs. Bodichon was about fifty, tall but plumpish, unself-conscious, and with a proud, intelligent face, her hair still golden though sprinkled with gray, her skirt rather short. Hans told me she was a good watercolorist, a pioneer for women's liberation, that Mrs. Lewes portrayed her in her novel *Romola*, and that she did not wear corsets because she viewed them as a symbol of male subjugation. How he acquired this last piece of information I do not know, but he liked such detail.

He was deep in talk with a tall, dark-haired young man whom I had not seen on previous Sunday gatherings and who, whenever I looked up, seemed to be looking at me. I rather wished I was in their company for I was curious about this stranger's manner and their intense conversation.

"So you're the intriguing Gwendolen," Barbara Bodichon said to me. "Mary Anne has talked a great deal about you." Apprehension as to what this talk might be must have shown on my face, for she added, "About your love for Daniel Deronda and your unfortunate marriage."

Your love for Daniel Deronda. As I heard those words, though time had passed and I had made such moves forward to life without you, a stab of pain and loss went through me so keen that I reeled, and to steady myself held the back of a chair. I then met the gaze of the tall young man, and for a moment, because I was thinking of you, I thought his gaze came from you. It had the same intensity of interest as yours at the Kursaal in Homburg when you drew me into you, and the same effect on me of fear that my will had surrendered. I looked away.

Mrs. Bodichon asked how I liked London and said she admired my courage in braving the city alone. I protested I could not claim courage, with Hans as my escort and attentive friend, Sir Hugo Mallinger caring for me like a father, my more than comfortable quarters at Park Lane, and Mama and my horse and the countryside only a day's drive away.

That was all to the good, Mrs. Bodichon said, now I was free and not trapped in the iniquity of a violent marriage. She pulled from her bag two pamphlets she had published, and handed them to me: *A Brief Summary in Plain Language of the Most Important Laws Concerning Women* and *Women and Work*. I thanked her but doubted I would read either. I was more disposed to live iniquity than read about it. (I still have all Mrs. Bodichon's pamphlets.)

She then gave me a little lecture on how wrong it was for men to hold the financial resources of the world and refuse to let women do decently paid work or have professional careers. To force women to marry for financial support was no better than legalized prostitution, she said. She spoke of a woman whose stolen purse was described in court as the property of her husband. "All professions ought be open to women," she said. "They should be employed as doctors, preachers, members of Parliament, watchmakers; trained as clerks, cashiers, and accountants; allowed to read all literature, including Rabelais, Fielding, and Sterne; allowed to swim in municipal baths."

I had read Charlotte Brontë's novel *Shirley* and thought her right to call on men to alter their laws so women might have lives other than through marriage, but though I wanted to be free or at least not chained, happy or at least not sad, mine was not a campaigning disposition. I told Barbara Bodichon I could not have great theories. I could only feel as I did. She said for us all it was how we felt that mattered. I had my life to live, and, like all women she met, I needed that life to be unfettered. "I love the courage of women," she said. "Had God existed, she would have been a woman."

OVER THE MONTHS that followed I learned about Mrs. Bodichon's eventful life. She came from a family of social reformers, Florence Nightingale was her niece, and William Smith, who worked to abolish slavery, was her grandfather, so it was perhaps in her nature to strive to make the world a better place.

I remembered dinner at the Abbey on that New Year's Day and the conversation about cotton plantations. I only half listened for all I had wanted was to hear your voice. Mrs. Bodichon told me of a slave auction she observed in America, of a girl, advertised as "Amy, a good cook, a good washer," who was holding her baby. A blackguard-looking man opened Amy's mouth, examined her teeth, felt her all

over, said she was expensive, and paid eight hundred dol-
lars for her. Another girl, Polly, twice sold, had her three
children taken from her, separated from each other, and
sold. Polly said to Mrs. Bodichon, "Mum, we poor creatures have need to believe in God, for if God Almighty
will not be good to us someday, why were we born?"

Mrs. Bodichon's politician father, Benjamin Leigh
Smith, never married her mother, a milliner like Julian's
mother, nor did she take his name. Barbara, eldest of the
five children she bore him, was seven when her mother,
aged twenty-three, died. She and her brothers and sisters
were then raised by Mr. Leigh Smith. He taught them at
home and supervised the building of a large carriage, like
an omnibus and drawn by four horses, in which he, they,
and the servants each year went on magnificent journeys
to Italy, Ireland, or Scotland. They took sketching materials
with them, and this gave Mrs. Bodichon her enthusiasm
for painting out of doors.

She spoke of Hans's paintings and said he had a con-
siderable talent. The man with whom he was talking was
Paul Leroy, an even more outstanding young painter. Had
I seen his work at Arthur Tooth & Sons in the Haymar-
ket? she asked. His canvases sold for as much as forty-nine
pounds. I apologized for knowing nothing of Arthur Tooth
or of Mr. Leroy and his art. "I am most ignorant," I told
her. "I have no more than a smattering of knowledge in any
subject and no particular accomplishments." She laughed,
put her arm around me, and said, "You shouldn't be so

competitive." I only half understood what she meant. I confided that in the past I had supposed I might earn merit and my living in the arts: by singing and acting perhaps, but I had been disabused.

Mrs. Bodichon said for herself she liked to paint but did not care about recognition beyond giving pleasure to friends. I thought of my disdain for middlingness and your praise of it, and of how accepting you said you were of that state for yourself.

"Paul's eyes haven't left you," Mrs. Bodichon said. "You must be aware of that." I was, she told me, *une femme fatale.* "Deronda apart—and he of course is a saint and too good for this world—I can't believe this monstrous Grandcourt has been the only man to try to win your heart." I did not mention Clintock or Middleton, for I thought them inconsequential, but I confessed I pushed Rex away because I could not bear him to make love to me.

She encouraged me to confide and seemed interested in all I said. I told her I would not marry again but since Grandcourt's drowning and your departure, I realized the importance of friendship, freedom, and adventure. I recounted how Hans and I went to the circus and how exciting it was that Juliette performed so convincingly as a woman and yet was a man. I tried to tell her how free I felt when I went up in a hot-air balloon and parachuted down to earth. Mrs. Bodichon was unsurprised. She told me of the French balloonist Nadar, whose real name was Gaspard-Félix Tournachon, who believed the future belonged to heavier-than-air machines. My flight followed his, she said. I too was moving from my land-locked present and reaching for the sky. I was a time-traveler journeying into the next century. Mrs. Bodichon had been in Hannover when Nadar crash-landed near a railway line. He broke a leg, and his wife hurt her neck. We aspire to the swiftness and ease of birds and angels, she said. It pains us to be earthbound.

She told me she found freedom through travel and journeyed far and often. When younger than I, she and a friend, Bessie Parkes, made an unchaperoned walking tour through Belgium, Germany, Switzerland, and Austria. *I come closer to Hester Stanhope each day*, I thought, and yearned for my own journey to unknown places.

Mrs. Bodichon liked to escape to the English countryside to paint. To do this she had built Scalands, a cottage on her father's estate in Sussex, set in three acres of woodland where, she told me, bluebells, nightingales, and cuckoos thrived. Would I like to visit her there, see her paintings, and meet her women friends? She could show me copies of photographs taken from Nadar's huge balloon, "The Giant." He called it "the Ultimate Balloon." A crowd of two thousand in Paris watched its first ascent. Sarah Bernhardt had flown in it.

Barbara Bodichon's courage and imagination inspired me. "I sense your readiness for adventure," she said. "You've had enough of genteel English life and the hypocrisy that writhes behind it. You need to ride into the distant hills and fly to the mountaintops. But first of all you must come and stay at Scalands. Let us fix a date."

When I looked toward Paul Leroy, he was looking at me. When I looked toward Mrs. Lewes, she was looking at me too. I was vain enough, for their benefit, to keep my back straight, my features composed. I could not know what either of them was thinking, but I was intrigued by their watchfulness and curiosity, as if defined by it.

Mr. Lewes came over, again took my arm in a way I found too personal, and said, "I must prize her from you, Barbara. Polly wants to quiz her more."

Mrs. Lewes praised my dress and complexion and said that given all that had happened, I looked remarkably well. She wanted news of my half sisters: were they studying, courting, working? Alice and Fanny were still at home, I told her, Isabel was courting Clintock, the archdeacon's son, and Bertha was working as a landscape gardener.

What of the face in the wainscot, Mrs. Lewes asked, was it still there? Was Miss Merry still overly fond of ginger biscuits? Would I remind her of the color of Jocasta's hair? Who exercised Criterion now that I was so much away from home? Whom did the Momperts employ as a governess after I withdrew my candidacy, and how was Mama managing with her rheumatic pains and shortness of breath? What news was there of the agent Lassman? Had Uncle and Mama received redress for his irresponsible business dealings that led to our losing such income as we had?

She asked so many questions. I could not understand

such curiosity about people whom she did not know. I would not ask her the color of her brother's bedsocks, whether cabbage gave her dyspepsia, or if Mr. Lewes snored. Her pursuit of detail was so unrelenting I concluded we were all research material for some book. Perhaps I would be her heroine or antiheroine and you her hero.

"Have you met Mama?" I asked, knowing she had not. I gave vague and equivocal answers to most of her questions, but I told her how Uncle ran into Lassman by chance at the Army and Navy Club in London and found him lacking in all contrition. With money borrowed from his bank, which he could never repay, this architect of our downfall set up as a property developer and built a terrace of houses in East London. Mrs. Lewes asked my opinion of him, and I condemned such ambition to profit at the expense of others. Her look was ironic.

Was Grandcourt's body ever washed ashore? she wanted to know. Where was Mrs. Glasher now? Did I still sleep in a bed beside Mama's when I went home to Offendene? And with that question I realized the hard transition I had made. I would never again be the child I was, the adored, assured, bright, witty girl. Yes, Offendene was the place I viewed as home, but Grandcourt took the innocent heart of it from me. I could not again be Mama's beloved daughter whose every word and wish were precious.

All I said to Mrs. Lewes was that Offendene, Pennicote, and Wancester now seemed to me small and used up. I had outgrown that life and must reach for the wider world. And even if I could not grandly succeed, I wanted to look forward, see new landscapes, meet new people, and be at ease with who I felt myself to be.

"You will not accept a small size for your woman's heart," she said, and laughed.

Then she told me how, when she and Mr. Lewes were in Homburg, they visited the Kursaal—only, she stressed, because of their interest in its architecture and history. She saw there a beautiful English girl, apparently Byron's great-niece, gambling feverishly, and she wept to see this young fresh face among the hags and brutally stupid men around her.

Again I had a sense of unreality, as if I was a work of fiction, a creation of her pen. Was she likening me to Byron's great-niece? Did she know I gambled at the Kursaal and lost? Was she colluding with your disapproval when on that decisive day you gazed at me? I could not countenance that she might know of that gaze, or how for me it was the moment of supreme connection against which I measured my downfall.

I tried not to show consternation. I said I did not see why occasional gambling was a crime. For myself I enjoyed the distraction of it and hated the duplicitous standards expected of women, particularly if they were young and unmarried. "Surely you know what it is to suffer the slavery of being a woman," I quoted your mother: "your happiness made as cakes are, by a fixed receipt." "Ah," Mrs. Lewes said, "the princess Eberstein. But she had a world-class talent to defend. When her voice failed in middle age, she married again: a Russian prince."

I supposed her to imply that my talent had no class and therefore, though still in youth, my best option was to find a prince. I said I found it hard to understand why Princess Eberstein chose to take a second husband after her declared abhorrence of marriage and admission she was unable to love. Nor did I understand her explanation that she gave you away to spare you from knowing you were born a Jew. Her father and husband died soon after you were born, and she then converted to Christianity. She could have raised you as a Christian without Jewishness being of significance.

Mrs. Lewes thought your mother would have kept you if she could have both cared for you and pursued her career. Giving you to Sir Hugo was perhaps an impulsive act. He was there and said he longed for a son like you. But I was mystified. Giving away your child was hardly like pawning a necklace. And she abandoned you entirely, evinced no interest in you, and although she remained unloving, she then remarried and had five more children, but did not part with them.

I WONDERED IF Mrs. Lewes had researched the lives of everyone in this room and beyond. I wondered if she dwelled on other people's lives to deflect attention from her own, and whether she denigrated me—my beauty, youth, lack of education, talent, or sound judgment—in order to elevate herself. Mr. Lewes was devoted, but her own arrangement of the heart was unusual. I suspect she was troubled by its unorthodoxy.

I began to view her as a fairground gypsy, a Madame Rose who could reveal my future, about which I was increasingly more concerned than my past, if I proffered the palm of my hand or if she felt the contours of my skull, or scrutinized the dregs in my teacup. I felt alarmed in her company. I surmised you or Sir Hugo must have given her much information for it certainly had not come from me.

She then mentioned my physical recoil at lovemaking and asked what was at the root of this aversion and if I preferred women to men. She said she had experience of that. I did not grace such questions with an answer. In her books, or the few I had read, she had not been candid about such issues. But I must have blushed, for she gave her knowing smile, then asked if I might marry again. I told her I would not.

Then she asked even more perverse questions: Was there a level on which I invited Grandcourt's assault on me? Was that the only way in which my coldness could be breached? "Relationship is formed from recognition," she said. "You knew of his cruelty, knew how unscrupulous and punishing he was to the woman who bore his children."

I could not check my anger. I was not, I told her, the flawed victim she perceived me to be. I said, "I am not like that. You don't know me. I am a young woman who has been unlucky and badly treated. My luck will change." I accused her of contriving a version of me, then condemning her own creation.

I felt questioned and cross-examined like a defendant on trial. It occurred to me that if ever I was to confide what Grandcourt had done to me, I would need Barbara Bodichon's outspoken warmth, not Mrs. Lewes's adversarial detachment.

"You hoped Grandcourt's wealth would save your mother and sisters from penury," Mrs. Lewes said. "Your motive was in part honorable but your course of action sullied."

She observed my agitation and became gentler. "I hoped Rex might marry you," she said, and again I had a fleeting intimation of how safe and, yes, happy my life might have been had that come about. I said it was enough that he and I had restored the friendship. Did she know, I asked, of his engagement to Beatrix Brackenshaw, his management of the Brackenshaw estates, and the gift he helped arrange of security of tenure at Offendene for Mama and us all? She looked surprised and said she knew nothing of that; the last she had heard of Rex was of his excelling at his law studies and his continuing devastation at my rejection of him.

Though she knew so much about us, it seemed the connection stopped at a point in time, like a broken love affair or a moving on from friendship. Or perhaps she viewed us as players on a stage for the duration of an evening, then abandoned us into the night and went home with her ugly little quasi husband, dogs, and toothache to other interests.

I wanted no more questions about myself. I wanted news of you. Had you loved me? I blurted the question unrehearsed.

"Yes," Mrs. Lewes said, without hesitation. "But perhaps he found you too like his mother, too willful and vain. I expect he thought you would hurt him. And you are not a Jew. You do not understand the essential allegiance."

And then I asked the question that if I allowed it choked my heart: did she think you would come back to me?

Her eyes looked shrewd but tired. "Gwendolen," she said. "I am not a soothsayer. But as you know, Mr. Deronda is married, his wife is adoring, they have a child, they are an orthodox Jewish family. Will he return to you? How can I know? I am sure, though, he carries you with him."

I thought of the Abbey and your English upbringing. You must carry that with you too. And I felt she did know. That she knew it all. Knew me from even before I was born. Knew why it was that the face in the wainscot broke my control, and why I shivered if touched by a man. I suspected she had been there in the room on my wedding night when I opened the box of diamonds, had seen Grandcourt tear at my clothes, pin me to the bed, and spoil me. Knew why I yearned for you to console me, counsel me, help me mend. Knew that were you to return, it would not be to me.

"But," I ventured despite myself, "were his wife to die?"

She made an exasperated sound and turned away. Her strange little husband, who was not a husband, sensed discord and came to my side. He spoke apologetically of Polly's fascination with the quotidian detail of all our lives.

Mrs. Lewes then took my hand in her warm hand and said in the kindest voice that I was often on her mind. The admission sounded like a declaration of love. I was unsure how to respond to this, or what to make of it, or what my relationship to her was. "Please come back next Sunday," she said.

HANS AND I took a brougham home. He was enthusiastic about the guests at the Priory, the stylish setting, the pleasing cakes, and vintage wine. He asked me about Barbara Bodichon. I said I found her warmhearted, interesting, quite unlike any other woman I had met, and how pleased I was she had invited me to her country cottage. He spoke of her fame as a feminist and a socialist, and I told him I knew that, but it did not matter; she was as interesting as if she were neither of those things.

Hans had talked to Paul Leroy and another painter, Edward Byrne-Jones, whose lover tried to drown herself in the Regent's Canal when he did not elope with her. She was his model, a beautiful Greek woman, but Byrne-Jones was married and there was drama and scandal.

Hans said Paul Leroy was smitten with me, had spoken

of my beauty, grace, the pathos in my eyes, and I do not
remember what, and had asked him to ask me if I would
model for him. Hans teased about love at first sight, said he
was aggrieved at such competition, feared his own chances
were now nil, and that with beautiful women he was always
destined to lose to men more talented, rich, and handsome
than himself. First he lost Mirah to you and now clearly
me to Paul Leroy. For himself, he would have to make do
with women of the streets.

Did he not consider it an impediment, I asked, that Paul
Leroy and I knew nothing of each other and had not spoken?
Hans said it was better that way, for then our illusions need
not be broken. As for his own pretense at self-denigration,
I reminded him how, for months now, at the mere men-
tion of the name Hans, my cousin Anna's eyes brightened.
Hans's view was that he and Anna were mere mortals, while
I had cast my spell on genius, intrigued the eye, and snared
the heart of a man who might prove the most important
artist of his generation.

Leroy had studios in London, Paris, and near Florence;
his work was bought by the cognoscenti and the rich. I
ought to be proud and pleased, Hans said. I was freed from
my persecutor and welcome at the heart of London intel-
lectual and cultural life. George Eliot, George Lewes,
Immanuel Deutsch, Barbara Bodichon, Paul Leroy—here
were the people who were shaping and changing our literary, artistic, and social destiny. And of course himself, he
said. Shining over us all. Was I not glad, he asked, that I

had left the little world of Pennicote behind? He would
wager that Leroy's destiny and mine were entwined.

I was flattered to be reminded of my power to impress
such glittering stars of Society but conscious of a familiar
sense of inferiority. It seemed I was not to contribute to the
transcendence of Art. I doubted I could unequivocally enjoy
Mrs. Lewes's beautiful prose, Mr. Leroy's inspired canvases,
Herr Klesmer's exquisite rendition of "Freudvoll Leidvoll
Gedankenvoll." Hans earned his place in the salon, while
I, rooted in uncertainty and, neither a man nor an artist,
was witness to a world from which I was excluded.

When staking my numbers on the red and the black,
or ascending the heavens in a balloon, I felt freed from the
snare of middlingness. At heart I feared I was, like Julian,
a daughter of Narcissus, and I feared being no more than
the reflected image of desire in an admirer's eyes or a pup-
pet in the hand of a stranger.

I lamented to Hans how Mrs. Lewes probed me with
questions and how it made me feel most strange that she
seemed to know everything about me.

"She is a novelist," Hans said. "Understanding people
is her trade."

"But she does not quiz you," I said. "And a novelist is
not a biographer. Why should she want to know about
Mama's shortness of breath and Rex's marriage and what
my sisters are doing and what became of Lassman and
whether Grandcourt's body was on the ocean bed."

I said I suspected she was going to write about me,

which made me uneasy. I wanted to live a free, adventurous, and happy life, not become a character in a book. Hans
said she would probably write about us all, that was what
novelists did, but the hero of the story would be you,
Deronda. You were the one she admired and lauded; she
was interested in the rest of us only insofar as we impinged
on you. Hans said he believed Mrs. Lewes was jealous of
your interest in me because I was beautiful and she was
not. She engaged with you intellectually over the history
of the Jews, whereas you were physically drawn to me and
desired me. As he spoke I felt the familiar yearning. I had
pushed you to the back of my mind, to the cold part of
my heart, but you were always there.

ALONE IN MY room, unnerved by the day, I conjured images
of the occasions when you and I met: your gaze in the gaming room at the Kursaal; at Diplow when I was engaged
to Grandcourt; riding beside you at the hunt; as you sat
with your back to me at your desk in the library at the
Abbey; when we stood by the window and looked out at
the moonlight; in the Mallingers' drawing room when
Mirah Lapidoth sang; when Grandcourt found us together
after I asked you to call at Grosvenor Square; at the Italia
Hotel in Genoa when I saw you on the stairs; when you
called at the White House to tell me of your impending
marriage and departure for the East. All those moments
and more were pictures in my mind, like treasured pos-

sessions. Each time I saw you I was surprised; as if I had found what I had lost and been searching for. Now there was no point in searching, though the ghostly feeling remained of what I wanted but could not find.

THE NEXT DAY Paul Leroy left his card with a request that he might visit me at five the following afternoon. As I prepared for his visit, I hoped with agitation that he did not intend making love to me. I dressed in pale green and pearls, placed the sheet music of Mozart's Piano Sonata no. 16 in C major on the piano, and an opened copy of George Eliot's *Romola* on a small sofa. I thought of wooings of me at Offendene: Rex's gauche declaration of undying love, Grandcourt's businesslike proposal, my appeal to you, and your apology that you could not help me.

Mr. Leroy arrived some minutes late. Tall and soberly dressed, he looked more like a lawyer than an artist. He did not appear vain, though he must have known he was handsome. His voice was quiet, pleasing, his English fluent, though with a light accent for French was his first language.

There was no flirtation. He displayed no anxiety or particular desire to flatter or please. He surveyed the room and me, thanked me for agreeing to see him, and asked if I would model for him. He said he would like the chance and challenge to capture in paint something of what I seemed to express. Mine, he said, was a face of subtle expression into which much could be read. Not only my conventional beauty intrigued him, but the divided emotions that showed behind my eyes. He spoke of a wish to paint nuanced portraits, which he hoped would show progression of feeling from one emotional state to another, from optimism to disappointment, for example, or pain to strength, or captivity to freedom. He wanted a classical face, as he called it, and said that when he saw me it was as if his theoretical idea met the living model. Portraiture is itself a relationship, he said, a reaching out from artist to model, a generosity from model to artist. I would be his muse. He could never reach who I was, but would like to offer his interpretation.

He had a direct way of talking, neutral but friendly. He said he also wanted to paint the shared exchange of emotional states as they registered on the faces of couples. What he called the split second of a realization. I wondered how my face and yours must have looked when you told me you were to marry Mirah Lapidoth.

The modeling sessions were to be at his Tite Street studio. He assured me he would pay me generously and not be demanding of my physical endurance or put pressure on me. If the work suited me, and if I had time, he hoped I would sit for him regularly. He could not begin for another month for he had to be in Paris for an exhibition of his drawings.

I was intrigued, though cautious. It seemed Paul Leroy viewed me as his inspiration. I thought of what men wanted from me. You perhaps saw my troubled soul and hoped to protect me; Rex admired my daring and beauty; Grandcourt saw a challenge to his viciousness; Sir Hugo thought me in need of a father; to Hans I was a caged creature whom he wanted to set free. But I did not want only to be a perception in the eyes of others. For myself I wanted to explore life more and take risks, though not of the marrying sort. Paul Leroy had come to my door; he offered another adventure.

I agreed to go to his Tite Street studio and try one session. I explained I was restless and found it difficult to sit still or do what I was told and that I preferred the outdoors: horse riding, swimming, walking, archery, parachuting. He laughed and said all those activities sounded inspirational and that if I indulged them, maybe he could draw them. As for sitting still, I must fidget as much as I liked.

There was a directness about Mr. Leroy. He was not guarded and cautious like you. He and I talked that afternoon in a personal way, an exchange of confidences. He had learned of my marriage from Hans and how my husband drowned in my presence. He too had been disastrously married. His ambition to be an artist formed when he was a child. His mother, like my father, died soon after he was born. He grew up with a stepmother whom he disliked, as I disliked my stepfather. His father, a martinet, owned hotels and casinos on the French Riviera and would not countenance his only son wasting his life dabbling with paint and canvas. To consolidate his own financial empire, when Paul was nineteen, he pushed him into an arranged marriage with a first cousin four years older than himself.

Paul felt no desire for her and had no interest in her but said it was worse for her because she was in love with another man.

After what he called four wilderness years of working for his father, he abandoned this wife and their small son, told no one where he was going, changed his name to Leroy, and traveled alone in Europe, Russia, and South America. At first he eked a living finding such paid work as he could and selling his pencil sketches. With money earned from these he bought oils and canvases. When his paintings sold, he rented a studio in Paris and hired models. Now his work was sought after and his income assured.

He had no contact with his family, and like Julian he seemed a self-creation. At ease with him, I felt no need to sparkle or use words merely to impress. He was serious and strange, but I had a sense of trust. He did not interrogate me, as did Mrs. Lewes, or woo me, as did Rex; I did not feel he wanted to control me or enslave me, as had Grand-court. I thought you would like him. He saw something in me to inspire his work; I was curious about what I might see reflected back to me through the mirror of his eyes. And I especially liked his assurance that payment terms would be generous. It felt indiscreet to ask what these terms were, but I was thrilled at the idea of earning money for myself, even if not in quite the way I had anticipated. I decided to spend it all on stylish clothes and gifts and outings for my sisters and Mama.

SCALANDS, BARBARA BODICHON said, was a house for
women from whose encouragement, wisdom, and experience I would benefit. The front door opened into the living
room, with a brick fireplace where those who visited wrote
their names; walls were crammed to the ceiling with her
paintings. There were books everywhere and pottery brought
from her travels in Algiers and other places. Some of the
women smoked cigars and wore jodhpurs or dungarees.

I often visited Scalands. I met artists, poets, writers, and
workers for social reform, but also women ill treated by
their husbands or victims of unjust laws. I met Anna How-
itt, a painter and petitioner for married women's rights;
Marie Rye, who in Liverpool housed girls from the streets
or the workhouse, taught them, helped them find employment; Elizabeth Garrett Anderson, who qualified as a doctor, but when she tried to pursue her training, the male
doctors complained to the hospital management.

I shared the scorn of these clever women at the way the
rule of men suppressed their lives, but though inspired by
them, I did not want to join their protest marches or sign
their petitions, and I fear I preferred novels to the sort of
books they wrote.

Mrs. Bodichon was outraged by all she heard of Grandcourt. It was bad enough, she told me, that a woman's
property should belong to her husband, but terrible for

her body to be claimed as his possession too. "I can imagine how you suffered," she said to me. "Mary Anne told me of it."

"Neither she nor anyone knows quite what happened," I said. "I cannot speak of that, even to myself." I remembered my conversations with Julian and his lack of surprise, but even with him I could not find words for what I endured from Grandcourt or how despairing and unclean he had made me feel.

"If you wish, you can try to speak of it to me," Mrs. Bodichon said. "My sympathy may be of use to you. I might be shocked but not embarrassed. I am as well able as anyone to understand suffering and disappointment. I am more often discouraged in my mind than exulting. I can't get what I want. My life is less than my aims."

I was disarmed and surprised to hear such an admission of weakness from a woman so confident and outspoken, who dared to flout all rules. "But that's how I feel," I told her.

"Friends help," Mrs. Bodichon said. "Every good friend one has is a fortification against evil, an extra arm for good."

Though joyous of her friendship and the doors she opened to me, I could not return even in words to that dark time with Grandcourt. I wanted to erase him from my mind. But I told her how, through that endurance, it was you who kept alive my optimism and gave me courage. I said I looked to you as my best and only friend, my confessor and hero, and that when you left for Palestine with your blameless Jewish wife, I felt devoid of hope. I admitted I yearned for you to fill my life when Grandcourt drowned.

"Deronda," Barbara Bodichon said, "is a good man. I have not met him, though I have heard often and in detail from Mary Anne of his exceptional qualities and extraordinary life. But perhaps his expectations are too lofty for a creature as impulsive and daring as you. Perhaps his opinions and ideas are too fixed. You did not know the price of your mistake when you married Grandcourt."

I confessed to her how much I did know. How I was warned by Lydia Glasher and had known Grandcourt humiliated and discarded her. Known too in my heart that those who wrong one person will wrong another.

Mrs. Bodichon would not condemn me. The marriage was intolerable, and had it continued, I would have endured a death within life. The worst of it, in her view, was that having realized my mistake, I could not extricate myself with sufficient money and the support of the law. I should not have been obliged to stay. The law should have protected me from Grandcourt's violence, allowed me to leave, and granted me the wherewithal to do so. I should not have been so ground down, so belittled as to have no choice but to withhold the rope when he drowned.

I spoke of the guilt I felt and the sense I now had of not knowing what direction to take.

"Good habits are important," Barbara Bodichon said to me. "And a routine life if you are in a weak state of mind. Don't despise little things if they make you cheerful. Dress helps, I find. When dispirited I put on a better and brighter gown." Then she said what gave her most strength was the sense that others relied on her. "If one leans on one side and one on another it gives strength to what is weaker than either." She said she built a rough wooden-scaffold bridge of life with the hope that one day she would see a perfect arch.

"I am one of the cracked people of the world," she told me. "I like to be with others like me." She said I was cracked too, and though I had never thought of myself in quite that way, I did not object to the notion.

THERE WAS MUCH laughter at Scalands on weekends. Mrs. Bodichon made each day fun. We all went horse riding, walking, blackberrying; we even went bicycling. Violet Greene, who specialized in fashion designs for modern women, offered to cut my hair short. Mrs. Bodichon thought this would be a rite of passage for me. And she favored my reverting to my birth name. She had kept hers as well as taking her husband's. She called herself Barbara Leigh Smith Bodichon. I was to meet this husband, Eugène Bodichon, when summer came. He was, she told me by way of under-statement, a most unusual man who hated England and the rain, so he stayed half the year in Algiers until the sun shone here.

I told Barbara how when married I would say my own name over to myself because I loathed to be called Grand-

court, and even to hear the name spoken provoked me into
remembering all I wanted to forget. You are Gwendolen
Harleth, she said. Abandon Grandcourt, never mention it,
and you will forget it, and others will forget it too. Men,
she said, by imposing their own names on women, enslaved
them and made their past invisible.

I thought how Mary Anne Evans, although not married, called herself Mrs. Lewes and wrote books as George
Eliot, though she was not a man, and how George Lewes
called her Polly, though I am not sure why. You were Charisi, not Deronda or Mallinger. Lydia Glasher would have
liked to be Mrs. Grandcourt. Princess Halm-Eberstein
called herself Alcharisi, Julian could transform to Juliette,
and Paul Leroy was I did not know who. I am Gwendolen
Harleth, I said. Gwendolen Harleth. I will not lose my name
again.

IN THE COMPANY of energetic women, who viewed the
world fearlessly, I dared make small choices, out of delight
in the present, hope for my unknown future, and in oppo-
sition to the prescriptions of the past. I recalled the day
when, as we toured Topping Abbey, you explained its architectural features, and you and Sir Hugo defended the min-
gling of the ancient and the modern. I did not have an
opinion, other than that I loved the horses stabled in what
once had been the choir and the way the evening sun came
through the stained-glass windows. Now, I thought I would

look for a new way of living and a modern view, while cherishing some things from my past: how safe I felt with Mama, the charm and romance of Offendene, my love and respect for you.

Looking at Barbara Bodichon's paintings, I hoped I too might have some talent for art. I excelled at drawing when at school, Bertha had a skill, so perhaps there was an inherited gift on the maternal side. Barbara found inspiration on her travels. She painted Swiss peaks, Lombard plains, and white Moorish houses, mountains, and cypresses in Algiers. As I looked at her work, she talked of such elsewhere places, and I felt inspired to travel to them, not like you to fulfill a mission, but to find a world outside of myself, as you recommended I try to do.

I told her I was to model for Paul Leroy. She approved and thought he would prove to be an interesting friend. There are men who do not fit the stereotype, men who are like women in their sensibilities, she said, and Paul was such a man.

I mentioned he would pay me generously for modeling. Barbara Bodichon too then offered me work: raising money for Girton, a Cambridge college for women she had founded, and for a school she had started, the Westminster Infant School, where pupils wore no uniform, were never punished, and there was no segregation because of belief or gender. Barbara and her friends taught boys and girls, Christians, Jews, and freethinkers. The fee was sixpence a week.

I was successful at fund-raising, with help from Sir Hugo, Lord Brackenshaw, and one or two of Uncle's connections. Barbara asked if I would like to teach at her school; I was emphatic I would not.

I WENT WITH trepidation to Mrs. Lewes's next salon, for it troubled me to have my life flashed before my eyes like images in a kaleidoscope. I wondered if I would see Paul Leroy again, but he had already left for Paris. I half listened to Hans and a curate, John Payne, talking about their doubts as to a future life, but I could not be interested in this weighty matter of eternity. I missed Offendene and you. I had heard that Mr. Payne mumbled his sermons. He wanted to talk to Mrs. Lewes about a poem she had written called "The Spanish Gypsy."

Mrs. Lewes, though surrounded by acolytes, again sought me out. I was able to tell her that Uncle had suffered a bad attack of gout; that Mrs. Glasher, or so I had heard from Sir Hugo, was now living in Italy with Giuseppe Fede, a Tivolian count about whom I knew nothing; that George Jarrett, the Pennicote carpenter, broke both his arms when he fell from a ladder while replacing a window frame for the Arrowpoints at Quetcham Hall; that Mrs. Arrowpoint had recently published a long article about Tasso's insanity, which had caused a small stir in certain circles; that Mrs. Gadsby, who had married the yeomanry captain and rode with the hunt, was now widowed, after the captain suffered a fatal heart attack while tending his bees; that Joel Dagge, the blacksmith's son who had found Rex on Mill Lane after Primrose fell on the day of the Bracken-shaw hunt, was now unemployed and not on good terms with his father; that Mr. Middleton, now a reverend, had a seat at Sudbury in Suffolk, was married to Florence, a seam-stress with an out-of-wedlock child, and that the responsi-bilities of family life had made him even more serious.

"And what of Clintock, the archdeacon's son? What had become of him?" Mrs. Lewes asked.

Clintock. Oh yes, Clintock. Croquet. I looked at Hans. I stopped wondering how she knew these people and just supposed she knew everyone in the world. Clintock was to marry my sister Isabel. They planned to live in Bath.

"And the young Henleigh?" she asked. "The now for-tunate heir. What was he like? Was he as arrogant as his father?"

I knew nothing of him, I told her. I had seen him hold-ing his mother's hand on Rotten Row and once before that at the Whispering Stones. He had looked cherubic and was pretending to play a toy trumpet. Perhaps Mrs. Lewes thought that heralded a musical career.

"Ah yes, the Whispering Stones." She ignored my flip-pancy, then said Lydia Glasher was well suited to Grand-court. Violence and ill treatment from her first husband, the colonel, had hardened her. She was fearless, having been so cast out by Society. Neither she nor Grandcourt cared about being disliked.

She then said she was disappointed Herr Klesmer could not attend her salon that afternoon. He and Catherine were giving a recital at the Wigmore Hall. She so fulsomely approved of their marriage you might be forgiven for thinking she engineered it. She told me they were much in demand for concerts in London, Europe, and New York and that Klesmer's compositions seemed to her on a par with those of Franz Liszt, whom she had met in Vienna in 1839 when he was living at the Altenburg with the Princess Carolyne Sayn-Wittgenstein. Liszt played one of his own compositions, and she said for the first time in her life she witnessed real inspiration: his face was beautiful, the music quiet, rapturous, triumphant. Klesmer, she thought, had something of this quality too. He and Catherine now had a child, a boy, who perhaps might prove to be a musical prodigy.

"One would expect no less," I said drily. She looked disapproving, and I returned to Hans and the Reverend Payne and their musings about the indestructibility of the human soul.

PAUL LEROY SENT a carriage to take me to his studio in Chelsea. He greeted me at the door wearing an artist's smock and declared himself delighted that I had agreed to be his model; more than his model, his muse. A young man with oriental features, pretty and delicate looking, shorter than I, took my cloak and hat. I was sure his eyes were lined with kohl and his cheeks rouged. Paul introduced him as Antoine.

The studio was grand with vaulted ceilings and light that flooded in from high windows; there was minimal adornment and a sense of order and calm: canvases stacked around the walls, easels and paints carefully positioned, a chaise where I was to recline, a curtained recess where I would dress for whatever part I was to play. It was quite unlike the chaos and mess of Hans's studio.

I had become accustomed to coincidence and strange insights. For our first session, Paul Leroy wanted me to model as Hermione from *The Winter's Tale*. He wanted to capture the look in my eyes of the statue who comes alive. Here was the perfect charade. No Klesmer to crash the piano keys. No death's head in the wainscot. No fear. When Paul walked across to adjust the set of my head, the turn of my hands, his touch was easy.

I liked looking at him and thought him as beautiful as perhaps was I. I liked the silence and ease of the afternoon. Paul Leroy turned me into art but did not seek possession. Antoine arranged the set, brought water, fruit, and cake. He wore soft slippers, moved silently, did not knock before entering the room, take orders, or wait for instruction. He seemed to anticipate whatever might be wanted, so there was no sense of master and servant or of fawning and scheming as with Lush and Grandcourt.

I was curious about their relationship, which was unlike

any I knew. The ease between them was of the sort that comes from long habit. They needed each other equally; the roles were defined, as with Mr. and Mrs. Lewes. Paul had money and talent, but Antoine was the impresario. Antoine made me think of Julian—the same desire to be beautiful, the same fascination with the performance of life.

Paul worked for two hours, said he had made a good beginning but did not want to tire me more. He would not let me look at his work until it was completed. We talked, ate food Antoine had prepared, and drank a glass of wine. Paul insisted he pay me a retaining fee and hoped fifty pounds a month was acceptable. I thought it excessive for what was expected of me, but he was adamant that those were the terms.

I spoke of Barbara Bodichon and my desire to travel and see something of the world: the Moorish architecture of North Africa, the sands of Egypt. "You must come with us," Paul said. In spring he and Antoine planned a three-month tour across Algeria, Egypt, Arabia. Everything would be arranged. I need bring only smelling salts, a fly swatter, and a sketch pad, he said. I would be Princess Gwendolen, and he and Antoine my retinue. With me heading the party, they could be assured of the best rooms in all hotels, the front of the queue at the watering holes, the liveliest camels across the desert.

My heart leaped with hope at such a prospect, but I felt compelled to jest. Did he not think it a problem, I asked, that he and Antoine had spent mere hours in my company? Given three days, they might despise me. Three months, and they might choose to sell me as a slave. Paul said that could not happen, he had observed me closely, he and Antoine were experienced travelers, and I would enhance any journey.

Anyway, he added, the proposed grand tour was not for six months. Before it I would have modeled countless times, we would have visited Paris and Florence, had days of adventures on bicycles and riverboats, and know all too well each other's peccadilloes and charms. I asked if Hans might come on some of these adventures. Of course, Paul said. To start, we must all go on horseback to the Lake of Landewin and bathe with no clothes on in green water under a blue sky with only sheep to watch and criticize. I said I thought the weather might be a little cold for that, and Antoine laughed and agreed.

ON MY SECOND or third visit to Scalands, Barbara's husband, Dr. Eugène Bodichon, was there. She had described him to me as the handsomest man ever, but I was not sure. I thought he looked like Moses. He had black hair and brown skin, his clothes were eccentric, he never wore a hat, and his English was scarcely comprehensible, even though he did not have much to say. Violet Greene told me that in Algiers he walked naked in the forest with a jackal. I found him more than strange, most eccentric, but I supposed that had the marriage been of a conventional sort, Barbara would not have made it.

She had first met him in Algiers, where he worked as an army surgeon and anthropologist. I was unclear what he was doing now. Barbara called him a lover of nature. "He is a man who gathers flowers daily for his own pleasure and walks twenty miles to hear the hyenas laugh," she said.

Their relationship had problems. Barbara hoped for children, but that did not happen. Dr. Bodichon hated England and the rain and wanted her to settle in Algiers, which she would not do, so they lived apart for months at a time. I thought of how I used to long for an hour away from Grandcourt.

At Scalands Dr. Bodichon did not appear before eleven in the morning, then breakfasted wearing a long white flannel burnous. He passed his days wandering in the woods alone, with an umbrella under his arm, and he liked to walk miles to see the sun set in the same place each day. At night when we dined, he wore a gray garment like the white one, drank eight or nine glasses of wine, and fed the dogs crackers and cheese, which made them excited and quarrelsome.

After observing him for a few days, I found it hard to think of him as sane. He would walk naked around the house to the alarm of many of us. Violet told me his bank had declared him incompetent to deal with his own finances for he gave all his money away.

———

I MODELED EACH week for Paul. Antoine attended to every detail of setting, dress, and comfort. The mood in the studio was always calm, Paul called me a godsend, and Antoine said I illumined their days. Their life was harmonious and ordered, I saw no discord between them, none was directed at me, and I did not question their relationship. Once when Antoine brought in a lavish display of flowers and fruit as adornment for a scene, Paul kissed his neck below the ear.

An occupation evolved for which I was paid and which I enjoyed. Within a few months my work extended to instructing galleries, purchasers, and framers. I talked to customers and arranged the carriage of paintings. Paul was sensitive to my uncertainty and concerned to spare me pain. He said I enhanced his life with Antoine. He did not make love to me or seek to control me. He wanted to hear what I had to say and to see through my eyes yet not intrude. Antoine cooked delicate food. Every meal with them seemed like a celebration. Each time I left, I knew they wanted me to return.

We went, Paul, Antoine, and I, to gallery viewings in Paris and Florence and for working visits to Portmadoc, Normandy, and Land's End. Paul seemed almost as doting as Mama and always wanted to hear what I had to say. Antoine showed no resentment. I always was accorded the more comfortable chair with the better view. If there was a thorn in my finger, it was Paul's care to remove it. Nothing was too good for me. Both men spoiled me. One night by a fire of applewood logs I told them something of my wedding night.

IN LONDON I went often to Barbara Bodichon's rooms at Langham Place. Her paintings were on the walls. The Ladies Reading Room there was open from eleven in the morning until ten at night. I paid my subscription of a guinea a year. One could read all the daily and weekly papers, there was a luncheon room attached, and it was a pleasant place to meet Mama, my sisters, Anna, or the Mallinger girls when they were in town for shopping. At the rooms women met to discuss and plan how to have proper schools, and the right to go to university and to vote. I heard the appeal of Emily Davies, who cofounded Girton College with Barbara. I heard of the views of John Stuart Mill, who had argued for universal suffrage.

I did not offer views of my own or go on marches or distribute leaflets. I preferred the opera, theater, shopping, walking in the forest, bowling, and horse riding. Nonetheless, the spirit of such freedoms settled in me. I was one of the cracked. I became unashamed.

One afternoon at Scalands, Violet Greene cut my hair. I was apprehensive but laughed as I shed my curls like the chains of the past. The shorter my hair, the freer I felt. Cropped, I looked young and daring. I rejoiced to think of my erstwhile husband's response: his horror at the gossip in the clubs, his wife consorting with feminists and suffragists, discarding her diamonds, shearing her hair. With my short hair and my name restored, I felt reborn.

PAUL TOLD ME he had a special request, which I must refuse if it caused me discomfort. He had accepted a commission to design a sculpture for a square in Toulouse. It was of Marianne, symbol of Liberty in France. *Liberty, Reason, France, Truth, the Republic* are all feminine nouns, he told me. He asked if I would model for him, with my breasts bare, holding the beacon of Truth in my right hand. He said I would symbolize the breaking with the old monarchy, headed by hereditary kings, and the heralding of the new enlightenment.

I had no hesitation or alarm in agreeing. I stood on a dais, a soft cloth wound round my waist, my head looking up, my right arm stretched high. My breasts were as much mine as my arms. Think of all you aspire to be, Paul said to me. Think of how powerful you are and the journeys you will make. Stretch as high as you can. Feel as brave as you are. He talked of the "Salon of the Rejected," of the need to move on from the old order, to discard the orthodoxies, trumpery, and inhibitions of the past and find the courage to be.

For many sessions I became Marianne, goddess of Liberty. I thought how proud Barbara would be of me. I concentrated and felt safe within myself and without

embarrassment or alarm at Paul looking intently at my
partly naked body. As I reached upward, my head back,
my muscles flexed, I thought how far I had traveled. Whatever the future held for me, no one, I vowed, would again
diminish me. I wished that you could have seen me, so
strong and free.

BARBARA ACCOMPANIED ME, Peter, Antoine, and Hans to
see Mama and my sisters at Offendene. We arrived with
flowers, sketchbooks, straw hats, exotic fruits, and special
Algerian sweets. Rex and Beatrix visited, and Anna. Bertha and Marjorie Millet joined us all for tea. I expected
Mama to be horrified at my new appearance, but she and
all the others thought me more beautiful than ever. Mama
was girlish and happy with my newfound friends. Barbara
flattered her and made her laugh. I thought how different
Mama's life might have been had she been shown a way to
determine her own path.

AND YOU, YOU receded but did not disappear. I carried you
in my mind. I thought of your compliant wife, her obedience and self-abnegation. I did not regret exclusion from
the world your faith imposed. Your orthodoxy seemed
another oppression, another man-made scheme. I could not
be a Jew.

    Nor could I reach the noble self-effacing ends you

advised. Each directive you gave seemed daunting, each aspiration beyond my grasp: I was not to gamble; I was to accept my suffering, nurture remorse, live to serve others. Others were no more to me than trees blowing in the wind. I chose instead to aspire to be myself, responsible for myself, to stand on my own feet.

ON SEVERAL OCCASIONS I visited Mrs. Lewes with Mrs. Bodichon, who always arrived with a gift: a jar of home-made blackberry jam, a basket of mushrooms, a sketch of a friend. Mrs. Lewes had several of Barbara's paintings on her walls. I observed the generosity of both women and the deep bond of friendship between them. They had been friends since Barbara was twenty-five and Mary Anne, as she called her, thirty-three. Mary Anne was then shy, awkward, suffered with her writing, and spoke of the pain and disgrace inflicted on her family because she lived with Mr. Lewes and her sorrow that her brother would not speak to her because he thought her shameful. Barbara's view was that it was not for others to say how she should live, but whatever her choice, she would stand by her.

Mrs. Lewes, I came to observe, had as warm a heart as Barbara. I reviewed what I at first mistook as her dislike of me. I don't think it was that. I think she was in awe of my appearance and suffered because such gifts eluded her, as her intellect and talent eluded me. And I believe she wondered what direction there could be for me if I had no particular ability or talent beyond my looks, and no strong or determined direction like you. She understood marriage would not suit me, but did not see how, outside of marriage, I might carve my way for myself. I could not be brilliant like Catherine Arrowpoint, capture the admiration and attention of Herr Klesmer, be rooted in a cause like you. I had to brave the world with my shortcomings and still believe myself worthy of an equal place with all the rich, clever people with whom I brushed shoulders, minds, and points of view.

Barbara would have liked her friend to take part in campaigns for justice, but though Mary Anne wanted to see women socially elevated, educated equally with men, and protected by fair laws, she was not going to write manifestos or make political speeches. Her contribution was to take a man's name while being truly a woman and to create Dorothea Casaubon, Maggie Tulliver, and Romola. Barbara said I would be surprised were I to read Mary Anne's latest book, which was with her editor, John Blackwood, for I would recognize many of the people in it. I said I would purchase a copy when it was published. I asked its title, but Barbara could not or would not say.

She invited me, Hans, and Paul, with Antoine of course, and Mr. and Mrs. Lewes to spend Christmas with her and a writer friend, Matilda Betham-Edwards. She rented a parsonage on the Isle of Wight. Eugène Bodichon was stranded in Algiers. Miss Betham-Edwards had been a friend of Charles Dickens, wrote poetry and novels, and loved France as much as England. She and Paul spoke mainly in French, and I was pleased to find I understood most of their conversations.

Mrs. Lewes played Beethoven on the parsonage piano, and Hans and Antoine played practical jokes. We had a goose and vegetables for Christmas dinner. Hans came in with a silver tureen, said it was a Christmas specialty, took off the lid with a flourish, and I screamed because of what looked like a snake; but it was only the vicar's scourge, which Hans had unhooked from a wall in the study.

I spoke of the forthcoming journey to the African continent, Arabia, and other exotic destinations and felt Mrs. Lewes was unconvinced that in the company of Paul and Antoine this was the right journey for me to make.

I was restless to leave England. Paul talked of the beauty and wildness of Africa, and I longed to be there. I wanted not to know what each day might bring, to walk and meet the unexpected, see other colors, distant rivers, a fiercer sunrise, to have if only for a while no fixed receipt. Barbara talked of blue mountains, waterfalls, dark cypresses, white houses among olive trees. I looked closely at her paintings of Moorish arches, white mosques, men in *thobes*, and Arabian nights.

I talked with puzzlement to Hans about why Paul wanted me to travel with him and Antoine. Hans said I screened them from too much visibility and eased their path, and perhaps they did the same for me. He said gently he did not believe Paul was my prince on a white steed who would capture my heart and carry me to the castle of eternal happiness. Perhaps, he said, I did not want such capture.

I HAD SAID good-bye to Mama, dried her tears, and promised her my speedy return. Then, on the eve of my departure, Mrs. Lewes arranged a gathering as a way of saying bon voyage. Rex was there with Beatrix Brackenshaw, Hans was with Anna. My uncle and aunt stood to one side like awkward onlookers. Klesmer and Catherine played a piano duet.

Mrs. Lewes quizzed me about our plans: where were we to stay, whom did we know, what were we taking with us? Paul and Antoine had arranged it all, I explained. I asked her to tell me if the journey would be a success and I would feel happy and free for a while at least. She laughed and said, "My dear Gwendolen, I must tell you again, I am not a soothsayer. I do not know what life holds for myself, let alone you."

"But you knew everything, everything, everything that impinged on my life," I said. "So surely you must know if I will, for a few months at least, be happy with Paul Leroy."

"My dear Gwendolen." Mrs. Lewes's voice was concerned, and I at last felt she truly cared about the quintessential me, and not just with the detachment of her novelist's mind. "I don't know what the future will bring you. Paul is a talented artist, wealthy but not tainted by wealth; he is good looking and cares for you with devotion. He is inseparable from Antoine, and I do not know the significance of that or whether their togetherness will disconcert you. I cannot see why you should fail to enjoy your journey. The omens are good. But I do not know whether you will be happy or how life will treat you. You know as well as I that nothing is forever, not the good times nor the bad, that our plans are often disrupted and our hopes diverted. I do not know, when you board the boat at Dover, whether the sea will be choppy."

And she looked beyond me, so I turned to see at what, and there you were. For a moment I thought I was hallucinating. "Yes," Mrs. Lewes said. "Daniel is visiting." She smiled and moved away to talk to a small, elderly, gray-eyed woman with nervous gestures and a hesitant smile who, I think, was a writer too.

It was as if the years snapped shut. There you were. Your quality of stillness. Your grave demeanor. Your gaze of persistence and containment as at Homburg, as if all I am was known to you. Your skin was darker, you had grown a beard, and you were wearing one of those little hats, a mark of Jewish orthodoxy, a *kippah* Hans said they were called. You looked biblical.

You asked, with all caring, how I was, your dark eyes searching, expecting perhaps the old unrestrained outpouring. I saw you had not forgotten me, that you held fixed our unchanging love, though we took it to no harbor. For a brief but eternal moment I could not speak. Then I told you I was going on a journey with friends and was leaving the next day.

You looked quizzical, disappointed, and as if you wanted to know more. Wanted perhaps to hear of the handsome prince, with the castle, carriages, and glinting sword of honor, who rescued me from suicide by drowning and helped me overcome the guilt of aiding my evil husband's death. "Your life . . . ?" you said, in a hesitant voice. I talked of an impending journey with untried friends, of kind Sir Hugo, Hans, the constant of Offendene, Mama's contentment, the new windows in the house, and the same returning swallows in the barn.

You wanted to go beyond detail and delve into my heart. So I told you that, for the most part, I was at peace with myself, that out of evil good had come, and that I had learned to take things as they are, not as I wanted them to be or how I was led to believe they ought to be. I said I could be reflective at whatever came to me, good or bad, sun or shadow, the best things about myself and the worst. "You'll be pleased to hear," I said, "that I have almost but not quite lost any wish to gamble."

You smiled but looked confused. Though I had gone no farther than to London, Paris, and Amsterdam, and you six thousand miles to the other side of the world, I had traveled in a way you could not understand. Your star was fixed. My journeys lay ahead.

Time and suffering had built a wall between us. You were now more entrenched in who you were, more sure of what was right and wrong, and I was less. I had seen how little it takes to drown. It was not that I learned to be more cautious, for to travel to unknown places with men to whom I was not attached was not cautious. It was more that I had learned not to suppose I could arrive at a destination.

You had taken your belief and its trappings with you from Wessex to Palestine: the Torah and the Tehillah, the Ten Commandments, the Day of Atonement, a day for rejoicing. I shunned any orthodoxy, Christian or Jewish, I had suffered confinement, and I would avoid it again: this you must be, that you must not be. I cared for the wide world and my brief and glancing view of it not defined by a man's commands. I was a free spirit like your mother, though I lacked her strength and talent. I loved you from the moment I first saw you; I love you now. I would always be thrilled, shocked, and delighted to go into a room and see you there. It would always be as if I had found what I had lost and was looking for. But I could not have converted to your beliefs.

You noted I was wearing the turquoise chain. You said you thought of me often. You had not written to me because you were uncertain what to say. Sir Hugo often sent you my news. You were disappointed I would be unable to visit the Abbey while you were there. Mirah was at home in Jerusalem with your son, Daniel.

And then you said it had long been on your mind to give me a memento. Something other than the turquoise chain. You took from your coat your mother's locket with her picture in it. I am wearing it now.

You and I, we were the life we did not live. The link between us remained untried, unbroken. Never together, never wholly apart. We were the figures on Keats's Grecian urn, questioning desire locked in our eyes and hearts. I was important to you like the unreal mother you once glimpsed but never knew. You were important to me like the love and happiness I yearn for still. I have so often thought of you and seen and felt your gaze—in the music of Schubert, in the night sky. In the melancholy of evenings alone I penned these fragmented memories to you in violet ink, not with a wish for you to read them, only so as not to relinquish you.

I MADE MY journey, the first of many. I made—and make—my travels of discovery and adventure with womanly courage, a pleasure in what is new and strange, an awareness of freedom and good fortune, and as a bulwark against past or future pain. I left Paul and Antoine in the Seychelles Islands, not in anger or with disappointment, but from a desire again to be at Offendene, walk the familiar lanes of Pennicote, see the bluebells in the woodland, hear the wind in the birch trees, see Mama, who I feared had grown frail. I journeyed home with strangers.

Next year I plan to journey to Ashkelon with Violet

Greene and two of her friends. I will try to visit you and your family. One day I am sure we will meet again. I would like to tell you of the journeys I have made, see your wise, kind eyes, feel the warmth of your hand in mine. I would like to tell you travel means most to me when it is in my mind. I would also like to tell you, but I will never dare, that you will always remain, though faded like an echo and locked away like a keepsake, my place of safety, my heaven on earth, the destination about which I will always wonder but can never reach.

Years Later

I consigned these pages to a drawer, time passed, memories faded. One afternoon my small daughter, Lucy, chanced on them and strewed them over the floor. As I gathered them up, before hiding them again I glanced at what I had written and was pained to be reminded of all I had endured.

I did not see Mrs. Lewes again after my return from Africa. She published the book about you in which I appeared. It was her last novel, and she gave it your name. I have not read it for I do not want harsh memories to surface, but I heard that she freely invented and omitted when it suited her so to do.

Her own story became more fantastic than either yours or mine. Mr. Lewes died of cancer not long after George Eliot's new book came out, and she then married a family friend, twenty years her junior, whom hitherto she had referred to as her nephew. She was about sixty by then. Mr. Cross—I think that was his name—was a city financier with a red beard. I do not recall meeting him at her salon afternoons. Mrs. Bodichon told me he had until then lived with his mother, who died, which left him desolate. Her view was that all love is different, but apparently he had had no previous involvement with any woman other than his mother. I wondered if Mrs. Lewes married so as to gain approval from her brother Isaac, who deigned to break his censorious silence and congratulate her on the wedding. He cared about the fact of it, not whether it would bring her happiness. Then on the honeymoon in Venice Mr. Cross jumped from the hotel window into the Grand Canal and had to be rescued from drowning by gondoliers and sedated with chloral. It did not sound like a propitious beginning to married life.

I thought how being hauled, or not, from deep water figured large in the stories of your life, Mrs. Lewes's, and my own. Mrs. Cross—I could not think of her as Mrs. Cross, though she liked to be referred to as such—within months of this marriage then died, I am not sure of what. A sore throat that turned into something else, I think.

I PONDERED THE news I had heard of some of the others who affected my life and wondered what of it was true.

So much and yet so little has happened and happens to

me and within me. Time leaks away, but I am not bound to the old rules, I am free, and I have my flight. I cannot be summed up or shown to have arrived. I could not reach the destination of your heart, but I have other loves, all different; my daughter is chief among them. I do not see her father, who already has a wife.

Mama has become rather vague in manner and rheumy eyed, but her face lights with radiance at the sight of me. And my true friends are there for me through good times and bad. Rex predictably is happily married and a respected judge. He always remembers my birthday, always invites me to dances, functions, and to soirées that I have no wish to attend. Hans and my cousin Anna are married. She bestows the same devotion and adulation on her husband as she did on Rex. In their company I recapture the picnic days of childhood, riding in the meadows, swimming in the lake.

Bertha lives happily with Marjorie Millet not far from Offendene in a thatched cottage. They are now acclaimed landscape gardeners, much in demand. They have created their own paradisal garden and talk hotly of birds and bees and how rigorously one should prune roses.

Isabel—Mrs. Clintock—so far has five sons. Mama worries there will never be enough money, on a clergyman's pay, to feed this tribe. Alice married a colonel and is proud of the aviary she has created on the grounds of their country house. Each time I visit, I with shame remember my slaughter of her caged bird. Fanny married a crofter; I forget how they met. They moved to Scotland, and she seldom writes home.

As for the rest: I heard from Sir Hugo that the young Henleigh Grandcourt eschews mammon, cares nothing for his inheritance, plays the saxophone, has grown his brown curls long, and writes poetry. Sir Hugo also told me how Lush endured an alarming death: he stepped into quicksand near Lyme Regis, was not hauled from it until the following day, there had been a storm in the night, and his chill turned to bronchitis then pneumonia. He lasted a fortnight. I shrugged when I heard this news.

Julian returned to America and wrote to none of us. Hans saw news that he fell from the trapeze wire in front of a huge crowd in Kalamazoo, damaged his back, then took poison because he knew he would never perform his wonderful acts again.

And from Uncle I heard that Mrs. Gadsby inherited a pig farm near Bristol from an unknown, unwed relative. It turned out to be a gold mine, so Uncle said.

About the Author

DIANA SOUHAMI is the author of twelve critically acclaimed nonfiction and biography books, including *Selkirk's Island* (winner of the Whitbread Biography Award), *The Trials of Radclyffe Hall* (winner of the Lambda Literary Award and short-listed for the James Tait Black Prize for Biography), and the bestselling *Mrs. Keppel and Her Daughter* (winner of the Lambda Literary Award and a *New York Times* Notable Book of the Year). She lives in London.